DeaD
BaBIeS

by the same author

Fiction:

THE RACHEL PAPERS

SUCCESS

OTHER PEOPLE: A MYSTERY STORY

MONEY

EINSTEIN'S MONSTERS

Journalism:

INVASION OF THE SPACE INVADERS

THE MORONIC INFERNO

DEAD BABIES

martin amis

HARMONY BOOKS
NEW YORK

Copyright © 1975 by Martin Amis

Published in the United States in 1988 by Harmony Books, a division of
Crown Publishers, Inc., 225 Park Avenue South, New York, New York 10003
Originally published in Great Britain in 1975 by Jonathan Cape Limited
HARMONY and colophon are trademarks of Crown Publishers, Inc.
Manufactured in the United States of America

Library of Congress Cataloging in Publication Data

Amis, Martin.   Dead Babies

I. Title
PZ4.A5174De3   [PR6051.M5]   823'.9'14   75-8216
ISBN 0-517-568667

10 9 8 7 6 5 4 3 2 1
First Harmony Paperback Edition, 1988

FOr JULIE

... and so even when [the satirist] presents a vision of the future, his business is not prophecy; just as his subject is not tomorrow ... it is today.

—MENIPPUS

contents

Part One: FRIDAY

    1: Let's Go: 3
    2: Routine: 6
    3: Sounds Funny: 10
    4: Nice Arrows: 13
    5: Appleseed Rectory: 16
    6: Fat Chance: 20
    7: Penthouse Cloudscape: 25
    8: From the Pain: 31
    9: Gin and Tears: 34

    X: QUENTIN: 37

    11: The Human Wigwam: 41
    12: Tall and Good: 45
    13: A Sort of Daydream: 47
    14: Out Here Somewhere: 49
    15: Meandered up America: 52
    16: A Heavy Fire of Eyes: 56
    17: Some Bush: 58
    18: Oh No: 60
    19: Collapsing Balloon: 61

    XX: DIANA: 64

    21: Down Unknown Paths: 73
    22: Who's He?: 79
    23: Drunk Space: 82
    24: Heavy Water: 84
    25: The Psychologic Revue: 86
    26: The Lugubrious Boogie: 92
    27: The Old Cops: 95
    28: Yanked: 98
    29: Silence and Day: 102

Part Two: SATURDAY

    XXX: GILES: 107

    31: Picking Up Speed: 111
    32: The Cool Doves: 112

33: But What's Perfect: 115
34: Breakfast: 116
35: Lagging Time: 119
36: The Real Thing Again: 120
37: Those Conversations: 122
38: Placements: 124
39: Cunning Stunts: 127

XL: WHITEHEAD: 129

41: His Lucent Girlfriends: 138
42: Plus Which: 139
43: Cruel Body: 142
44: Wars and Shit: 143
45: The Billet-doux: 146
46: Wan Windows: 147
47: A Bit Permanent: 148
48: These Days: 151
49: Hell of a Place: 154

L: CELIA: 155

51: Just Checked Out: 160
52: Tear-Tracks: 160
53: The Lumbar Transfer: 163
54: Too Good to Waste: 164
55: Don't Be Disgusting: 168
56: It Started Strangely: 170
57: Old Dreads: 172
58: Everything Will Be Mad: 174
59: Something to Do: 176

LX: ANDY: 179

61: Into the Middle Air: 183
62: Ghostly Periods: 187
63: The Antidote: 189
64: High Tea, or Here We Go Again: 190
65: Seems Silly Now: 192
66: No More Games: 196
67: Spring Clean: 197
68: White Room: 198
69: Wrong Yesterdays: 199

Part Three: SUNDAY

    LXX: JOHNNY 203

      71: The Coming Lights: 204
      72: That Sad Welcome: 205

main characters

THE APPLESEEDERS:

THE HON. QUENTIN VILLIERS: tall, blond, elegant, urbane.

ANDY ADORNO: tall, dark, rowdy, aggressive.

GILES COLDSTREAM: smallish, fair, rich, anxious.

KEITH WHITEHEAD: very tiny, very fat—court dwarf to Appleseed Rectory.

THE HON. CELIA VILLIERS: robust, mousy, straightforward, wife to Quentin.

DIANA PARRY: dark, angular, shrewish, girlfriend to Andy.

THE AMERICANS:

MARVELL BUZHARDT: small, hairy, authoritative, Jewish.

SKIP MARSHALL: tall, sallow, slow-talking, Southern.

ROXEANNE SMITH: full-formed, red-haired, American.

OTHERS:

LUCY LITTLEJOHN: silver-haired, jovial, a golden-hearted whore.

JOHNNY: a practical joker.

AUTHOR'S NOTE: *Not only are all characters and scenes in this book entirely fictitious; most of the technical, medical, and psychological data are too. My working maxim here has been as follows: I may not know much about science but I know what I like.*

DEAD BABIES

part one
FrIDAY

1: LET'S GO

There were five bedrooms.

In the master suite, on knees and elbows, Giles Coldstream was crawling around the floor in search of the telephone, both hands cupped tightly over his mouth. The curling green cord eventually led him to a heap of spent gin bottles beneath his desk. With his left palm still flat over his lips Giles tugged at the wire, hobbled into a crouch, and dialed two digits.

"Get me Dr. Wallman. Quickly. Dr. Sir Gerald Wall—"

But even as he spoke, a tooth the shape and hue of a potato chip slopped over his tongue and fell with a hollow rattle into the bakelite receiver.

"Please, quickly."

"What number do you want?" *asked a female voice.*

"Please. I'm—they're all—"

And now, in strips, like an unstrung necklace or rippling piano keys, they begin to cascade from his mouth.

"What number do you want?" *the voice repeated.*

Giles dropped the telephone. His hands fidgeted frenetically inside his mouth—trying to keep them there, trying to put them back. His face went glossy with tears as a bubble of blood welled from his lips.

"My teeth," *he said.* "Somebody please help me. They're all gone."

The bedroom across the passage was not, perhaps, as grand as Giles's, but it was spacious and well appointed, commanding a decent view of the village street and the soft rise of the hills beyond. At the table recessed into the alcove of its bay window sat the Honorable Quentin Villiers, blond and lean in a pair of snakeskin sexters, coolly shrouded by a dome of dust-speckled light from his angle lamp, which in turn threw charcoal shadows along the room behind him, half disguising the naked body of a girl asleep on the bed. Diderot's *Le neveu de Rameau* nestled on his golden thighs. Quentin closed the book, extinguished his cigarette and took a white pill from the snap-open box on the table. He flicked it into the air, throwing his head back to catch the bright little cylinder in his mouth. He gave his saliva time to wash the taste away.

The Hon. Quentin Villiers stood up. Through the partly drawn curtains he watched the village road turning gray in the quiet dawn. His reflection began to melt from the window-pane—the wavy fair hair, the thin mouth, the abnormally bright green eyes. When he switched off the lamp the rest of the room seemed to lighten.

"Darling, darling, wake up," said Quentin, massaging his wife back to consciousness. "It's me . . . it's me."

Celia Villiers stirred and blinked, her face flexing with recognition. Quentin carefully folded back the sheet and gazed with reverence at her breasts, caressing her throat with imperceptible fingertips.

"I love you," he whispered.

"Thank you. I love you too."

After a few minutes Quentin rolled over onto his back. Celia's brown-maned head disappeared in its slow sacramental journey down his chest. Then, with an expression of exaggerated calm, Quentin turned to gaze at the ceiling as she wettened his stomach with her tears.

The third and smallest of the first-floor bedrooms was separated from the one we have just left only by a slim sandwich of plaster and hardboard. Accordingly, the sound of the Villierses' lovemaking came through the partition with reasonably high fidelity, waking Diana Parry, the lighter sleeper of the adjacent pair.

Having resumed consciousness, then—a state she seemed never to be very far from—Diana propped herself up on her elbow and stared with an involuntary pang at the back of Andy Adorno's head, coated with hair no less dark and shiny than her own, and at his broad, gypsyishly birthmarked shoulders. While Celia's yodels of appreciation increased in volume and frequency, Diana began to enumerate the blackheads between Andy's shoulder blades. Diana did this in a hostile spirit, because Andy had not made love to her the night before. The noises from the other room became more jarred and ambiguous. It was always a frightening, rather inhuman sound, Diana thought.

Still asleep, Andy rolled over, causing a smell of moist towels, Andy's smell, to glide up the bed. Diana noted with transient satisfaction that his face was the color of vanilla and his breathing stertorous. She lifted the top sheet to look at Andy's whiskey paunch. It swelled and subsided peacefully.

Diana dropped the sheet back into place. Andy had had a coltish, alcoholic erection. Diana sneered at him.

Climbing cautiously from the bed, she picked up her cerise silk caftan and cuboid vanity case. She stepped over a broken guitar and weaved between the drum set and microphone stand. Next door, in the bathroom, she positioned the case on the closed toilet seat and drew a basinful of water. With hands like stiff little flippers, she started to wash her face.

The second-floor bedroom was as yet unoccupied and so need not detain us long. A conventionally low-ceilinged attic, it had a derelict and melancholy air for all the recent work that had clearly gone into its reclamation. The two single beds had been pushed together beneath the small window and made up with fresh double sheets. On the bedside table stood a bottle of Malvern Water, and *three* glasses. As a kind of token, a large turquoise-haired gonk rested against the pillows, its limbs spastically askew, its mouth fixed in a mad, idiot leer.

In the fifth and final "bedroom"—actually a fetid nine-by-nine box situated between the garage and the boiler room—Keith Whitehead lay on sandpaper blankets farting like a wizard.

Let's go.

Whitehead is an almost preposterously unattractive young man—practically, for instance, a dwarf. Whenever people want to say something nice about his appearance they usually come up with "You've got quite nice coloring," a reference to his dark eyebrows and thin yellow hair. That granted, nothing remained to be praised about his unappetizing person —the sparse straw mat atop a squashed and petulant mask of acne; the dour, bulgy little torso and repulsively truncated limbs; the numb, cadaverous texture of the whole.

The more clothes you took off him, the more traumatic the spectacle became. His (equally fat but better proportioned) sister went into hysterics when she once surprised him in the bath. As he entered the Wimbledon municipal swimming pool two teenage girls spontaneously vomited into the shallow end (on being questioned, they said it was the quiffs on the nipples of Keith's D-cup breasts that had done the trick—Whitehead was subsequently banned from the

baths). At school physical checkups, doctors habitually refused to lay a finger on him, and the PT master threatened to
hand in his notice should Keith ever set foot in his gymnasium
again. As if in reply to these bodily shortcomings, Keith's
nature is one utterly lacking in wit, generosity, and charm.
Whitehead is, moreover, keenly appreciative of this state of
affairs, well aware that by almost anyone's standards he
would be better off dead.

He reviewed it now, as he extracted himself from between
the blankets and sat rocking on the bunk in his pungent
pajamas, waking for the hundredth time in this house full of
tall and affluent people. Keith was hungry; his stomach was
rumbling so loudly that he kept yelling at it to shut up. It was
eight o'clock. Probably the others weren't up yet and the
kitchen would be his. He got to his feet and, after some consideration, put on his dressing gown, a tweedy brown horror
that his parents had bought him the minute they were sure
he wasn't going to grow out of it. Mr. and Mrs. Whitehead
had allowed for, indeed banked on, their son growing a few
more inches; this had turned out to be a needless precaution,
and the heavy material now swilled amply in his wake. But
Keith was hungry, and he was even more appalled by his
clothes, grubby little items that he knew he was too fat for,
than he was appalled by the risk of being found short-arsing
round the house without his high-heeled boots on. In slippers,
then, Keith Whitehead opened his "bedroom" door and crept
across the garage into the house.

2: routine

And so when Giles Coldstream came into the kitchen Whitehead was already there. They looked at each other in mo-
mentary alarm. Keith sat flushed and breathless at the table,
having just finished beating up The Mandarin, Celia's
bronchitic Persian cat.

"Hello," said Giles, struck not for the first time by the
relative adequacy of Whitehead's teeth.

"Hi," Keith gasped.

Giles sat down carefully next to Keith at the table and
looked into his face for a few seconds; then he looked away.
"I had my really heavy recurring dream last night, actually,"

said Giles. Giles said this with some surprise; he had never mentioned his dreams to anyone before. Why, then, had he told little Keith? It wasn't as if the morning so far had been anything but humdrumly routine. Giles had simply woken, sent his tongue slithering like a fish round his mouth, checked off his teeth in the bedside shaving mirror, and raced across the room to the huge, shuddering fridge where his early morning jug of Bloody Mary awaited him. Giles decided that he should have drunk more before venturing downstairs. Sobriety always made him indiscreet.

"What happened?" asked Keith, ". . . in your recurring dream?"

"Oh. All my teeth fell out again."

Whitehead frowned pleasantly. "I believe that's to do with fear of sexual failure. It's a sex dream—when all your teeth fall out."

"No, it isn't," grumbled Giles. "Not with me."

"What's it about with you then?"

"It's about all my teeth falling out."

"Ah. How do you know?"

"Because that's all they ever do."

"What?"

"Fall out."

Giles got up and walked across the kitchen to the draining board, which he clutched with both hands. He glazed over.

"Oh. I see," said Keith.

Giles shivered briefly. "But let's just not ever talk about it," he said. "Ever again. If that's all right by you."

Keith shrugged. "Fine," he said. "Fine by me."

The electric kettle began to come to the boil. Giles slowly backed away as the steam condensed on his arm.

"Ah. There goes my coffee," said Keith Whitehead.

Keith had been rinsing out a coffee cup when The Mandarin prowled grandly up to him. Whitehead sighed as he heard its friendly meow. He knew that all The Mandarin was thinking about was Jellymeat Kat. Disdainfully Keith polished the mug with a dishcloth. He was fucked if he was going to feed Celia's pet.

It was then that The Mandarin made her terrible mistake. With a chesty purr she nosed in under Keith's tweed truss and started to flow in figure-eight patterns round his feet, sending wispy fur tickling up his legs.

Whitehead's armpits came to life. "Right," he said.

Gently trapping The Mandarin between his thick white calves, Keith looped the dishcloth and held its end under the running tap. Next, he parted his gown, The Mandarin peered up at him with moist, affectionate eyes, and Keith caught her a good one right on the nose. From then on it was a scramble. As The Mandarin slithered out in terror from the tweed wigwam, Keith pivoted, kicked her into the corner, and came in with his waterlogged rag swinging. Two minutes later, having clouted and dribbled The Mandarin round the kitchen, Keith hoisted her out of the door on the end of his slipper, too winded to continue.

"Are you going to have anything, Giles?" asked Keith.

Giles played with the idea of having a lightly boiled egg. The idea did not attract him. He was off solids at the moment. "No, what I came down for, actually, was a *lime*." Giles intended, rather, to use this fruit in the preparation of some Gin Rickeys, a new drink he had read about.

Keith was going to have something. He thought it likely that he would die if he did not. He hadn't eaten for three days and the timpanist inside his stomach grew more importunate by the second.

"There's a lot of bacon," Keith coaxed. "It says on the packet that it's due to go bad tomorrow, so we might as well finish it. Want any?"

Giles started back, as if from a physical threat. *Bacon* was one of the foods he disapproved of most—not only for its toughness but also for its texture: those little knots of gristle and hide which could so easily be mistaken for escaping crowns, caps, bridges, or (who knows?) actual teeth. No. Giles liked to know what was going on in his mouth, thank you. We're sorry, but Giles had swallowed a cap or two in his time and wasn't about to let it happen again. (Once, stranded in Blackfriars on a rainy March afternoon, ravenous and without his credit cards, Giles had stolen into Trims, a health-food cafeteria, where it took him an hour and three-quarters to eat an almond rissole, sorting and grading each item with his tongue before letting it pass down his throat.)

"No I *won't*," he said. "No, I really don't feel like anything."

"Well, I'd better have some then," Keith said fatly.

"Now where would one find . . . a *lime*."

"I'm not sure." Whitehead peeled five strips of bacon onto the grill. "Giles—have you any idea who's supposed to be coming for the weekend?"

"No. I didn't know anyone was coming. Besides, what day is it today?"

"It's Friday. Yes," Keith went on, "some friends of Quentin's. American, I believe. And also . . . Lucy Littlejohn."

Giles was under the dresser, burrowing among the wooden boxes. "Oh, really?"

"Apparently," said Keith. "I don't know anything about the Americans. Do you, do you know Lucy Littlejohn?"

"Mm, a bit," Giles muttered.

Keith jabbed at the bacon with a fork. "I hear she's . . . Quentin and Andy tell me—"

"Look, here's The Mandarin!" said Giles, turning on his haunches and running a hand along the Persian's arched, silvery back. "How are *you*, Mandarin. Have you fed her, Keith?"

"Yes."

"Oh. No, you've *been* fed, Mandarin. Yes, Keith's already *fed* you."

Whitehead shifted his weight from one foot to the other. "Because Quentin and Andy say Lucy's really something. She's really . . . quite a nympho."

"What do you mean exactly?"

Keith coughed. "Just that she'll fuck anyone."

"Ooh, I don't know about 'anyone,'" said Giles, dubiously, having fucked her himself.

"Andy's fucked her, Quentin's fucked her—"

"—*I've* fucked her," Giles weighed in.

"Brian Hall and all that lot have fucked her."

"Bob Henderson and all that lot have fucked her," said Giles. "Yes, I suppose she does fuck quite a lot of people. Cy Harling and all that lot have fucked her."

Whitehead, who had hardly fucked anyone, hadn't fucked her, and it was his dream to do so this very weekend. Thus, he said abruptly, "I hear she's got some sort of venereal thing"—a wheeze of his to put Giles off fucking her himself.

"Is that so?" Giles asked mildly, his head still invisible beneath the dresser. Normally this intelligence would have caused him considerable retrospective alarm. But he found that he was losing interest in sex these days.

"So they say," said Keith.

"Well," asked Giles, straightening up, "who hasn't nowadays?"

At length, Giles found his lime and Keith cooked his bacon. As they shuffled past each other Giles halted on his way to the door and looked the tiny Whitehead up and down.

"Hey," Giles pointed out ingenuously, nodding his head, "you're really a lot smaller without your boots on." Giles looked him up and down again, seemingly impressed by his own powers of observation. "Fatter, too. You know, I never really realized," he said, as if telling Keith something he would be intrigued with and grateful to learn, "just how small and fat you actually were."

When Giles was gone Keith smacked his plate down on the table, kicked the attentive Mandarin, closed his eyes, and, lips flapping, let out a long, frowsy sigh.

3: SOUNDS FUNNY

Celia sat up suddenly in bed, hugged her knees to her breasts, tilted her head to one side, and asked, "What shall we do with them when they arrive?"

Quentin Villiers rearranged the sheets to cover the lower half of his body. He did this rather fussily, but his voice remained genial and melodious. "I should prefer to wait and see what sort of state they're in. They'll have been driving all night and will doubtless be racked with amphetamines."

"I think I'll make them a cooked breakfast," said Celia.

"A cooked breakfast? A 'cooked' *breakfast*? My sweet, sometimes you are too deliciously *outré*. Eating a cooked breakfast—it would be like going to bed in pajamas, or reading an English novel."

"Darling, you're not to tease me."

"Well, my dearest, *really*. No. I rather thought a picnic. It might amuse them. . . ." Quentin opened a hand toward the light that was gathering behind the bedroom curtains. "It promises to be a fine day and, besides, I should like some air myself."

Celia flopped back to her husband's side and nuzzled his neck with her large bruised lips. "You've been up all night, haven't you?"

Quentin released a mouthful of smoke and nodded slowly.

"What doing?"

"Cultivating the life of the mind."

"You hardly ever sleep now, do you?"

Quentin drew in a mouthful of smoke and shook his head slowly. "I do try to avoid it. It bores me so."

"Quentin?"

"Celia."

"Is it true that the three of them have scenes together?"

"Naturally. Why, haven't you ever joined in a threesome— or what I believe they call 'a troy'?"

"Never," said Celia. "Not even in my dissolute days. Have you?"

"No, I haven't either, curiously enough. They're sure to try to enlist us, by the way."

"But we won't, will we," said Celia, cuddling nearer.

Whether through regret or impatience, Quentin concealed a sigh in an emission of cigarette smoke. "Of course not," he said.

"Will the others?"

"An excellent question." He arranged the pillows behind his head to still greater advantage. "Andy most assuredly would, if given the ghost of a chance. Diana, I'm undecided about. I don't think Giles could really be bothered to. Little Keith would probably be prepared to be unseamed by Marvell and Skip if he thought that might win him an opportunity to make Roxeanne his own, which, again, I'd have thought it wouldn't. Roxeanne is fairly 'catholic' in her tastes, but in Keith's rather unsavory case . . . ?" Quentin flapped a limp wrist.

"What about that character Lucy Littlejohn?"

"Character. My sweet, you talk as if she were forty-five. She's a colorful personality but she's hardly a character."

"She's an old flame of yours, isn't she."

"A spark, a mere cinder," protested Quentin.

Celia relaxed and the moment passed. "It sounds funny, doesn't it, darling," she said, "two men and one girl? Two girls and one man seems more on the cards . . . but. What do the three of them *do*?"

"They do most of it on a chair, I rather gather. Marvell, the little one, sits on Skip's, the big one's, lap, thereby impaling himself, and then Roxeanne impales herself *front*ways on Marvell's lap, so that she may kiss them both in turn. Frightfully eventful for Marvell, one imagines."

"Mm."

"There are some rather baroque variations, what they call *soixante-neuf et six*, but that's the main theme." Quentin gave one of his rare yawns. "They're terribly straightforward about it all. You can ask them for details when they come."

"Mm. It does sound funny, though, doesn't it?"

"Yes," said Quentin, "I suppose it does."

Next door, Andy Adorno peeled back his adhesive eyelids and focused with some degree of reluctance on Diana, who was lying on her side, facing him, the cerise caftan resting here and there on her perennially olive skin. She turned a page of her magazine and glanced at him. Andy closed his eyes again. The taste of dusty stone steps which lay coiled round his senses was augmented by a noisome wave of eau de cologne.

"Jesus fuckin' Christ," he murmured.

Diana turned a page. She said, "There's some coffee and toast I've brought you."

Andy correctly guessed that these nutriments were intended to moisten his mouth and sweeten his breath. Out of the corner of one of his narrow red eyes he looked at Diana again, noting the tactful makeup and the vigorously brushed black hair, through which Diana now ran a hand as she turned another page.

"What's with the glamour?" he asked.

"Just had a wash."

Andy sat up a few inches, his dark face creased with remorse. He said, "Jesus . . . coffee." He sighed. "And I suppose you want me to fuck you now, don't you?"

She passed him the cup, shaking her head.

"That's good. Cos *I*," said Andy putting his mug on the bedside table and sitting up, "feel like *shit!*" He juggled his face between stiff-fingered hands. Then he turned to her and added in a softer voice, "And anyway, I never do what I don't want to do. Okay?"

"Okay."

"Aw, my fuckin' *head!*" roared Andy, as he sprang from the bed and stumbled from the room. Diana heard him battering violently on the bathroom door. "*Christ!* Who's *in* there?"

Keith tensed on the lavatory seat. He had been on it for fifteen minutes, soggy with constipation. "It's Keith."

"Keith! Don't you *dare* use this bathroom again." Andy wriggled with impatience. "Now move your arse!"

Keith's buttocks, by way of response, gave a loud yell as a pint of air rushed out between them. Both he and Andy gasped with fright.

Why, this dreadful shout from Whitehead's rear was heard by everyone in the house, by Giles as he squeezed lime juice into a frosted glass, by Celia as she marshaled her cosmetics, by Quentin Villiers as he zipped up his faded denim shirt, and by Diana as she lay on her bed, staring at the wall with cold, unblinking eyes.

4: nice arrows

Let us, then, illustrate our difficulties.

Within half an hour, three conversations were in progress.

one

En route to the kitchen for another lime, Giles Coldstream saw little Keith in the smaller of the two partitioned sitting rooms, flicking tiredly through the copy of *Television Weekly* which had been delivered that morning. Giles popped his head round the door.

"Hey, Keith, anything good on today? I can't remember."

"Yes, lots," said Keith.

Giles and Keith would often sit together, silently, like old men, in front of the television during the late mornings and afternoons—Giles because time and time again he found himself not thinking about his teeth, Whitehead on the broader principle that it must make useful contributions to his sanity.

"There's *Imbroglio* at eleven, of course," said Keith. "You didn't see it yesterday, did you?"

"Yes I did. No I didn't," said Giles. "I missed that one, actually. What happened in it?"

"Well, the guy the photographer's wife didn't fuck went back to his son's mistress."

"Ah, I see. But . . ." Giles frowned gradually, "what about Jimmy?"

"What about him?"

"Jimmy. The mistress's daughter's boyfriend."

"I know who he is. He ran away from home again on Wednesday."

Giles seemed relieved. "That's right, of course he did. So all that was all right then."

"Why didn't you come down yesterday?"

"Um, sleeping or something, I think. Yesterday . . . was that *Round the House, Chuckadoodledoo, Brumber and Alphonse,* and *Tammy*?"

"No, that's Tuesday."

Giles cocked his head. "Are you sure?"

"Yes."

"Well, what was on yesterday. Apart, of course, from *Imbroglio*?"

"*Young Scientist, Vespa Newtown, Cooking Without Tears,* and *Elephant Boy*."

"Oh, of course. When does it start today, actually?"

"*Know Your Pony*'s on at ten-thirty," said Keith.

Giles smiled without opening his mouth. "Well, see you down here for that, then?"

"Right you are."

TWO

"How big's his cock, for instance?" inquired Diana, settling herself on the windowseat and placing the tea tray on Celia's crowded dressing table.

Celia winced as she strained to unscrew a jar of face cream. "Pretty big. Well above average. Ah, thank you, Diana. How big's Andy's?"

Diana sighed. "Enormous. When he's not on anything, of course." She sipped her tea, and asked, peering over her cup, "How often does Quentin fuck you?"

With white-plumed fingertips Celia dabbed at her variegated, spot-sprinkled face. The clear fact that Celia's complexion was so much worse than her own slightly mitigated Diana's disgust when Celia said, "Once a night, at least. And usually in the morning."

"Even when he's on something?"

"Especially then. That doesn't seem to affect Quentin. Sometimes when he's speeding he can go on for hours."

"Really?"

"Oh yes, hours." Celia stopped kneading her face in order to glance alertly at Diana. Then she resumed. "Once literally all night . . . How often does Andy?"

"Oh, every night—or in the morning. And sometimes at odd times during the day. How good is Quentin?"

Celia went vacant. Then she said: "Fantastic. And Andy?"

Diana couldn't go vacant so she went knowing. Then she said: "Fantastic."

There was a pause.

"One of the most beautiful things Quentin does," said his wife, "is talk."

"Big deal."

"No, I mean when we're making love."

"Oh," said Diana briskly, "Andy does that too. 'I'm going to fuck your fucking cunt till—' "

"Oh no. Not like that." Celia shook her head. "Quentin, Quentin says poetry."

"Oh. No." Diana shook her head. "Andy doesn't do that."

THree

Quentin and Andy were in fact playing darts in the garage. Between shots, they sipped Irish coffee from pint-sized mugs and passed thin, one-paper joints back and forth. Their tall bodies swayed indolently to the music from Andy's portable tape recorder. Whenever they were alone together there was always a pleasant tang in the air; it was not sexual tension so much as a mutual, agreed narcissism.

"Christ, what's that smell?" said Andy.

"It's the fungus on the boilers," said Quentin, "though no doubt deriving further piquancy from the aroma of little Keith's 'room.' "

"It's like bad chick." Andy accepted the darts Quentin offered him and walked to behind the chalk mark ten feet from the board. "Or like stale come—which figures."

"Why? What could little Keith possibly have to masturbate about?"

"Nothing," said Andy. "Nothing at all. But he's got plenty of visual aids."

"Oh, really? What's he got in there?"

Andy took his three throws before replying. "Just a great load of cunt magazines."

"What genre?"

"Yeah, he page-fucks the models. Banana shots. Guys with bent rigs being gobbled. Open beavers. One's with the cameraman halfway up the girls' bums."

"Oh. Just straight stuff then?"

"Beat me, beat me," said Andy warmly as one of his favorite LPs wound onto the tape. He strolled to the wall and plucked his darts from the board. "Nice arrows. Yeah, mostly. Diana took a look in there the other night. Says he's got one or two of dogs buggering some old woman."

"That sounds *very* sexy," said Quentin. "Oh, dear, poor little Keith."

"Yeah, he's a mess, isn't he?"

"Sort of baby's face on a dwarf's body."

"Like a sort of wrecky little doll."

"Breath like a laser beam," mused Quentin.

"Or an oxyacetylene burner."

"Fat as a pig."

"Smells like a compost heap."

"Or a dotard's mattress."

"Be bald as an egg by the time he's twenty-five."

"Or twenty-four."

"Or twenty-three."

"Or twenty-two."

"He's that now."

"At least."

"Yes," said Andy. "It's amazing, when you come to think of it, that he's so cheerful."

"Especially with us handsome bastards about the place."

"Check." Andy nodded, his eyes closed. "Check."

5: appleseed rectory

Are we presenting characters and scenes that are somehow fanciful, tendentious, supererogatory? Not at all. Quite the contrary. The reverse is the case. By the standards that here obtain Giles and Keith could be dismissed as pathetically introverted, Quentin and Andy as complacent and somewhat fastidious, and Celia and Diana as sadly, even quaintly, in-hibited. The household, indeed, considers itself a fortress for the old pieties, a stout anachronism, a bastion of the values it seems to us so notably to lack.

For we have gone on ahead a small distance in time. Our subjects are now mere adolescents, quite unaware of the shape their lives have begun to take. Let us glimpse them, then, in their transient innocence.

This summer, as we write, *Giles Coldstream* has just passed his Common Entrance and, following this coup, is holidaying victoriously at Monkenvale, the family seat, whose forty apartments are occupied by Giles, his mother, and a staff of thirteen. Giles is a radiantly unselfconscious little boy, rather undersized, brown-haired, eversmiling, the cossett of the house staff, the darling of the village, and shyly in love with the gardener's eldest son, who takes him fishing most afternoons and to the local cinema every Saturday and on alternate Wednesdays. Giles is accurately described by the cook as "such a sunny little thing"; he has moments of fore-boding, brief but intense, only when his mother wheels herself into his room at night and when he visits the dentist.

It is being a glorious summer also for *Andy Adorno,* who is no less enjoyably whiling away his vac as an assistant sorter in the Notting Hill post office. By law, Andy is too young for the job, but he looks older than he is and the people at the post office like him as much as most people seem to. They have agreed to pay him £22 per week, cash, with the conse-quence that Andy is buying a fair amount of cocaine on Friday evenings. Despite his experiments with this and any other drug he can get his hands on, he remains cheerful, rowdy and energetic. Furthermore, at what he calls "the vague commune in Earl's Court" where he has always lived, Andy encounters lots to eat and drink, plenty of friendly guys with all sorts of amazing musical instruments, and a con-tinuous stream of girls who keep on successfully trying to go to bed with him.

As usual, *Celia Evanston* is being toted round Europe by Aramintha Leitch, her stepmother, who is, as usual, between divorces. They are at this moment checking out of La Traviata in Monte Carlo and waiting for the Mercedes that will shortly take them to the Cannes Hilton. Lady Leitch, a small, ath-letic blonde, is being importuned variously and without success by the hotel manager, two hotel waiters, the janitor of the hotel swimming pool, and the *maître de* of the hotel dining room. The first wants Lady Leitch to settle her bill; the other four want to know when Lady Leitch will return so that they can all sleep with her again: to each the noblewoman gives her Hebridean address. Celia can be made out in the corner of the foyer sitting amid a pile of luggage and hatboxes. A hideous bellboy crouches beside her; their conversation is in French and has the cadences of recrimination and denial. Finally, the girl stands—small, fat, shock-haired, but with a certain assurance—glances at her stepmother, and says, *"Dix minutes."* The hideous bellboy spreads his hands, as if this is all he had asked, all anyone *could* ask. The couple disappears arm in arm.

Celia's future husband, *Quentin Villiers*, is thirty miles away, by the side of the Italy road. He is on a walkabout-hitchhike tour of Europe and this is his first real holiday without elderly chaperones of one sort or another. Thus, although he has little money and few contacts, his green eyes are perpetually bright with pure hedonistic anticipation. He stands in a lay-by with his duffelbag, dressed only in faded Rob-Crusoe jeans cut off well up the thigh. Quentin is already six-foot, tanned and aquiline; the traffic practically concertinas when he sticks out his thumb.

Diana, *Diana Parry*, is a mere shadow of her future self, a tall-for-her-age, severe-looking, badly coordinated girl with a narrow orange mouth and a sheet of black hair that hangs on her head like a paper-thin cowl. At present she is on her way from her mother's flat in London to her father's flat in Amsterdam. Her demeanor at Heathrow Airport is characteristic: she fumbles with her documents, drops her handbag, splinters fingernails on the suitcase handles, and is painfully conscious of the men's malevolent stares. Diana is particularly on edge today, having received a letter from her best friend Emily containing the ebullient postscript that Emily has just that minute begun to menstruate; this intelligence establishes Diana as not only the smallest-breasted but also the one nonpubescent girl in her coterie. While Diana is not at all sorry to leave her mother she is not especially anxious to see her father. She opens a magazine as the airplane accelerates along the runway.

And *Whitehead*? Thirteen years of age, Keith is at present

the subject of experimental (and, in the event, deleterious) gland-correction surgery in the Research Wing of the St. Pancras Hospital for Tropical Diseases. Since the age of five Whitehead has had always to observe a starvation diet to avoid grotesque obesity; with adolescence has come an explosion of fatty tissue, a hormonal influx that has alarmed even the most experienced of the hospital's dieticians. His three-strong, seventy-stone family trudges along two evenings a week; it sits and swears at Keith for half an hour ("The operation will be a complete bloody disaster, you realize," foretells Whitehead, Sr., enviously), then trudges off again, without good-byes. Little Keith excited so much revulsion in the public wards that the consultants were forced to move him into a private room. He will be discharged in five weeks' time; the doctors will pronounce him more fat-prone than ever but "as sane as can be expected." For the time being, Whitehead lies in pulsing, hot-faced, glandular silence by day and at night is the weeper of unreflecting tears.

These are the six that answer to our purposes, and we have taken them on ahead a small distance in time to Appleseed Rectory, a three-story structure which stands in the outskirts of the Hertfordshire village of Gladmoor. Gladmoor is still a village. It has survived the northern thrust of the London suburbs partly because of its inconvenient remoteness from the main intercity highways and partly because of its taxing proximity to the Luton Airport approach routes. Gladmoor has been conserved too, perhaps, by its capacity to astonish: straying down the one gray-brick road, seeing the wonky Edwardian streetlamps, the warped and splintery sign over the coach house, the great oaks which bend back toward the hills, visitors find it hard to expunge the sense of unreality, of suspension, which even the drumming aircraft cannot break, an aura of peace and sweetness almost as palpable as the integrity of the stone.

Approaching Appleseed Rectory from the direction of the village could be a particularly dislocating experience. When Quentin had sent directions to his American friends, for example, he had written: "Immediately after the hump-backed bridge, stop, get out of the car, and look hard to your left, and the house is inset twenty yards from the road. *It's there!*" With good reason: it was commonplace for regular callers at the house to speed down the road past it, U-turn, miss it again, and oblige garrulous locals to redirect them. Appleseed Rectory always seemed to be the color of the sky against which it was set. The off-white brick made it look like something in a monochrome photograph, or like a painting glimpsed through net curtains. It was exceptionally narrow, windowless at either end, and seen from the road it would sometimes melt back to a bodiless shimmer. In hot weather the sun would draw thermal gradients from the roadside stream, corrugating the house like an image on a rippling banner. On rainy afternoons it would appear completely to recede into the vaporous, hospital-gray medium of the sky.

And inside the house itself perspective seems no less unreliable. Everyone is always blacking out at Appleseed Rectory, and they can't remember farther back than a few days. Everyone tends to be either drunk or stoned or hungover or sick at Appleseed Rectory, and they have learned to be empirical about all sense perceptions. Everything is out of whack at Appleseed Rectory; its rooms are without bearing and without certainty. The inhabitants suffer, too, from curious mental complaints brought on by prolonged use of drugs, complaints that can be alleviated only by drugs of different kinds. And so Appleseed Rectory is a place of shifting outlines and imploded vacuums; it is a place of lagging time and false memory, a place of street sadness, night fatigue, and canceled sex.

More in a moment.

6: FaT CHaNCe

Keith was still wallowing on the sofa in the smaller Rectory sitting room when Quentin and Andy appeared in the doorway. Ten o'clock, Friday morning.

"It's drug time!" Andy announced.

"Oh, God," said Keith.

One among many of Whitehead's domestic posts was that of drug-tester. Two or three times a week Andy and Quentin would approach him with a pill, or a scrap of blotting paper, or a sac of powder, or a vial of fluid, or a sachet of crystals, or a moist sugar lump, which Keith would then be required to swallow or suck or sniff or (occasionally) inject. Quentin and Andy would tell him how long they expected the drug to take and would disappear for that period. On their return Keith would either be giggling and leaping about, or shaking his head and saying, "Nothing yet," or shivering with terror beneath the sideboard, or enjoying agreeable hallucinations, or asleep, or crying, or cleaning the kitchen, or locked in the broom closet, or vomiting crazily, or unconscious and very white. Sometimes, if the effects of the drug seemed to be irresistibly efficacious, Quentin and Andy would personally join Keith in the experiment. If the converse, they would take seats and, in a spirit of detached inquiry, watch; they would note how little Keith's pupils bulged and throbbed, discuss the way in which he would twitch and pant, observe how, in the final stages, his skin paled, his tongue went lizard-green, and his lips gashed gold-vermilion.

"Nothing very special today," Andy went on. "Just a pound for three from the black guy in the canteen. He's pretty reliable—for a Pakky—so it should be quite mild and won't last long."

"Up or down?" asked Keith warily.

Andy glanced at Quentin and said, "Down. But not far." His brisk manner returned. "Pins-and-needly feeling after half an hour or so—we think—then you ought to feel a bit sleepy, dizzy, queasy—but nice. A thing of the past within a couple of hours."

Whitehead narrowed his eyes. "No side-effects?"

"Absolutely not."

"It doesn't make your piss go all black like that stuff the other week?"

"Uh-uh."

"I won't have all that green gunge coming out of my ears?"

"Promise."

"I won't be up all night trying to crap?"

"No way."

"And, look, they don't make your cock retract like that powdered stuff you—"

"Actually," digressed Andy, "one guy's eyes came out on stalks when I hit him with some bad MDA, and his tongue went all—"

"Are you *sure* they don't muck up your cock, because I . . ." Keith stirred in his seat, settling on his buttocks as if they were cushions. "When's Lucy coming?"

"Lucy? Who knows?" said Quentin, appealing to Andy.

"Sometime this evening." Andy's gaze steadied. "Why?"

Whitehead sat up straight. "I'll give you three guesses!"

Quentin and Andy regarded each other uneasily. For Keith had said this in one of his "funny voices," an Americanized treble, as it might be Jiminy Cricket challenging Pinocchio with some pedagogic taunt.

"What?" said Andy.

"Cos I want some of the old *dippy-dippy-dippy!*"

Keith smiled at the silence as his words swung out into the room and hovered in the air above the round glass table. Each of them simultaneously became aware of a lone bird gurgling doggedly somewhere among the branches that swathed the sitting room windows.

"Dippy-dippy?" said Andy.

Keith strove on in a precarious Yogi Bear falsetto: "Dippy-dippy—the old in-out, in-out—dunking the dagger—some of the other—a bit of the old . . ." Whitehead trailed off.

Andy looked at Quentin again.

"Does he mean fucking, or what?"

"That's right," said Keith defeatedly, in his normal voice.

"Fucking Lucy?" asked Quentin.

"Mm. That's right. I only thought . . ."

Just then the telephone peeped and Quentin swayed across the room to answer it.

Andy joined Keith on the sofa. "Well, why the fuck didn't you say so, Keith?" Andy's tone grew earnest. "Keith, listen."

"What?"

"Don't ever speak in that voice again. Okay?"

"Okay."

"Christ, Keith. I really got the horrors for a moment. Thought you were going mad again."

"But I've used that voice before?"

"I know that," said Andy, "but don't ever use it again. Or any other of your funny voices. Okay? Now." He took a handful of pills from his pocket and sprinkled them onto the coffee table. "We'd really like you to take two, but they're semi-barbits so you won't be able to lush much, so one's okay, though I'd prefer it if you could handle two. I'll give you some for a present, but you—"

"Hey!" cried Quentin, muffling the telephone. One blue-jeaned leg emerged from the folds of Quentin's satin house-coat to rest on the arm of a nearby chair. "It's Lucy herself. Hello Lucy! And whose bed might you be in?" he asked, and started chuckling grandly at her reply.

Keith looked wildly around.

"Well, Lucy, if you *will* bathchair-snatch . . . Yes, once—for a dare. One moment, Andy should like a word. And when *are* you coming?" he added in an aggrieved voice. "Very well, see you then. No, I'm a one-girl guy now. The same to you."

As Quentin whisperingly handed the telephone to Andy, Keith took a pill from the small mound and rolled it thought-fully in his palm.

"Luce? Andy! Incredible. How many? Yeah? Mythical. And"—he turned and winked at Keith—"we've got a little surprise for *you*, too. Someone very anxious to make your acquaintance. You wait and see. Keith Whitehead. Well, he's tall, dark—ooh, about six-one, six-two?—chiseled features—"

Whitehead gave a groan of protest.

"—thick black hair, absolute dynamite in the cot, I hear, rich as Croesus—"

"Andy, please."

"—thin as a blade, but, what with his height, you know, really *built*—"

"An*dy*."

"—take him in yourself tonight. Okay, kid. Bye!"

The telephone chirruped faintly as Andy replaced the receiver and turned grinning to Quentin. "That's what they call a soft sell," Quentin remarked.

"You appreciate," said Keith hoarsely, "you appreciate what you've just done, don't you?" The shape of Keith's mouth was such that his upper front teeth were always partly exposed; now the semicircular stripe of chapped red rubber virtually obscured his nostrils.

Andy hurried across the room and crouched blinking in front of him. "What?"

"You've just, you've . . ."

"What? Now you take your pills like a good little boy. What have I done?"

Keith waved a hand impotently.

"C'mon, Mac, fill me in."

Keith rested his head against the back of the sofa and swallowed something deep in his throat. His voice was speedy and distant. "If you hadn't said those things to Lucy I might have had a slim chance—"

"Slim chance? Slim chance? Fat chance, boy, fat chance."

"I might have had a . . . Oh, *Christ*, I might have had a chance to make . . . Ah, how could *you* conceive—"

"To make a good impression?" interjected Quentin, who had been watching the squat pair with twinkly disinterest. "What Keith is trying to say, Andrew, is that he harbors doubts about living up to the rather stylized picture of himself with which you have just furnished Miss Littlejohn. That lady now expects to be welcomed by a tall, slender, dark, handsome stranger and—"

"—And all she'll get is fat, fair, rough, little Keith. Yeah, of course, but I was only fucking about—she knows that. Christ, where's your sense of humor?"

"Well, Keith. Satisfied?"

Whitehead wasn't. "I was hoping you'd sort of talk to her, Andy, use your influence." He gestured at the pills. "I do you all these favors, couldn't you ask her to do me one?"

Andy seemed genuinely puzzled. "Why not just try her, like anyone else?"

"Look at me." Keith spread out his arms. He appeared to be about to cry. "I'm not like anyone else."

"I can't . . ." Andy clicked his tongue and stood up. "*Okay*. I'll, you know, I'll—*Christ* I hate all this pervert talk. Now fuckin' take those pills, Keith, and let's have no more of this shit."

When Andy had left the room Quentin walked over to the sofa and sat down on its arm. "Try not to be hurt by what Andy says," he murmured. "I dote on him, as you know, but I'm afraid that—if he has a fault—it might be a certain parsimony of imagination."

"Pardon?"

"I mean he tends to assume that everyone is very much like himself. Keith, are you all right?"

Whitehead sniffed and ran a finger along the isthmus that separated his nose and his mouth, collecting a bubble of snot which he wondered vaguely where to deposit. Quentin held out his fringed silk sudary and Keith blew into it with grateful enthusiasm. It had occurred to him, working on the assumption that insensitivity must have its limits, that Andy had seen no important connection between Keith's ill looks and his ability to attract Lucy, that it might be all one to her, that she was as undiscriminating as people regularly suggested she was; but Quentin's compassionate words had burst even this tiny pimple of expectation. Keith sniffed again. "I don't care any more, anyway," he said.

"Keith, you must never talk like that," said Quentin.

The room paled as a cloud passed between it and the sun, then brightened again. Quentin leaned forward and gently tousled Keith's hair: the artfully posed strands scattered beneath his palm to divulge a broad area of unoccupied scalp. Quentin's fingers retreated.

"Don't worry," he said softly. "I'll make sure something unusual happens to you this weekend. Something or other, if not with Lucy."

7: PENTHOUSE CLOUDSCAPE

Lucy Littlejohn lived in a top-floor Knightsbridge maisonette with three other girls. It was not by any means an atypical household and we would do well to look at it closely. On a normal day they rise between one and two in the afternoon either for long Badedas ablutions in the luxury bathroom or scathing showers in the downstairs closet. Then, while the color television flashes and rumbles in the background, they sprawl about the sitting room in nighties and dressing gowns, angelically aglow in the penthouse cloudscape, sipping coffee from French-style bowls and talking about their respective nights out. At four they wander off to shop in Sloane Street and Beauchamp Place, returning at six for glasses of Tio Pepe and further chat before drifting upstairs to change. Between telephone calls they flit in and out of each other's rooms to borrow scent, swap tights, crave advice. Their voices glide out from brightly lit bedrooms to congregate in the dusky landing; the conversation might lead one to believe that they are restaurant critics, nightlife pundits, gossip columnists, incognito bailiffs; they are not. At nine, the taxis and limousines start to arrive.

All the girls have what they call "daytime lovers," but only Lucy habitually sacrifices her financial affairs to her amatory ones, a tendency apotheosized and, ironically, terminated by the handsome, insolvent Adorno. They met the summer before. Andy had run up to her in Pont Street and said, brushing the hair out of his eyes and not smiling, "Hey—why don't you let me come home with you now?" "Yes, all right," Lucy had said at once. They walked to her flat in silence, with tight chests and almost equal shares of surprise. "I wouldn't have asked," Andy said diffidently as he entered Lucy's room, "but you looked so nice."

And she was nice. Short brown-and-blond hair, big violet eyes, her innumerable saris, veils, beads, jewels, belts, garters, scarves not entirely obscuring her friendly figure, a forty-tooth smile and a deafening laugh, areas of mild grease showing through her elaborate though hastily applied makeup, worn-thin shiny patched jeans, lucent orange skin visible beneath her stained and holey blouse, immaculate white underwear. For fifty-five consecutive evenings Andy appeared, smudged and steaming from his holiday job in a Westminster timber yard, bearing a bottle of wine, some hash perhaps, and a toothbrush. For eight weeks Andy talked to Lucy about politics and the American novel, played her the derelict guitar he had restrung and unwarped (Lucy found this embarrassing at first but soon got not to mind it), told her about his life, and made high-powered love to her two or three times a night. And for two months Lucy paid no rent.

On the fifty-sixth evening Mitzi and Serena were waiting by the intercom when Andy let himself in. "Who're you seeing tonight—Louis Quinze?" he said, sweeping past them into the sitting room, where he was hushedly informed by Lucy that her flatmates' plans for the evening might well have fallen through and that he wasn't to vex them further, particularly in view of the fact that she was a little bit behind with the rent. But Adorno, biting the screwtop from a double liter of wine as he flicked off the television and picked up the guitar, wasn't listening; he had seen "the plastic trio" (his sobriquet for Lucy's friends) only once or twice and had betrayed no interest in them whatever. Ten minutes later the intercom whined, there was renewed activity in the hall, and Andy peered round to see a tiny Burmese gentleman dressed in gray military uniform. "Fucking with soldiers now, are they?" he said. The midget relayed to Mitzi and Serena someone's compliments and apologies and held up a huge floral wreath over which the two girls fluttered apathetically.

Swearing and grumbling, the girls staggered in from the hall. Mitzi made for the telephone as Serena flopped down splay-legged in an armchair. "What's with the midge?" Andy asked. "Here, try this wine." Serena shook her head. "Euch," said Mitzi. Andy looked curiously at Lucy before dipping his head in fierce accompaniment to his guitar.

"Look," Mitzi told the telephone, "if you don't want to fuck just say so. It'll be a good fuck. It'll be a very good fuck." The telephone replied but Mitzi, who was in the process of accepting a cigarette and a light from Serena, could respond only with an angry hum of negation. "No—no—no cash! Two good fucks just for something to *do*. Yeah, Serena's here, so are there any, you know, is that . . . Heimito, or whatever the hell his name is . . . ? *Oh no, oh* no—you *send* a cab. . . ." Mitzi appeared to be on the point of authentic fury when something the telephone said calmed her. "Okay, okay, hon. Come get us. Ciaow." She hung up, spreading her palms at Serena, who shrugged.

"Everything together?" asked Lucy.

Mitzi must have caught irony in Lucy's tone. "Yeah," she said, "and you better get *your*self together pretty soon. This place doesn't run on buttons."

A faraway murmur quite suddenly became a roar as the sound of a low-flying helicopter battered against the windows before receding again into the distance.

"Who was that?" snapped Mitzi. "Bob?"

Parting the curtains, Serena consulted her watch. "Uh-uh. Too early. Must be Gary."

"Right. He said he'd be going late this weekend. Christ, that Jap."

"No, he was from Burma, wasn't he?"

"Yeah, well what the fuck difference does it make?" asked Mitzi.

"Not a hell of a lot."

Simultaneously the girls became aware that Andy's strumming had ceased, that Andy was staring at Lucy, that Lucy had curled up on her chair and was swaying from side to side with her arms wrapped tightly round herself. Mitzi and

Serena stirred, but Andy directed his gaze at them with such venomous contempt that they were both silenced by a rush of physical fear.

Andy shuddered. Then, with a relaxed, almost negligent wave of his arm, he splintered the guitar on the steel coffee table in front of him. "Lucy," he said, when the silence had quietened, "is this the way you are? Are you like this?" He sighed. "Lucy, go upstairs and pack a bag and come home with me. If you owe these dogs money, I'll pay it. If you're in trouble, I'll take care of it. Pack a bag and let's get the fuck out of here."

Lucy crumpled a bit into her chair, of course, saddened perceptibly and grew smaller and shook her head in token distraction; but she knew she wasn't going anywhere. She shook her head.

Awed as much by his offer as the fact that Lucy had refused it, Andy stood up, toyed momentarily with the idea of kicking Mitzi or raping Serena, looked round for more things to smash, saw nothing, and so contented himself with upending the table, spitting on the carpet, and breaking the lock of the front door as he left.

All this—or very nearly all this—Diana knew. And as she moved about the bedroom methodically assembling and pairing off Andy's drumsticks, stooping to pick up plectrums and harmonicas from the floor, righting the stack of guitars in the corner, restoring flutes and penny whistles to their boxes and records to their sleeves, bundling together his boyishly stained underpants and pleasingly aromatic T-shirts, blinking at moments of surprised emotion when she noticed his gym shoes placed side by side in the wardrobe or his beloved horse-brass saxophone strap laid out on the desk, Diana attempted to organize her responses to the history. Although she had screwed the above information out of Andy in a playful, bantering spirit, and with due reverence for his potent outrage and sexy disgust, it was with genuine and lasting pain that she thought about these early days with Lucy: equally, although she had screwed the following information out of him in a reproachful, judicious spirit, with due condemnation of his vengefulness and cruelty, it was with genuine heart-quickening glee that she thought about these later episodes.

Diana swayed to a halt, turned, and met her eye in the wardrobe glass.

A week later, the following Friday, Andy went round to the flat, apologized to Serena and Mitzi (and also to the tanned Isabella, who had just flown in from Morocco), led the tearful, bewildered Lucy upstairs, made sarcastic love to her ("I think I Mailered her, actually—up her bum"), slapped her about a bit, and stalked off, leaving his unopened pay packet on the dressing table. The next night he appeared with Quentin, very drunk; he led Lucy up to her room again, made her strip at fistpoint, summoned Quentin and urged him to copulate with her while he watched from the corner, drinking wine and chuckling malevolently; Quentin said a lot of things like "Andy, really," and "Isn't this all rather . . ." and "Honestly, I *do* think . . . ," but a combination of lust, alcohol and an anxiety not to seem a killjoy persuaded him to go ahead, and he did so with style and virtuosity. Lucy was then required to perform fellatio on Andy, who from time to time offered to knock her fucking head off whether she swallowed it or not, while Quentin dressed.

"No, man, it's creative," Andy told Quentin as they stumbled together down the stairs, "—radical rape, for her own fuckin' good. Anyway, I paid her yesterday."

Before leaving, the pair looked in on the sitting room. Andy exposed himself to each of the girls in turn, asked a television producer if he would like his face beaten to pulp, burst into tears, exhorted the entire company to go eat shit, and blacked out.

Andy's pranking continued just as engagingly when term started at London that September, though his visits became rarer and much less virulent. Once a fortnight or so, he and his friends would club together for the necessary £20 (it was Andy who insisted on this token, not Lucy) and roll round to Pont Street for some laughs. Customarily Lucy would do an elaborate strip for them, masturbate some of them, go to bed with one or two perhaps, and ask for a few minutes with Andy. Lucy seemed to have entered into the spirit of things by this time; she cried every now and then when Andy made love to her personally, alone, but on the whole she was resigned to the status Andy kept insisting was her true one.

She didn't know why she had refused Andy's offer yet neither could she claim that she regretted her refusal. The exuberance of her character insulated Lucy for the role; as soon as Andy's vindictive hostility appeared to have dissipated, after his first few raids on her person, there was nothing abject in her displays and nothing cringing in her submissions, merely a kind of inevitability.

But next it was Giles's turn, and here Andy's scheme suffered its first major reverse.

The sickly waif was shoved into the flat one navy-blue November night and beamingly introduced by Andy: "Here she is—do anything for fifty quid." They sat smalltalking in the kitchen. GILES: How long, in actual fact, have you lived here? LUCY: Ooh, nearly a year. GILES: Oh, really? Because it's really . . . very nice, actually. LUCY: It ain't a lot, but it's home. GILES: In fact, how long did you say you'd lived here for? ANDY: Look, man, you don't have to do all that. They're all whores here.

Giles and Lucy were duly cheered up the stairs. Once in her room, Lucy went confidently over to the bed, smiled, and began to undo her shirt. "Actually," said Giles, producing an enormous flask from his hip pocket, "do you mind if we don't do anything, actually? I'll still give as much money as you like. I've got money, but I'm a bit . . . nervous. I mean, please don't think I'm a pervert or anything." "How old are you, Giles?" "Twenty and a half." "Have you had girlfriends?" "Oh yes. Only I just don't feel like it these . . . Though I think you're jolly attractive: you've got awfully nice . . ." (Giles was going to say "teeth"; but this merely reminded him of why he didn't feel like it.) "Okay, love, you can just lie here for a bit—don't worry, I won't sneak on you—and then go." "Gosh, thanks." Which he did, writing her out a blank check as he left.

What Andy had so tragically forgotten was that in many respects Giles was the dream man for Lucy: kind, pleasant if rather vacuous in appearance, amusing in his way, gentle, affectionate, and quite extraordinarily rich. Having instructed his solicitors to pay off all her debts, Giles entrusted Lucy with his billfold and gave her a free hand, happy to go to any restaurants, cinemas, or clubs she suggested, to take a pullman to Brighton or a Daimler to the Lakes, and vetoing only overtly teeth-imperiling enterprises. After their eleventh night together Giles awoke with (i) not too much of a hang-over and (ii) an erection, with which he shyly confronted Lucy and subsided trembling in her arms. They were inseparable all that winter.

The affair ended, as did so much else for Giles, when he wobbled down the staircase of the Old Compton Street Wheeler's, lost—co-instantaneously—his footing and Lucy's hand, tripped, fell, and smacked out his front two caps on the Soho pavement.

During Giles's three-month convalescence in various rural sanatoria, Andy cautiously remade Lucy's acquaintance. They agreed to contact each other whenever they felt sad or lonely, to confide in each other, to help each other in times of need, to be friends.

Diana's face was beginning to darken when Andy came into the room.

"Amazing," he said. "You've cleaned up all my stuff. My harps, too." He went over to his desk. "That's a bad horse-brass," he said approvingly, nodding his head.

Diana did not look up. "When is she coming?"

"Yeah, she rang. This afternoon sometime, early this evening."

Andy knelt, stroked back a handful of Diana's expensive black hair and planted a kiss on her temple. "Thanks, man," he said.

Although Diana was aware that this was Andy's "way" of apologizing for his earlier shortness, and also that by his standards it was an act of almost obsequious gallantry, she still felt the need not to respond, and turned away.

"Well," suggested Andy, "fuck *you*."

8: FROM THE PAIN

Quentin pursued little Keith into the kitchen. Behind them came Andy, in some distress.

"C'mon, Keith," he said, "any *action*?"

Keith woggled out a chair from under the table and sat down, the better to face the huge beauties who prowled round in front of him. He glanced at his watch. "How long—?"

"I know how long, you little spaz." Andy clapped his hands together. "An *hour*. If there's—"

A loud crash from the slammed back door was followed by the familiar fat-thighed shuffle of Mrs. Fry, the woman who charred three mornings a week for Appleseed Rectory, as she made her grunting way down the passage toward the kitchen.

Asway with frustration, Andy gripped the back of a chair and began to plead, "Look, if they're not fuckin' working now, they're—"

"Hey hey hey," interrupted Quentin, making compassionate, pacific nods with his head. "Not in front of the servants, Andrew."

Andy leaned back against the dresser. "Okay," he said in a strained voice. "*Okay*."

"Morning all!" A face that resembled that of a cruel pig wearing an onion-shaped blond toupee flashed with unsettling speed around the door.

"Good morning to you, Mrs. Fry," said Quentin. "How may we assist you?"

"Just want the mops, Mr. Villiers, thank you." There was a silence. Mrs. Fry stared at Quentin for a moment with what might have been appalled desire then barged past Keith's "outstretched" legs toward the broom closet. A smell of Domestos, baby powder, and aged sweat flew up into the air.

Whitehead looked at Mrs. Fry askance, largely due to the fact that he had made a highly unsuccessful pass at her the month before. Keith had been lying on his bunk, wondering what use to put to the early morning erection which he so painfully nursed, considering whether to reach down for a handful of the magazines that glistened beneath his bunk. Mrs. Fry had called from the garage that she wanted access to the brushes stored in his room. Whitehead bade her enter and, when she knelt down with her back to him, leaned forward in hot pajamas to cup the gauzy pink bosom of her apron. Mrs. Fry turned around and hit little Keith so hard on his right ear that he immediately burst out crying—not out of shock or frustration, merely from the pain.

"Got everything, Mrs. Fry?"

"Yes, thank you, Mr. Villiers." She smiled to reveal false teeth of perfect whiteness. " 'Scuse!" she hooted at Keith, who smartly wedged his legs under the chair.

"Fuck," said Andy absentmindedly to himself, adjusting his heavy groin with both hands, "these jeans don't half get to your snake."

"Allow me," said Quentin, holding open the door past which Mrs. Fry disappeared. Quentin turned to Andy. "Well, I think you showed admirable restraint, Andy." There was perhaps the tiniest hint of real disapproval in his voice?

"Mm? Oh, that," said Andy. "The fuck, she just licks the floors around here." Anger returned to him like a jolt of electricity. He swooped down once again on little Keith. "Nothing? Not even dazed, hazy, not with it, vague, loose—"

Keith, who had protruded his lower lip ominously from the word "hazy" on, said, "Not a thing, Andy."

Andy shook his head as if to clear it. He started back, spun round full circle, and returned his gaze imploringly to Keith. "Take two more. Take four more. Take—"

"Slow down, Andy," said Quentin. "You've just been burnt, that's all."

"You'd better not be fucking with me," Andy told Keith hopefully.

"They just don't work, Andy."

"That *fuckin'* *boogie!*" Andy began to windmill his arms in incredulous rage. "Jesus! 'Yey, man, is forking good, be my fren, forking con your ass.' Forty pounds!" Andy took the flat, one-ounce tobacco tin out of his pocket and crashed it on the table, over which it slid to belly-rattle on the kitchen floor. Andy straightened, and said with abrupt calm, "I'm going to go beat him up. Coming?"

"Yes, I'll just get my coat," said Quentin. "Keith, if Celia asks tell her I shan't be more than twenty minutes."

"What are you intending to do to him, Andy," asked Keith when Quentin had left the room.

Andy held up a large-knuckled, many-ringed fist. "Either he's going to give me my money back *and* all the drugs I can carry or I'm going to kick the absolute shit out of him. I tell you, he's going to be one sorry boogie when I . . . *Quentin!*"

Andy's motorbike snarled into life. Keith heard the door shut again, the motorbike letting go with a whirl of gravel, and the gears changing eagerly as it raced down the village street. With slightly agitated movements Keith leaned to retrieve the tin of pills, which he snapped open. He stared at its contents for several seconds.

9: GIN AND TEARS

"Glug glug glug," whispered Giles to himself, swirling the lime juice in its prefrosted beaker and holding it up to the light. "Glug glug glug glug glug."

Seen from outside his window Giles Coldstream might have been mistaken for a crazy scientist were it not for the amiable blandness of his face. The desk over which he was hunched was a fizzing, gargling laboratory of martini shakers, electric stirrers, corkscrews, siphons, ice buckets, glass coolers, lemon peelers, spoons.

Without taking his eyes from the misted beaker Giles reached out gropingly with his right hand until it settled on the lumpy green bottle of Gordon's gin, which he then unscrewed, upturned, and frowned at. "Ah. Empty," he said.

Giles sauntered the length of the room, opened the double doors of his vast teak drinks cupboard, selected a bottle of gin from the off-license-sized rank on the top shelf, and returned to his desk. Giles filled the tall beaker almost to the brim, adding, by way of an afterthought, scolding himself for his forgetfulness, a squirt of tonic. He sipped quizzically. "Delicious." Giles sipped again, more candidly this time, and ambled back to the bed. A creased Penguin of Iris Murdoch's *The Black Prince*, the tale of a sixty-year-old man's romance with a twenty-year-old girl, lay open on his pillow. He read a few more pages before disappointment at Miss Murdoch's continual shirking of the question of the protagonists' difference in teeth caused him to toss the book scathingly under his bed. "You can't 'suspend disbelief' forever," he remarked. From the pile of hardbacks which *The Black Prince* joined— *Teeth, Oral Hygiene: The Facts, The History of the Denture, A Dentist's Day, The Tooth*—our good Giles selected one at random and sank with foreboding into the deep pillows.

Twenty pages later there was a firm rap on his bedroom door. "Giles?"

He peered woefully over his book. "Yes?"

"Telephone."

"Who is it, actually?"

"Some old woman."

"No. I meant outside the door. Who are *you*?"

"Celia."

"Ah. Now Celia—couldn't you just sort of—"

"What? Look—" Celia fought with the handle. "—I can't—".

"Hang on." Giles swung his body off the bed and toddled over to the door, whose three bolts he threw back and which he opened a few millimeters.

When Giles saw Celia he screamed.

"Gosh, sorry about that," he said afterward. "I didn't really recognize you." Celia had a lardlike cream pack on her face and had brushed her hair out tangentially from her big square head. She looked like an anemic golliwog. "Look, um, uh . . ." Giles snapped his fingers weakly.

"Celia."

"Celia. Look—Celia—it may be my mother. In fact, it is. Do you think you could very kindly tell her I'm ill?"

"No, I'm afraid I couldn't. I've already told her you're well."

"I see. Am I right in thinking you've got a telephone in your room? May I take it in there?"

Celia swiveled and after a moment's hesitation Giles followed her across the landing.

"What's happened to your telephone?"

"I cut the wire," said Giles, not without pride.

Celia preceded him into the room and pointed to the telephone on the windowseat. "Whatever for?" she asked.

"The sudden ringing gives me such a fright sometimes. I thought I might fall over one of these days and knock out . . ."

Giles was going to say "some teeth," but he fell silent, blank and becalmed in the doorway.

"Well, you'd better answer it now you're here."

"Oh! Thank you . . . Celia."

Celia repaired to her dressing table. She took up the hairbrush with a roll of her eyes. "You stink of gin, you know."

"Do I?" asked Giles, faintly intrigued. "No, I didn't know that." Giles then gave Celia one of his smiles, which is to say he compressed and elongated his lips. "Hello? Mother? Oh, hello. This is Giles here. I'm very well, indeed, thank you —awfully well. Ah, no, now, today *isn't* a good day, actually. Oh, I've got lots of things I must do. Jolly busy indeed. And tomorrow, do you see, is Sunday, and one can't very well— If it were *Saturday* tomorrow then nothing would be simpler than to . . . Are you sure?" Giles muffled the receiver and looked up groggily at Celia. "Today wouldn't be Friday, would it? Oh, dear." He contemplated the telephone unhappily. "What? Yes, mother, you were right. Saturday it is then. Perfect. Well! I suppose I shall be along to see you then. Good-bye. And I love *you*."

Giles stood up; he gazed out of the window for a few seconds. "Look. Here come Andy and your husband on their motorbike," he murmured. He turned to leave.

"What's the matter with your mother these days, anyway?"

"Only mad. Just mad. Mad as anything."

Back at his desk Giles quickly prepared, and as readily swallowed, a tall, refreshing glass of lime, tonic, ice, gin and tears.

So now everyone else is beginning to gather in the kitchen.

Adorno, still loosening up after his exertions with Kashdrahr Khoja, lumbers hungrily round the room, jogging, ducking, feinting. Diana, dressed in a white vest-and-panty scants suit, smoking a gold-tipped menthol cigarette, watches him with mild distaste. Little Keith sits at the table; he has a profound, all-pervasive testicular stomach ache, for which he thanks the corduroy trousers that miraculously contain the lower half of his body; he sports also a beige fishnet Fred Perry which smells of old cars, and boots so high heeled that he was required to lower himself into them from a chair: when the opportunity presents itself, little Keith pays his undivided attention to Diana's breasts. Owing to her pains at the altar of her dressing table, the wide-boned face of Celia Villiers enjoys a sleek, vinyl radiance, as fortuitously does her body, roped in a complex of floral bands which splay at the waist into a leather-lined jungle skirt. She halfheartedly berates her husband for vanishing just when his friends were due to arrive. Quentin, for his part, argues that Andy was in no state to be left alone with the mischievous blackie—whom he had half killed as it was. "Relax," says Andy, shadowboxing in the corner. "I only batted him around a bit—keeps the boy in line." It's midday, exactly twelve o'clock. The sun sends planks of light in through the ribbed kitchen window.

The battered '78 Chevrolet sweeps up the pebbled, semicircular approach and drifts dustily to a halt, sending a squirt of gravel into the oblong rosebed five yards from the front door. An ironic hush falls as the three Americans detach themselves from the car. Stretching, and now straightening up, hands on hips, to assess the house, they turn to one another with squinting smiles until a sudden movement from the kitchen alerts them to the presence of their observers. Three faces grow shrewd.

Everyone except little Keith moved instinctively out into the hall.

"The weekend starts here," said Quentin.

X: QUENTIN

"The only remotely vexing thing about the aeroplane crash that killed my parents," the Honorable Quentin Villiers is fond of saying, "—the only thing about the news that didn't make one simply weep with joy—is that my brother Neville survived it. . . . Apart from vacs I led a rather somber and enclosed childhood—Christ's Hospital, Winchester, The House —and I knew Neville only as the overweight and generally hopeless young man who paid biannual visits to the seat in order to bore and rob my parents—who anyway deserved no better, I don't think I need add. Happily, though, Neville is eighteen years my senior, a homosexual, and an alcoholic. I was mightily cheered to learn recently, too, that while holidaying in nubile Indonesia (he pretends to be an agronomist), Neville contracted an admirably tenacious strain of syphilis, fore and aft, a strain which frequent calls on a reputedly rather depressing venue far south of the river have done nothing whatever to arrest, let alone cure. I dine with him as often as I think anyone well could at White's where I note his deterioration with a potent joy. He suffers appallingly also from gout, of course—a great Villiers infirmity, gout, an attractive complaint on the whole, though one that I have so far been spared. His blood pressure is alarmingly high; his heart capricious; I hourly await news of his death." (At this point Quentin usually takes Celia's hand or glances at her silkily.) "I shall inherit, then, in the none too distant future. At least—thank God—Neville had the gumption to wrest my father's money from him a decade before his timely death. I don't imagine for a moment that my brother will see out another decade, so these ghastly death duties are sure to be levied this time. The estate should nevertheless be enough to keep us in tolerable comfort for the rest of our lives, and a title still helps. I wonder if I shan't fight to reverse this pernicious ten-year ruling when I come to sit in the Lords. . . . But until then I shall continue to live, firstly, off my wife—who has some money of her own, thank heaven—and, secondly, off my own modest salary, which, as everyone here knows, I never tire of finding means to supplement. Cheers!"

Obviously Quentin was an adept at character stylization, a master of pastiche, a connoisseur of verbal self-dramatization —and he needed to be. Although affiliated with London University Quentin was the only member of the household who wasn't supposed to be taking a degree there. Instead, he ran— more or less singlehanded—the university newspaper, a satirico-politico-literary magazine called *Yes*. Acquiring the editorship had been a singularly painless business. Quentin went along to the interview carrying a portfolio of anonymous learned articles which he hadn't written, a stack of laboriously forged references, and a mawkish panegyric from the homosexual literary editor of a Sunday newspaper. He needn't have bothered: the reviews were never checked, the references never taken up. When Quentin walked into the board room, a silver Lycidas in a clinging white chamois suit, a sigh of longing was heaved in unison by the entire committee. While Quentin outlined his editorial plans the delegates could only gaze meltingly into his champagne eyes; when he finished, a languid exchange of nods and smiles took place and Quentin was offered thanks for his attendance. No further candidates were seen.

And Quentin's editorial work was a *jeu d'esprit*, a personal *tour de force*.

To begin with he wrote most of the book reviews himself. He would allow a cooling-off period after publication, collate and synthesize the notices of rival journals, find the points on which they agreed, and rewrite them in the inimitable *Yes* style. Hence, the unanimous verdict that the prose of a novel was ornate and self-conscious would lead Quentin to write:

So-and-so's sentences read like a frenzied collage of George Eliot at her most sententious and James Joyce at his most abstruse.

And when drunk:

> So-and-so's book reads like a drunken compositor's rendering of the maddened yelps of Henry James and Gertrude Stein locked in verbal *soixante-neuf*.

Or, if a biographer were generally held to have been insensitive in the handling of his subject's private life, Quentin would remark:

> So-and-so's dirty little fingers rifle through his subject's private life like a hick detective investigating a pimp's account book.

When stoned:

> So-and-so cavorts through the dignified hideaway of his subject's private life with all the tact and discretion of a lobotomized orang-utan which has just sat on a hedgehog.

Or, if a literary critic were widely felt to have been overgenerous to his chosen author, Quentin would note:

> If so-and-so were anyone to go by, Shakespeare would be reduced to an imitator of McGonagall when compared to the writer on whom he so shamelessly fawns.

And on speed?

> So-and-so's drooling idolatry of his author makes Tennyson's praise of Wellington look like a neck-scissors and body-slam followed by a forearm-smash.

And so on. The reviews, seldom more than a couple of hundred words, didn't claim to be definitive; but they were, as you see, "lively," together with being basically "sound." Quentin inserted formidable bylines, such as O. Seltnizt and D. R. S. M. Mainwairing, names that tended to correspond to numbered bank accounts here and abroad. On the rare occasions on which Quentin felt bound to commission reviews he would get Celia to type them out and return them with a printed slip reading:

> Dear Sir/Madam: The Editor regrets that he is unable to use the contribution kindly submitted to him and returns it herewith.

Quentin never bothered to cross out the *Sir* or the *Madam*, and yet he always bothered to write on the back:

> I've seen some shitty pieces in my time but by Christ your ———— really takes the cake. Unimaginative, sloppily written, poorly reasoned, ill-informed—I could go on. Were you drunk when you wrote it, or is the whole thing a joke? Either way, I shan't be needing any work from you. QV.
> Return the book immediately.

Two months later the review would appear, usually in the Round-Up columns, partly reshuffled and totally rewritten. The contributors often suspected malpractice but they were too young, baffled, and ashamed to take the matter further. The fierce esteem in which Quentin was held quickly silenced any direct complaint to the university and in most cases the only reprisals Quentin received were sheepish letters asking for another chance.

As regards the political side of the paper Quentin filled his pages with hate pieces too scabrous and extreme to be printed elsewhere; his correspondence columns were acknowledged to be the most compelling in modern journalism. The writers didn't care about payment, and besides Villiers explained that *Yes* was nonprofit-making. The remainder of the magazine was bulked out with vicious gossip about imaginary persons ("Anthea K. tells me that Henry W.'s erection problems continue to torment them"), rather good satire, exposés culled from celebrity acquaintances, Andy's erudite though often loosely argued contemporary music page (unpaid, but he wanted the records and concert tickets), and Quentin's excellent film and theater reviews. Production was handled, for a derisory wage, by little Keith, who had been brought several times to physical collapse with printers' errands and whose eyesight had been reduced from 20–20 to partial blindness by the speed-perpetuated galley-reading sessions that Quentin forced him to complete.

Yes was an astonishing success. Quentin charmed the big names into contributing and everyone else into subscribing. Circulation tripled, and, after a turquoise-suited Quentin was photographed on the front cover (caption: Yes *Editor Quentin Villiers talking at conference to James Altman and Professor English Hoenikker, both off camera*), the magazine won outspoken praise from William Burroughs, Gore Vidal, Angus Wilson, and a quorum of distinguished intellectuals.

Quentin is a superman. The versatility of the fellow! He can talk all day to a butcher about the longevity of imported meats, to an airhostess about safety regulations in the de Gaulle hangars, to an insurance salesman about postdated transferable policies, to a poet about nontypographical means of distinguishing six-syllable three-line stanzas and nine-syllable two-line ones, to an economist about pre-war counterinflationary theory, to a zoologist about the compensatory eye movements of the iguana. Just so, he can address a barrow boy in rhyming slang, a tourist in yokel French, a Sunderlander in Geordie, a Newmarket tout in genteel Cambridgeshire, a gypsy in Romany. He can mimic not only types but intimates too. He can bring Giles out of his room calling "Mother?" send Whitehead scurrying into the garage with a cackle from Mrs. Fry, cause Andy to rebuke the wordless Diana from going on at him, convince his own wife that it is not he who sits in a darkened room. These imitative gifts are matched by the astounding versatility of his physical presence. Quentin can silence a cocktail party just by walking into it or, alternatively, cruise around the room for half an hour and listen to people complain about his nonarrival. He can swank into the Savoy in T-shirt and jeans or sidle dinner-jacketed through the Glasgow slums. He can halt a conference with a movement of his little finger and yet sit so invisibly that directors start to discuss his salary without realizing he's there. "Or so it seems," Quentin is fond of saying, "—and that's all it needs to do."

Watch Quentin closely. Everyone else does. Stunned by his good looks, proportionately taken aback by his friendliness and accessibility, flattered by his interest, struck by the intimacy of his manner and lulled by the hypnotic sonority of his voice—it is impossible to meet Quentin without falling a little bit in love.

11: THE HUMAN WIGWAM

Does he know, for instance, what I'm feeling now? wondered Whitehead, as Quentin, glancing back into the kitchen before unbolting the front door, favored him with an oddly piercing, oddly meek, smile, the corners of his fine mouth curving downward at either end.

Did he know what it was like to be introduced to a girl a foot taller than oneself, the dwarfish humiliations involved in shaking hands with somebody practically twice one's height, the sneaky web of tensions that obtain when a person measuring four-foot-eleven (or "five-one," in Keith's parlance) meets a fellow human being who has cleared the magic divide of five-foot-six? For the Americans, Whitehead had established by peering in tiptoed apprehension out of the kitchen window on the way to the hall, seemed to have been selected to illustrate the elementary differences possible in the standard Earthling hominid: one rangy pale giant with cropped white hair and plasticene limbs; one tuft-faced goblin whose plaited brown braids extended to his waist; and . . . Roxeanne, it must have been, one of those terrifying, genetics-experiment, centerfold American girls—well over six feet in her platforms, a bonfire of lambent red hair, breasts like zeppelins, large firm high backside, endless legs. During his buildup to the ordeal, Keith had had a prayer that he would be able to suffer it in a sedentary, and thus unexposed, posture. Now, watching Quentin gambol out with a cheer to embrace the newcomers, and watching Celia approach the four in a solemn, formalized step, Whitehead began to see the full horror of what was in store for him.

Quentin held out a hand to his wife and turned to his friends. "Marvell . . . Skip . . . Roxeanne," he said huskily, gazing from one face to another, ". . . take my wife in."

There was a pause. Celia then moved forward to join the circle of arms, where she was embraced by each in turn and kissed on either cheek by Roxeanne and firmly on the mouth by Skip and Marvell. Grouping in a circle, the quartet leaned inward and touched foreheads. Besting his emotion, Quentin looked toward the porch, within which Andy, Diana, and Whitehead were uncertainly arranged. Quentin's voice was lusty, brave: "Come on!" he cried.

"Fuck this," sighed Diana.

"C'mon, it's only tender," Andy told Diana before striding out into the drive.

Queasily Keith watched Andy kiss Roxeanne—with in-decorous relish, he thought—and link arms crossways with

Marvell and Skip. Five foreheads touched. Whitehead looked up at Diana. "To hell with this, eh?" he pleaded.

Diana, more out of a reluctance to be with the loathsome Keith than a desire to be with the others, glanced at him in tired contempt and left him alone at the front door. A rather stiffer version of the Celia ritual was enacted, then the entire pyramid of legs, arms, and faces turned expectantly toward the tiny boy.

Keith was still reviewing various gambits—run screaming to his room? fall on his face? start crying? go mad again?— when he found himself skipping corpulently across the drive, piping out, "Room for one more inside?"

"Right here," said Marvell immediately; "There you go," said Skip, separating his arm from Celia's to allow him entry; "Oh, you're so *small!*" shouted Roxeanne in evident delight. As Keith craned his puckered mouth up at the seven grinning faces, Roxeanne, supported by Quentin and Andy, craned hers down to kiss it. She never got there: Quentin's foot slipped on the gravel, Roxeanne's right brick was whipped out from beneath her, the human wigwam swayed, wheeled round a quarter circle, tottered, and collapsed to shrieks of mirth on the ground.

Gradually they staggered laughingly to their feet. ". . . Drugs now," said Quentin, still trying to catch his breath, laughing again. "Much drugs."

The Appleseeders' stance on that topic found eloquent recapitulation and support a few minutes later from Marvell Buzhardt, the small, owlish American, postgraduate in psychology, anthropology, and environment at Columbia University, underground journalist, filmmaker, and pop-cultural entrepreneur. Dr. Buzhardt sat rolling joints at the kitchen table with Quentin and Andy, sliding round a bottle of duty-free liquor, while the girls made snacks for the projected picnic. Skip was unloading the Chevrolet, Whitehead running errands to the mini-market. Marvell had, in fact, recently published a short monograph on this theme in conjunction with the Berkeley Alternative University Press, a copy of which he promised to dig up for them before he left.

"What's the book got to say, man?"

"Simplistically, Andy, *The Mind Lab* has this to say," Marvell began. "For some time now it's been clear to all the genuine people studying this thing that the brain is a mechanical unit and that its aberrations aren't down to environmental, psychological contexts but to purely *chemical* reactions—that's all, nothing more. This idea has had a lot of trouble getting through because people won't let go of the belief that *no* part of us is divine. You go crazy, right? It's because you've got shit in your head, lousy chemicals. Anyhow, that's just the lead-in to the main polemic of my book."

At this point the Doctor ceased all activity with grass and cigarette papers in order to clench his hands pensively on his crown—to the secret boredom of Andy, who was less interested in talking about drugs than in getting a lot of them down him in the shortest possible time.

"Okay. So if you go crazy now," Marvell went on, "they give you good chemicals to counteract the bad ones in your head. Or electrics. The only mysterious thing about the brain is its complexity. Nothing cerebral about it, man, just one mother of a terminal of chemicals and nerve ends, and science can keep up with it now. So: why not apply this positively?"

"I don't know," said Andy, in moonish response to Marvell's interrogative, though in fact rhetorical, stare.

"No reason! Look—fuck—we're agreed that life is a rat's ass and that it's no fun being yourself all the time. So why not do with your brain what you do with your body? *Fuck* all this dead babies about love, understanding, compassion— *use* drugs to kind of . . . cushion the consciousness, guide it, protect it, stimulate it. We have a fantastic range of drugs now, Andy. We have drugs to make you euphoric, sad, horny, violent, lucid, tender. We have drug combinations that will produce any kind of hallucination or sense modification you want. Alternatively, we have drugs that can neutralize these effects instantaneously. Not the old Leary line—no 'religion,' no false promises. We have chemical authority over the psyche—so let's use it, and have a *good* time."

"Piss," said Diana. "What about brain damage? False memory, street sadness?"

"Well . . ." Marvell rocked his hairy head from side to side. "There's kind of an appendix dealing with—"

"And anyhow, most of that," said Roxeanne, "is media hysteria."

Quentin: "How was the book received, Marvell?"

"*Pig* and *Smeg Sunday* raved. The only straight press things I've seen, of course, tried to dismiss it as psycho agit-prop."

"Of course," said Andy, picking up Marvell's grass kit. "They would. Well, what have you got in mind for us today, then?"

The Doctor smiled. "Uh-uh. What have *you* got in mind?"

12: TALL AND GOOD

Quite overwhelmed by the colossal impression he seemed so far to have made on the guests, Whitehead stole tremulously across the garden. Keith's mission was to consolidate his feelings of well-being, and he proposed to do this by paying a call on the only people he had so far encountered in his life who made him feel flash, cool, grand, a pop-star, a Mohawk, one-up, stylish, sexy, brilliant, rich, tall and good. They were the Tuckles.

The Tuckles?

The Tuckles. If Quentin and Andy were at a loose end—or if they were under the auspices of some particularly electrifying drug—they used often to race out across the lawn to give a bad time to Mr. and Mrs. Sydney Tuckle, the wrecked dotard pair whom they were trying to evict from the Appleseed annex, a single-storied, two-room structure built into the corner of the garden wall and screened from the house by a bank of flowerless rhododendrons. The Tuckles had been installed there half a century earlier as factoti to some previous owners and had, insufferably, refused to budge since. Legally they were immovable, but Quentin and Andy, claiming to have dreams of converting the lodge into a studio/guest house/rumpus room, argued that if they could make life nasty enough for the couple they would leave of their own accord.

Quentin had once set up, for example, a polyethylene-covered loudspeaker outside the Tuckle front window, through which he relayed at glass-shattering, eardrum-puncturing volume such sounds as road crashes, cannon salutes, airplane takeoffs, advancing mobs, heavy breathing, tank battles, ambulance sirens, elephant charges, shouts, screams, obscenities. When this gave no clear reward Quentin transmitted a high-pitched sonic hum for three days and three nights; on the fourth day Mr. Tuckle was seen groggily repadding the windows with blood trickling from his left ear, at which point Quentin good-humoredly gave in to domestic pressure and discontinued his broadcasts. Andy's ruses tended on the whole to be more atavistic in conception. He once peed through the keyhole and then, to Quentin's roars of laughter, defecated down the chimney onto the Tuckle hearth. In similar moods he had playfully blocked up their sewage outlet, cut off their heat and water over the Christmas weekend, fused their electricity circuit, and restricted their comings and goings by, variously, camping outside with an ax, blacking up their windows with hardboard (so they didn't dare come out), and training the pressurized garden hose on their door for ninety-six hours. Although it was at their peril that the Tuckles staggered out of the back gate to visit the shop—liable to be menaced, spat on, jostled—Quentin and Andy were of course far too cavalier to mount a systematic campaign. Indeed, we suspect that if the old pair ever did move on Quentin and Andy would miss them sorely.

Whitehead rapped on the toytown front door. He rapped again and backed off a few paces. "Come *on*," he said. "It's Keith Whitehead."

Suddenly the letterbox creaked for a split second. There followed the sound of bolts, many and elaborate, being thrown back. The door opened slowly. Mr. and Mrs. Tuckle edged out into the strange sunlight.

"Mr. Whitehead! Thank God!" Mr. Tuckle swayed so wholeheartedly on his feet that Keith reached out and balanced him against his wife. "I beg your pardon for the delay, sir," Tuckle pursued, "but Mr. Villiers must have seen you when you came down here on the Tuesday—because he stood outside the door here yesterday and called up that he was you and everyone else was out. We could have sworn it *was* you, sir. We could have *sworn* it was you. He said it just in the way you say it, sir. Why, I opened the door without really thinking. And there was Mr. Villiers, with the dark-haired one standing beside him with a dustbin. He hurled it—he hurled it at us and we flew back into the house. Mrs. Tuckle took the lid on her neck. He would have charged in here on top of us, sir, but Mr. Villiers held him back."

"It was your own bloody stupid fault for not looking first," said Keith.

"You're right, of course, sir, it was. Very rash."

"Well, what the hell do you expect me to do about it?"

For the first time Mr. Tuckle's voice showed real agitation. "No, sir, please. We don't expect you to control them. You can see they don't know what they're doing themselves half the time. We're grateful for what you do do, sir. Deeply grateful." Mrs. Tuckle confirmed this, her eyes damp with trust. Mr. Tuckle swallowed. "And could you tell Mr. Coldstream that we're deeply grateful for his gift."

"If I remember to," said Keith. (On hearing of the Tuckle plight Giles had asked Whitehead to take along a liter of gin the next time he went to see them, which Keith had done that Tuesday, adjudging the present too fattening to intercept.) "About shopping. And by the way, Mrs. Tuckle, it's no bloody use asking me to get Beenies at the mini-market. You know bloody well they don't stock them there."

"I'm sorry, sir, I didn't—"

"Anyway, you can do it yourselves today for once. Some guests of mine have arrived and I've decided to take everyone out for a picnic. It should be clear from one till at least three."

"Thank you, sir, thank you."

"Yes, and in future when I knock I'd better say 'Whitehead.' I won't say 'Keith' or 'Mr.' Then you'll know it's me. 'Whitehead.' "

Whitehead didn't seem as pleased by this innovation as he thought he was going to be, but when the Tuckles started to say "Thank you, sir, thank you—" again, Keith was off, striding back over the lawn, feeling far too flash to say good-bye.

13: a sort of Daydream

"Away from the drill!"

"What? I say, Giles, are you all right?"

Giles had been lying on his bed, bent double with psychosomatic toothache. His strangled shout had been a semi-delerious reply to Quentin's courtly knock. By 12:30, Giles had consumed five Gin Rickeys, four gin and tonics, three gin and its, two gin and bitters, and one gin.

"Oh, hello, Quentin," said Giles when he had unlocked the door. "I'm sorry I cried out at you like that, actually. I was just having a sort of daydream."

"Sorry to disturb you. Only we're all off on a picnic and I've come to get you."

"Literally 'all'?"

"Yes, I'm afraid so."

"Ah." Giles didn't want to go anywhere, but he knew that being alone in the house was something he would never be able even to contemplate. "I see. Well, I think I'd better come then."

From behind his back Quentin produced two vast cardboard boxes. "Celia has prepared lots of food," he said. "We'll need some drink, however."

Giles expressionlessly accepted the two boxes and turned to open his teak cupboard. He knelt. "Hang on. Mostly red or mostly white?"

"Let's see," said Quentin. "We've got beef, steak sandwiches, chick—"

"Stop! . . . Uh, sorry. But actually—could you just say the *wines*, actually. Okay?"

"Of course, Giles. Mostly red, please. Why not half a dozen St. Emilion '74 and half a dozen Châteauneuf-du-Pape '77," Quentin said simply. "Oh, and some Pouilly-Fumé for the girls."

"There . . . we . . . are," said Giles some minutes later. "Now . . ." He took a liter of Napolean brandy from the lowest shelf and (after a silent consultation with Quentin) *two* of Glenfyddich Irish from the one above. Finally, having gone over to the desk to establish that his bottle of gin was at least half finished, Giles included a fresh Gordon's. "That ought to do it," he said to himself.

"Splendid. I'll get Skip up in a minute to lend a hand. No, you haven't met everyone yet, have you?"

Giles did not react to this question. But then, all of a sudden, as he was being led from the room he whipped around and clutched Quentin's jean jacket. "Mrs. Fry's not down there, is she?" he asked wildly.

"No, she's gone. Why? Why does she bother you. She's a good soul, really, a treasure."

Once again Giles glazed over. "She's got . . . it's just her . . ." Giles was going to say "false teeth." He had been present when Mrs. Fry sneezed out her dentures onto the draining board and laboriously reinserted them; since then he was subject to dizzy spells and retching fits whenever he saw her.

"Come on, Giles," said Quentin. "My friends have brought something that'll make you feel better. Everything will soon be all right. Come."

Giles looked around as if for the last time at his empty room, sniffed, gave Quentin a zestless smile, and moved with awkward caution out of the door.

14: OUT Here SOMeWHere

"We can't go in there," he said.

"Why not?" asked Diana.

"Just look at that." Giles pointed to a large sign which stuck out at an angle from the barbed-wire fence. The sign had this to say:

FUCK OFF

TRESPASSERS WILL
BE PROSECUTED

"What about it?"

"It says," Giles explained, as if Diana might only recently have learned to read, " 'trespassers will be prosecuted.' "

"So?"

"Relax, Giles," said Quentin. "I know the man who owns this spread. Oofie Worthington. He said I could use it any time."

"Really, darling?" said Celia. "I didn't know you—"

"What about that barbed wire, then?" said Giles, abruptly taking a step backward and fastening a hand over his mouth.

"No problem," said Skip. The three Americans had loomed up on them. "I just hold it . . . right here, and—hey, man, handle the other thing, okay?" Stamping their boots on the lower wire, Skip and Marvell elevated the upper one with their hands. Marvell grunted and winced a good deal while he was doing this but Skip's small, boyish face remained blank, almost dead. "Okay," he droned at last.

(Unnecessarily—buckling his body, the hamper in his

arms) Whitehead went first. One by one the girls followed. Quentin and Andy steered the twitchy Giles through, ferried the alcohol across, then hoisted Skip and Marvell over.

Quentin Villiers hastened to help unfurl the blankets with his wife. They kissed fleetingly and crouched to open the hamper.

"Is everyone going to eat now?" asked Giles vaguely, raising the gin bottle to his lips. "Because I think I shall just drink a lot instead, in fact."

At this juncture Skip paced up to Giles and grasped his free hand. "Hi, Giles," he said in his monotone bass. "I'm Skip."

Skip was showered with a spray of high-octane saliva as Giles gurgingly removed the gin bottle and tottered backward, arms lifted to protect his face. "Careful! Uh, sorry . . . Skip? I just didn't see you coming. My name's—" Giles sank to his knees. "Actually . . ." he said.

Now, in a complicated semi-embrace, Quentin, Celia, Marvell, and Roxeanne moved away from the picnic site the better to admire its surrounds. "I like it," said Marvell, attaching tufted hands to either hip. He let his eyes scan the curved field with the kneeling willow in the middle of it, the sturdier file of birches that lined the distant fence, the far hill, the sky. "I like this planet."

"Beautiful," said Roxeanne. "Beautiful, Quentin, truly."

"When we married," said Quentin, "I said that we should have to live out here somewhere." He turned to his wife. "Somewhere where there was still some England."

"Yeah," said Marvell.

"It's not a question of rapport with nature—what a horrid idea that is!—rather, a question of solidifying one's sense of oneself. I'm an Englishman. This is England. There's nothing English about London any more."

Celia and Roxeanne gazed up at Quentin with joy and wonder respectively. Indeed, Villiers' extraterrestrial good looks were very much in evidence that day. His frostily faded jeans and revealing denim shirt contrived to make him appear at once rugged and civilized; his damp-sand complexion contrasted favorably with the etiolated pallor of his housemates and the rather coarse suntans of the Americans; the gusty breeze curled but did not tousle the strands of his silvery blond hair.

"You shun your spirit," he murmured, "every time you agree to sell your days to the city, to measure out your life at the city's pace."

"Right," said Marvell. "You feel like a cog, a sort of robot that's got to—"

"Hey, you lot," called Diana, "stop talking piss and come and help me with this fucking hamper."

Andy was urinating noisily against a nearby tree and Giles had curled up with the gin bottle. The fact was that little Keith had been lending catering assistance to Diana, who happened to object both to his revoltingly pudgy fingers occasionally skimming her own and also to being bracketed implicitly with the least attractive person present.

"For Christ's sake, let's break out some of that Irish," said Andy.

"Yes," said Quentin, "and let's take in some of this sun."

Marvell and Roxeanne arranged themselves on and around Skip's outstretched form—an arm here, a leg there. It didn't look self-conscious, somehow or other.

"Now," said Marvell. "I want you all to give this drug thing some genuine thought. I don't want to get too mechanistic about it but I've done this sort of project before, in controlled conditions, and I have some sort of article or possibly a pamphlet in view. Names changed; conjectural in idiom." Marvell yawned, and nestled further into the nook composed by Skip's chest and Roxeanne's shoulder. He looked like an unwholesome potentate, propped up against his friends' long bodies, his face shadowed and beady under its trellis of hair. "I don't know about you guys," he went on, "but I'm pretty fucked and I don't want to be flashing all night on this thing. We take off around seven, should be right. Think it over and give me your specifications when we get back. I'll be interested to see what you people choose."

It had taken Giles the last two-thirds of this peroration to crawl the five feet to where Andy lay spreadeagled on a blanket. On arrival, Giles poked Andy's shoulder.

"What?" said Andy.

"Hey, Andy," Giles whispered loudly. "What's that chap saying?"

Andy stretched. "Says he's got drugs'll do anything. Anything you like. You tell him what you want to happen to you and he'll make it happen."

"What, anything? He—he could even make you stop worrying about your . . ."

"Anything, man," said Andy, searching for a more delicious posture in which to drowse. "Anything."

When Giles had removed the swimming green of the gin bottle from his lips and settled himself also on the ground, there lingered in his mind the afterimage of what had snapped into focus from the smoke between everything and his eyes, the three smiling faces of the Americans.

15: meandered up america

The Americans constituted a "triad," a "troy," which meant, more or less, that they got to fuck and bugger one another indiscriminately. It was their habit, too, to rope in another personage to form a "rectangle," or another couple to make up the full "star." And are we to believe that sexual excursions outside the group were censured? On the contrary, they were encouraged, applauded as adding further imaginative declensions to normal activity. The threesome had flourished for two years and showed lively signs of continuing to do so.

Their story went something like this.

Skip's father, Philboyd B. Marshall, Jr., a horrible human being, used to run a hot, dirty garage on the outskirts of Tara, Tennessee. Philboyd had done so many appalling and traumatic things to his son that anyone who heard about them spontaneously congratulated Skip on his apparent sanity. Philboyd had once *raped* him, for instance—not (we hasten to add) in a libidinous spirit, but because he had caught Skip emptying the latrine with a shovel rather than with his bare hands, as Philboyd had requested, this being itself a punishment for an earlier mischief. "Kitch you at that kind of non-sense again, boy, and you're in real trouble."

Father and son relations worsened. What with the gas station not doing so good these days, the way all the guys were moving out of Tara and all the niggers moving in, the fact that a man couldn't take a beer at Kramer's without getting jostled by the longhairs . . . Philboyd's life became a depressing series of grousing sessions, drunk bends and violence jags. The old mechanic died a little every time a Rican or a Jeeew pulled into his station, expecting gas what's more;

every time he saw the boogies come across the railway line, seemingly unharmed; every time the sun went down over the Coke sign back of the house, causing his evenings to be dimmed by a premature vault of shadow. When Skip became physically unable to take more of his motiveless beatings, Philboyd bought from the glue factory a three-legged mule, which he installed in an enclosure and went out to visit torments on twice daily with kitchen knives, meathooks, branding irons. This helped some, but not for long. The animal fell down dead on him two months later.

And so then of course some Vanderbilters get along from Nashville and Skip starts to hang out with them. They're all between twenty and thirty and Skip hasn't seen seventeen yet, but he has this peculiar facility with older boys. For Skip is what used to be called a "slag": he'll do anything; there's nothing he won't do. "Skip, see if you can dive from the cooling tower into that tank right there." "Every time." "Skip, take the shit buckets down to the trash pile, willya?" "Uh-huh." "Skip, go steal us some beers from Kramer's, okay?" "Right on." "Skip, eat that slug." "No sweat." Certain menial sexual chores fell also to the lanky boy, which he performed with care and avidity. As a student once remarked, "Skip'd rim a snake so long someone held its head." There were lots of drugs, too.

One day Philboyd motored past the Kampsite in his dump truck, saw Skip lying on the grass with a crew of whores and hippie fags. To his hopelessness and grief, Philboyd could not act immediately; time was—when there'd been enough tubby little rednecks like himself still living in Tara—they could have pitched right in there and whomped up a storm. This reflection saddened him further. As it was, on Skip's return that night Philboyd clubbed his son around the kitchen with a frypan for three-quarters of an hour. "Ah, let the boy be, Philb," came Mrs. Marshall's sickly voice from the adjacent bedroom. "Trying to get some rest in here." "Shut the fuck up," replied Philboyd, who had in any case decided to take his wife's advice, being too old and fat to go on. "Skip, next time I see you which those queeahs again," he panted, "I'm goan bust your head."

And, to be sure, the next time he saw Skip with those queers again Philboyd attempted to keep his promise. He could hardly believe his good fortune. There was Skip with a solitary student, drinking beers in a downtown penny arcade. Philboyd slapped open the door and strode over to them, eagerly unhitching his belt. "This is it, son. I'm gonna kill your ass." Without reaching any kind of decision, Skip rose, made a circling motion with his right fist and then offered it up to Philboyd's chin at high velocity. Philboyd seemed to stay perfectly still for at least two or three seconds, his face frozen in unbelieving disappointment, before being snatched up into the air and cannonaded against the wall, down which he easily slid to collect in a fat puddle on the floor. With slow-motion fear his son scooped him up and straightened him against a fruit machine. "Dad . . . ?" Skip's hands were shrugged off. "Ah, let me be, son." Philboyd stumbled home, hair matted with sawdust, blood, and beer, and dejectedly hosepiped his wife to death.

Seemed like Skip's life had fallen apart all around him. Ma was dead. Philboyd had a manslaughter charge to face. Marshall Mekanix was closed down. The authorities didn't appear to give a shit what he did. And he had always hated Tara anyhow.

Skip found employment in the automobile plant on the far apron of the second cloverleaf off the third spaghetti junction along the subsidiary expressway running westerly out of Nashville, Tennessee. He worked sixteen hours a day, without ambition and without boredom, taking off in borrowed cars at weekends for St. Louis, Memphis, Oklahoma, 'Pulco, Mexico City, where he participated in various nihilistic debauches, scrogging and getting scrogged, taking large quantities of mescaline and cocaine, the roller of middle-aged cowboys, the occasional witness of optimum sex tortures and genital mutilation profiles, a blank figure in the tumescent heat-hazed carscape, silent, unreflecting, and alone.

After two years of punching out automobile steering-column shroud toggles Skip threw everything he owned into a beatup '75 Plymouth, meandered up America just rolling like a stone nobody throwed—*and* Omaha, *and* Minneapolis, *and* Salt Lake City—until he hung an impulsive right off the interstate thruway and idled toward the fine town of Prescott, Arizona. Halfway there he killed a bottle of paregoric and blacked out in a rest stop; he awoke a buckled mess at the bottom of the roadside ditch, his car and money gone, his nose, ankle, and five ribs broken, his left pinkie missing, a portion of his right ear bitten off, and a bad hangover. It took him forty-eight hours to regain the road.

"The first time we saw Skip?—enough to make a maggot gag. Roxeanne and I are out researching locations in Arizona for an existential Western I never got together, we're making for the nearest town to pick up some food, come around the bend in the Chev, and there's this sort of twitching heap by the side of the road. We slow up. Never in my life seen a human being nearer the state of nature. We pull over. Clothes half ripped off, face a pool of blood, body broken, random. I still have the photographs."

"Mar was cool but I was shaken up. Kept thinking, uh-oh, Popeye, some Trogs have been having fun, let's get out of here before they have some more, but Marvell said we'd better get him to somewhere and he was right. I put a blanket down for him in back and we like shoveled him in? We thought he might go stiff on us right there but then he started to groan and struggle, even saying things—like, 'I'm all fucked up . . . I'm all fucked up.' Marvell gunned it into Prescott, see what they could do there, said we could go on to Phoenix if his condition necessitated it. Bastards in Prescott Casualty said they couldn't even take his fucking temperature without State Reg.—and this guy doesn't have *any*thing, no ID, no cash. He was like nobody. So it was LA, not knowing whether we'd have a stiff in back when we got there. LA they kind of roped him together again but they still wouldn't take him in. So we had to."

"I got some medic friends along. No problem. Skip was delirious for days, wriggling around in bed, moaning about his father and beer cans and stuff. When he came to he didn't appear to have any recollection of what had happened to him or of anything before it—found myself in there explaining that we were on the planet Earth, a spherical body revolving around the sun. The Sun? big fire in the sky? Most of it returned to him, though the stuff about his father comes and goes. It was strange, you know? Like bringing a new human being to life, like creating something. You feel strong things then. And, Christ, if you'd seen the way that guy responded to affection. Made you sick to think what his life had been."

"He used to tell these positively prehistoric stories about his father? Some animal. Skip's eyes would practically come out of his head when we told him about our parents—you know, mine are all house-on-the-hill and Marvell's used to be very heavily Yiddisher—that they were rich, affectionate, indulgent. Totally alien to his thought-style. He was kind of relieved when we told him they were all divorced now and that we only saw them for cash. Marvell explained to him about control, about how you don't need parents for much or for long, that you phase them out soon. If only Skip could have."

"Right. I don't think he thinks about his earlier life at all now. The father's still around, however. The authorities forwarded us a letter when we put Skip on Californian Reg. just before we came out here. Shit, what a document. I'll show it to you. We never handed it on to Skip. It would wreck his head to be taken back to those days again. Want to see someone go really wild? Ask Skip about his father. I don't recommend it. Anyhow, so it goes. It was no sweat for us; we had the cash and the space, he helps around the apartment, helps me on projects, fixes the car. . . . He's happy."

"We're like his mother and father as well as his lovers."

"Yeah, and he's . . . let's just say he does things for us."

16: a Heavy Fire of eyes

Whitehead had just drained his first glass of Pouilly Fumé, had just turned down Celia's disdainful offer of a piece of crispbread topped with smoked salmon and, alas, butter, had just agreed with Roxeanne that Capricorns seldom got along with Leos (a proposition that Andy, a self-elected representative of the latter sign, began to pooh-pooh), when a ghastly bark sprang from between his lips, bringing all conversation to a halt.

In a tone of mock-heroic formality Keith begged the picnic's pardon, and the conversation cautiously resumed, what time awful quickenings started to occur inside his stomach. It hissed, whooped, spat—Keith whistled popular tunes in an attempt to drown its loud awakening; he was moreover obliged to squirm about on the blankets in order to contain the balloon of air that romped friskily around his colon. As the picnickers began actually to raise their voices to make themselves heard, little Keith decided that he wouldn't wait to see what his metabolism was going to pull on him next. Hardly caring what sort of spectacle he made of himself, he slipped some paper napkins into his pocket, stood up, and looked quickly about him.

"Saw some interesting—I've got to go, to see . . ."

No one stirred as Keith took his leave, as he trotted down the hill under a heavy fire of eyes.

Whitehead picked his way through the outskirts of the thicket, wading through not particularly long grass, his trousers creaking in alarm every time he lifted a foot to clear a log, his high heels wobbling and bending on each anthill and tuft of grass. He walked a tormented half mile, becoming ever easier to please as regards possible sites, but only after he had twice been brought to a kneeling position by the wedge of pain that rocketed from his coccyx to his perineum did he turn and stare back through the tent of nervous leaves. First removing his boots, then his trousers (which required him to lie on the ground and wriggle out of them like a snake shedding its skin), Keith crept in between two dense bramble bushes and melted backward against a severed trunk. A tight-chested grunt was followed by a moan of ecstasy.

"Hi."

Emerging silently from the trees Skip had come to a halt about five yards away. He now closed that distance and un-elongated himself into a crouch, his knees almost touching little Keith's. A grass stem remained motionless in the corner of his mouth as he said, "You like threes, Keith?"

Whitehead would have answered if he could.

"Threes," Skip ponderously repeated. "You and two guys. You and a guy and a girl."

When his voice did appear Keith was, retrospectively, most impressed by its performance. It did not gurgle or whimper, neither did it jump octaves or turn into a corky burp of adrenalin—all things Keith couldn't have blamed it for doing. In fact, it sounded urbane, detached, almost bored.

"Well, you know, Skip, I haven't really got strong views on the subject, although of course I try to be tolerant about that kind of thing."

"Mm-hm. You like getting head?"

". . . Sorry?"

"Head. Getting blown. Getting sucked off."

"Oh! Well, not *mad* about it. But again of course it's all part of the basic . . . Yes, I'm for it, on the whole."

"Mm-hm. You like to be fucked?"

". . . Well, as I say, it's not one of the things one customarily . . . but you naturally try to keep an open . . ."

"Mm-hm." Skip swayed languidly on his haunches. "Mm-hm."

"Look— Skip— I don't want to seem abrupt but do you think we could finish this chat another time?"

"Pardon me?"

"Another time. I am on the *toilet* here."

"Sure you are," Skip said reassuringly. But then he rolled his eyes so that his pupils disappeared upward, revealing two sacs of glistening blood at the base of either socket. "Oh, sure, man. Another time."

17: SOME BUSH

"I must say, Roxeanne," Celia observed briskly, "you have got the most marvelous breasts."

"But they're so awfully big," said Roxeanne. "I think Diana's are so pretty? Really the perfect size."

At this Diana curled her lip slightly, as if to suggest that she had heard that line before. Celia resumed, "Yes, Diana's are pretty too. But yours are so enormous and so marvelously . . . solid. Look at mine. Yours seem to point upwards. They don't sag in the least."

Roxeanne shrugged, corroborating this. "Well," she said happily. "Hey, Quentin, is it cool if I take off my pants?"

As the afternoon sun had intensified, had seemed indeed to bear down on them with an invidious strength, Diana and Roxeanne had spent a lot of time—Diana shrewdly, Roxeanne vaguely—wondering which of them would be the first to remove her top. In almost any other company Diana would have had few reservations about taking the lead: her breasts, as Celia had pointed out, may not have been large but they were pretty; they covered a fetchingly disproportionate area of her chest, were smoothly rounded, and rose to neat orange nipples which were soon tinted and hardened by the wind's

gentle ministry. Diana was, nevertheless, banking on Roxeanne's being a good deal more punctured than they looked
under her smock and had even assumed that she must, in
the nature of things, be wearing a quarter or half-brassiere
beneath it. As it was—having both muttered something about
wanting to get a tan—the girls bared their treasures simultaneously. Except Marvell, who gazed on with complacence,
and Giles, who was apparently unconscious, the fearsome
glory of Roxeanne's breasts filled everyone present with utter
consternation. They seemed to shoot upward out of her
collar-bones (forming a ledge off which, had it occurred to
her to do so, she could have not inconveniently dined), U-
turned over symmetrical cupcake nipples, and repaired to the
commodious launching pad of her rib cage without marking
this junction by so much as a crease. Diana had looked at the
vast tenement then back at her own diminutive cups with
scarcely concealed incredulity, and only on the appearance
of Celia's breasts—depressing items that flatly splayed in the
direction of her armpits—did she begin to regain her equanimity.

"I beg your pardon, Roxeanne," said Quentin, "I didn't
quite catch that."

"If I take off my pants?"

"Ah, a common ambiguity when colonials are of the company. Now, do you refer to your trousers or to your panties?
Which?"

"How about both?"

Quentin glanced at his wife. "Well, old Oofie is in
Kuwait, so far as I know. As long as you don't mind the odd
wayfarer or rustic?" He laughed, holding out his hands. "By
all means."

Laughing also, Roxeanne said, "They're very welcome," lay
back, hooked her thumbs into the waistband of her jeans and
eased her seemingly infinite legs out of them. Her (anyway
otiose) panties followed. "Okay," she concluded, "no smart-ass
remarks about natural redheads."

"Certainly not," said Quentin sincerely.

Diana stared hard at Andy as he rolled over, propped his
head up on his palms for a few seconds, his face perhaps six
inches from Roxeanne's alabaster midriff, and reassumed his
original position. "Christ," he mused softly. "Some bush."

18: OH ПО

Oh no, surely they can't all be at it already, can they?

Whitehead posed this question to himself while emerging from the thicket and beginning to make his way up the incline toward the picnickers, all by now in varying stages of deshabille. From his vantage, the sections of bare, mottled flesh lost their outlines in the dusty summer air; as he traipsed toward them their bodies seemed to shimmer and merge, to resolve and separate, to flow together and then to cease. Twenty yards away, quite suddenly, they regained their distinctness, becoming again immobile and discreet. Whitehead slowed with relief.

Then—more—he came to a halt, still unnoticed by the eight further up the slope, and sank, without emphasis and without any sense of irony, to his knees, a tubby supplicant of the warming wind. The keen anxiety he always felt on approaching any group of people now quietly allied itself to a deeper, more settled foreboding. Keith had once, when tranquilized, told a friendly dietician that he hadn't minded discovering that he was small, fat, and ugly half as much as he had minded discovering that he would always be those things, that all of it could never change now. Would it ever—just a bit? Although Whitehead didn't consider himself a highly sexed person—his masturbatory career, for instance, he had come to regard as an increasingly disturbing and ghostly adventure—he felt it highly likely that if he failed to have a definite sexual experience this weekend he would make some sort of attempt to kill himself. It was not release he craved, far less pleasure, merely a token withdrawal of the insult of ugliness. Little Keith picked up a blade of grass and twirled it in his fingers. The action returned blood and self-consciousness to his features, steadying him somewhat. He smiled furtively as he recalled the incident with Skip. Christ. There really wasn't anything people wouldn't do any more. Being, so far as he could ascertain, a heterosexual, Whitehead had found the approach dramatically unsexy, but it was quite flattering all the same, and it went to show that a lot was in the air. The weekend would, in any case, be unlike any other.

On rejoining his friends Keith's anticipations were strengthened and elaborated. If he looked to his right, he could see—for what they were worth—the breasts of the square-faced girl called Celia, wife to the gorgeous Villiers; if he turned to his left he could admire Diana Parry's dinky navel and compact stomach; practically under his nose was a square foot of tawny pubic hair. Keith didn't dare look at anything, of course. He had never had so much sex in his life. But as the newly returned Skip smilingly caught his eye, a whole range of sexual possibilities couldn't help opening itself up for little Keith Whitehead.

And, both less and more straightforwardly, a whole range of them opens itself up for us, too. We could—let's see—we could have Diana take his hand and shoo him off to the woods, have Celia lean over and tenderly unbuckle his thin plastic belt, have Roxeanne shinny beneath him there and then. Of course, we can bring this about any time we like— but *Keith* can't, oh no.

19: COLLAPSING BALLOON

"Look," said Andy, "there's some cows over there. How casual."

"Yeah. Coming on pretty authentic," said Marvell.

Giles, who had shown no sign of life whatever for the past ninety minutes, lifted his head and narrowed his eyes over the lip of his gin bottle. "How do you know they're not bulls?"

"Because," said Andy, "bulls have horns and cows have tits. They've got tits."

"No," said Skip slowly. "That's not so."

"How come?" Andy asked.

"Some cows don't have tits. Some bulls don't have horns."

"Oh yeah?"

"That's right. For example, a cow might not have had calves yet."

"Is that a fact?"

"Sure."

Andy sank back. "Well what the fuck difference does it make anyway?"

As if in answer to this query a black heifer detached itself from the ambling herd, trotted up the dip in the field, paused, arrived at some sort of decision, and came bowling down the slope toward the picnickers in a firm-legged gallop.

Approximately four seconds later they were lying in a

bloody, groaning heap on the other side of the barbed-wire fence. In an electric, hair-triggered scramble they had climbed, jumped, dived over, under, and between the barbs—clawing one another out of the way, springing from flattened torsos, pulling each other's hair for leverage—to subside like a collapsing balloon of flesh in the adjacent field. Whispered obscenities broke the silence as the wheezing tangle of limbs gradually came apart and a dazed cataloguing of injuries began.

All three girls bled not very profusely from abrasions sustained on their shoulders and bare breasts. Skip had a vent of skin flapping on his wrist, Andy a deep and dirty gash on his cheek. Only Quentin was entirely unscathed.

Keith, who was still severely winded, having been used as a trampoline by everyone else, had a cut nose and lip and a four-inch stripe running across his forehead like a second mouth. More material to his desire, though, was the fact that his only good trousers were irreparably torn and that the six-inch heel of one of his boots was nowhere to be found. Giles squatted with his back to the carnage; one hand held a pocket mirror to his mouth, whose interior the other frenetically enumerated; the cap on his left incisor came away without any fuss between his fingers; with a distracted cry he flopped twiching to the earth.

"Jesus," said Marvell, "we've got our ancestors to thank for that."

Skip leapt to his feet. "Eat shit, eat shit!" he roared, his mouth whitening.

The heifer now stood a few feet from the fence, staring at the disarray in companionable wonder. Its instincts had programmed it to run up to the picnic in that fashion, but they had programmed it also to swerve away at the last moment and trot off wondering what to do next.

"Motherfuck, motherfuck," said Skip. He uprooted a brick from the base of the fence and moved along the wire calling out softly, waving his hand.

As the animal frowned, dipped its head and moved forward, Skip brought the brick down on its pate with a long-armed swing. There was a dull crunch.

The heifer remained motionless, then jerked backward. It turned, skipped into the field, ran about in untidy decreasing circles, and keeled over onto the grass.

There was a silence.

"You've killed it," said Andy. "It's all fucked up."

"It does seem to be totally buggered," agreed Quentin.

"I'm gonna go kick it some," said Skip, stepping forward.

Female voices were raised in protest. Andy stood in Skip's path and a halfhearted scuffle took place before Quentin lent his support. Whereas Andy restrained Skip with dislike, and because he didn't particularly want him to kick the heifer, Quentin restrained Skip considerably, in the spirit of a wise man preventing a fellow Jew from attacking a platoon of Nazis, with due respect for Skip's wrath. At length Skip relaxed.

"Just get the whiskey, man," said Quentin.

"Yeah," said Andy. "Let's get *drunk*."

"Yeah. *Yeah!*" screamed Giles.

Within half an hour the nine were re-established on the near side of the barbed-wire fence. Nobody's injuries had proved to be more serious than anything handkerchiefs and saliva wouldn't relieve—except Andy's ripped cheek, which he claimed to have "cooled" by emptying a bottle of Glenfyddich over it. This move exhausted the supply of spirits and the wine was therefore started on in earnest. Weightwatchers Celia, Diana, and Whitehead didn't object to the switch, having been on Pouilly Fumé all along, but there was loud complaint from the others about the inability of wine to do much for them these days. (Giles, face downward at the corner of the blanket, had made no response to demands for his bottle of gin.) "I guess this'll keep us up till we get back," said Marvell, boredly unwrapping his hash kit. The food, also, was partaken of gingerly: pieces of meat were picked up between finger and thumb and held aloft like live worms before being quickly dispatched; offending portions of salad and cheese were disgustedly spat out on the grass; water biscuits, apples, celery, and radishes enjoyed fair popularity, but little truck was had with such greasy and malodorous dishes as sardines, liver sausage, and anchovies. The company snorted when bananas were mentioned and actually gagged in unison when boiled eggs were produced ("No," said Celia, putting them away, "perhaps that wasn't a good idea"). Twenty minutes with a bottle of wine apiece, however, and loquacity returned, mainly in the form of piecemeal self-congratulation about the recent escape. Quentin then began a speech on the writings of the late Alain Robbe-Grillet; its length, periodicity, and range of reference held in thrall everyone but Keith (anyway groggy enough with heat, the memory of Roxeanne's body, and his triannual deliverance from the costive state) and Andy. The restless Adorno rolled over in front of Diana and started to stroke her hair and whisper sexy things to her neck. Diana turned away toward the curved field, where without comment she saw the injured heifer climb uncertainly to its knees, its feet, then zigzag away. When she looked back at Andy she noticed that some blood from his cheek had dripped onto the downy white scants of her pantie suit. "Keep away from me," she said quietly. "Just keep, the fuck, away from me," said Diana.

XX: DIANA

Diana spends a lot of time wondering what the hell she's doing in Appleseed Rectory. Occasionally—when the attentive Villiers pours her a Tio Pepe at 11:30, or while she drives to the shopping center in Celia's I-type Jaguar, or as Giles's unsteady hand appears round his bedroom door with a wad of £20 notes to settle the quarterly accounts, or during the moments after Andy has made love to her—Diana feels, well, a sort of fleeting satisfaction with the stage her life has reached. But most days she sits there hating everything, the place she's in, the people she's living with, the light around her, the time of day it is.

For this there are excellent reasons. Diana's background may not in itself be illustrious, but it has an unquestionable luster. Always she has mingled with the great. At the age of six Diana spent the first of many summers at Moreley Court, where her ermine waterbed was maintained at body temperature and where every night she found her toothbrush pre-pasted in the ormolu bathroom. Two years later she wintered with the Beresford-Parkinsons in the famous Ariadne Palace on Lake Geneva, down whose hanging-garden avenues unsmiling dwarfs ferried her breakfast to the aviary swimming pool. As a teenager she was the perennial houseguest of the Rudolphes, the Perths, of the screen personalities Murray and Elspeth Krane, of the Balfours, the Grizes, of Sir Henry and

Lady Doorlock, of the motion picture producer "Tubby" de Large and his lovely young wife, Lurleen. And, a little later, she is marriageably to be seen on the west patio of the Castello Pinero near Padua, basking naked on the glossy decks of Logo Lesbos' schooner among the Seychelle reefs, quaffing champagne in Giovanni Raffini's dune litter at the topless beaches of Acapulco. Youngish, well-connected, cosmopolitian readers can expect to see her about the place in six or seven years' time. At cockail parties, soirees, premieres, and so on, she will usually be accompanied by one or other of her parents, but after a few months she will begin to arrive alone, still a rather hesitant figure, slightly ill at ease about the aggressive sexiness of her catsuits and leotards, continually on edge about her appearance, until, during her second year of social immersion, she will be widely celebrated for her aplomb, verbal asperity, and daring and expertise in bed.

Diana's half-vicarious celebrity can be explained, on the one hand, by her mother's editrixship of "Nell's Notebook" in the pages of the distinguished glossy *Euroscene*, and, on the other, by her father's position as Assistant Chief Casting Director of Magnum Cinematic Promotions, Ltd., Paris and New York. Examples of that matrimonial tendency whereby unlike poles attract, Eleanor is practical, intelligent and cunning, a sharp-faced woman and angular, while Bruce is foolish, guileless, and benign, a shaggy middle-aged boy with a demeanor of nonspecific, goofy good will. Their Parisian idyll spanned Diana's conception and gestation, and survived her birth by two months, at which point Eleanor decided that she didn't much like Bruce and got on an airplane to London, where she embarked on a continuing series of compact, knowing little affairs with persons flourishing in the media; the hopeless Bruce meanwhile staggered around Paris getting drunk for six months, then took up with a Breton ingenue of such ingenuousness that she has since forgotten French and failed to learn English. Between these hearths the young Diana was patted like a listless shuttlecock for the first fifteen years of her life.

From the beginning Eleanor Parry policed her daughter's social life with astuteness and dedication. She enrolled Diana at the sort of schools where the children of the fashionable were likely to gather—Eldahurst Kindergarten, Laura and June Bateson House, The Hendlebury Association for the

Furtherance of Girls' Education, Hampstead Comprehensive—
then withdrew her once the requisite circle of acquaintances
had been made. Selflessly Mrs. Parry attended all parents'
meetings, liaison projects and school bazaars. A brief perusal
of the register furnished her with remarks like, "Oh, of course,
you're little Sarah's parents! My Diana absolutely adores
Sarah," or, "Then Bettina's *your* child. Oh, dear, I'm afraid
poor Diana must pester her dreadfully." Parental invitations
soon followed and were as readily accepted by the young
columnist. Host and hostess would then receive, consecutively,
a flattering profile in "Nell's Notebook" and a long letter from
Eleanor about what difficulty Diana had in making friends.
And Diana was such a ferociously immaculate guest (an
excellent gauger of mood, correct forms of address, prompt
thank-you missives, tips for the maids) that it seemed churlish
not to ask her again.

For his part, big Bruce Parry saw to it that Diana's
thrice-yearly holidays with him in Paris and New York were
varied and eventful. As was the case with his ex-wife, everyone was to some extent in Bruce's debt and his social standing
was thus providentially enhanced. Unflappable and always
eager to please, old Bruce had given many one-line parts to
talentless mistresses of superannuated company-owners, had
often found employment for loafing sons of neurotic lighting-
cameramen, had regularly steered hysterectomized vamps
through mid-career crises, was prepared to put in unpaid
overtime to cover up for menopausal assistant directors and
alcoholic production managers, had been known to work
around the clock to appease coronary-prone producers, depressive financiers, and apoplectic entrepreneurs. And—heck—the
guy just likes kids. Confidentially known in Magnum House
as "The Nursery," the apartment of Bruce Parry and his
alingual consort is an indulgent, eventempered Disneyland of
sweets, crackers, and party games. Accordingly, little dark-
haired Diana is a feted personage whenever she visits her
father, the receptacle of much guilty hospitality.

Unfair. There *is* genuine warmth and feeling in the childish
Diana. Although she is deeply unresponsive to her parents,
there is much that remains—for she's the girl who writes
thirty letters a week, who gives you her old handbags and
makeup, who spends three hours a day vocally marshaling her

dolls' house, who steals stockings from the boutique, who'll tell you about sex, who likes the tanned boy in ragged socks and sandals and chucks the yobs' caps under buses, who kicks the matron and shows her pants to the gardener, who'll offer you up to 20p. to shout FUCK OFF outside Miss Granger's study, who'd rather come with you than go home, and who bursts into tears without knowing why. Diana is as baffled as anyone by her cold envy for her mother, her cold contempt for her father, and by her fear of being alone.

A word about Diana's sex life.

Nine days after the first menstrual bloodstain had been sighted on her sheets Diana was successfully, and very painfully, seduced by a thirty-five-year-old stuntman at a Bruce Parry shindig. High time too, she thought, dispatching letters to her friends the next morning. When she got back to London she told her mother about it. Mrs. Parry, who would never stand any nonsense from Diana, marched her straight down to the gynecologist's and put her on the pill. Diana could be said never to have looked back: an intelligible procedure—at what, anyway? If someone neither sordid nor unattractive seemed to want to go to bed with her, Diana went to bed with him. Along they came—tramp tramp tramp—slowly and sporadically at first, then in steady Indian file. Unlike many of her friends, Diana never felt that she had "let herself down" in these *affaires*, no matter how brief and pleasureless they might have been. She had never slept with anyone who wasn't rich, well-groomed, and halfway civilized; the ubiquitous venereal maladies which she could not but occasionally complain weren't, in her case, of the chronic variety and her tolerance to antibiotics was happily low; on no account would she entertain gentlemen friends at home and her bedroom remained a silent, pink retreat of dolls and paper tissues; up until the age of nineteen, up until Andy, Diana hadn't once spent an entire night with a man, would leave unfussily when the act was completed, had never woken up to new skin and breath.

For Diana, sex was not a fleshy concern; it was a dial in the machinery of her self-regard, a salute to her clothes sense, applause for her exercises, a hat tipped to her dieting, the required compliment to her hairdresser, the means socially to measure herself against others. She quite enjoyed it, too, now that most people were good enough at pressing the right buttons to give her clitorial orgasms of admittedly varying quality. If anyone happened to be particularly rich, handsome, or accomplished in bed, Diana would perhaps see them more than once, and, if they were moreover kind and/or amusing, she might even get quite to like them. But sexual lassitude and disgust seemed to be everywhere among the young, and two-night stands were becoming a rarity. The party, the man, the dinner, the flat, the fuck, the taxi, the scalding bath. Besides being good exercise in itself Diana found that it helped her to eat less. She would get out of bed the next morning and complete her callisthenics program with fresh verve.

Diana and Eleanor Parry were sunbathing by the Reina Victoria swimming pool one August afternoon when Andy Adorno boomed down the Seville Road into Ronda on his 1,225 cc. Harley Davidson Hurricane, stripped to the waist, his gout of black hair driven back from his face, his heavy body dusted and sweatstained in the mountain sunshine. He pulled up at the traffic lights adjacent to the hotel driveway, and, revving hugely in the empty road, glanced round about him, enjoying the heat, the noise, the new town. Twenty yards away, Diana and Eleanor looked up from their magazines. "Why aren't there any Spick laws about scooters," said Mrs. Parry. "I don't think he's Spanish," said Diana. "Mm, too tall." Adorno turned and met their eyes; he smiled, apparently pleased that he was the theme of their irritation. "You English too?" he shouted. Removing her sunglasses, Diana nodded. "Catch you around," he said as he hurled the bike forward with needless violence into the town, causing the tan-suited *patrones* of the hotel to watch the thinning sprays of grit with cardiac disgust.

They saw him every day—punching the pintables that lined the cafe terraces, shooting pool with the soldiers in the main square casino, lurching out of side roads by the bus station on his bike, bellowing past the hotel to El Hondon swimming pool with some bikini-ed Swede or American clutching his waist. Diana and Eleanor would mention Andy from time to time. "Saw that hooligan with the motorbike this morning in Bar Oliva drinking Anises . . . the yob on the motorbike was in the Telefonica with some dagos today . . .

the bike oik almost ran someone down in the market square
. . . I wish the bike oik wouldn't go around half naked all
the time. . . ."

Parry *fille* and Parry *mère* were alike convalescing after a
long run of abbreviated affairs. In particular, Diana had recently tired of a set of spendthrift stockbrokers which she had
found herself going to bed with; Eleanor had recently been
spurned by the young director of a new radio company, who
had waived her frank entreaties at a crowded after-dinner
party. For Mrs. P. the cure was relatively straightforward—
she needed a rest. The younger Diana, on the other hand, was
suffering from the inevitable attack of night fatigue; night
fatigue, with its languor and apathy, an indefinite series of
one-directional days over which the dusk hung like the promise
of extinction. So they gave themselves up to silence, dark
glasses, and sun, to a period during which they would re-
invigorate their bodies and conserve their sexual energies,
going to bed early, sober and alone.

With two weeks of the holiday still to run Mrs. Parry decided that she didn't much like Ronda and got on an airplane
to London. The evening before, over dinner in the starched
chill of the Reina dining room, Eleanor complained of a slight
restlessness, and when Diana went to her mother's room the
next morning she found her gone.

Diana had, she supposed, intended to stay out the month,
but as she ate lunch that day and reread her mother's note a
familiar tremor came over her. The night fatigue was passing;
she felt active, envious, neglected again. At two she walked
down to the Iberia office and booked a flight for the next day.
She spent the rest of the afternoon drinking up the remaining
sun, every now and then anxiously examining her bikini
marks. She returned to her room, did her exercises until her
thighs were as stiff as steel rods and her breasts felt like
little fists of muscle, and then, as a sort of token, put on her
short white Pucci dress, checking in the mirror that her black
pubic triangle was just discernible beneath it as she left for
the hotel bar. She was there bought champagne until 8:30
by a perspiring American called Dexter, with whom she
dined. "Let's look in at Coca's afterwards," Dexter then said.
They drank more champagne in a discotheque alcove. Dexter
was putting his hand up Diana's dress a good deal; Diana re-
taliated by not uncrossing her legs. At eleven, when Diana

was wondering whether she could be bothered not to sleep with Dexter—it was, after all, the simplest way of terminating the evening—Andy came in.

Andy came in, stripped to the waist as usual, a bottle of twenty-peseta wine swinging from one hand, a length of bread in the other. He waved and shouted hellos at the bartenders and turntable operators, kissed two waitresses, and took the floor, dancing alone under the throbbing strobes with elaborate martial-arts movements. Ten minutes later he started to saunter round the club, nodding to his friends, peering closely but offhand at the prettier girls, until he came to Dexter and Diana, at which point he paused. Three feet from their table Andy came to an emphatic halt and began to stare at them both, declining to reply when Dexter uneasily asked what he could do for them. Andy inserted the last wedge of bread into his mouth and chewed on it for what must have been half a minute, meanwhile dusting his palms. Diana soon forgot her embarrassment as she concentrated with rapt distaste on the loose movement of his jaw, the swilling and munching of his large square teeth, the moist swipes of his thick tongue. "Hey there!" said Dexter with simulated amusement when Andy reached out for the half-full champagne bottle, held it up to the light, and swallowed its contents in one long pull, his adam's apple pulsing like a geyser bubble in the intermittent light. Andy dragged his bare forearm across his mouth and burped immensely. "Most refreshing," he said, replacing the bottle and moving round the table toward Dexter, at whose side he knelt and into whose large red ear he started intently to whisper. Andy and Dexter stood up. "Guess I'll be getting along," said Dexter wonderingly. Andy watched him leave and then, with a complacent air, turned to Diana. He held out a hand toward her.

Ninety seconds later Diana was being driven at speed by Andy Adorno down Ronda's main street. Her mind had been full of good things to say to Andy—"Wow, if big boy want, big boy take," "Look, hippie, I don't go for mysterious strangers," "OOoo, aren't you oddly compelling"—but there was something about his manner, something at once single-minded and negligent, which suggested to her that he was on some crappy drug and was liable to get ugly. Now she could think only of her immediate physical discomfort. Using one hand to keep the hem of her dress somewhere in the vicinity of her navel, she put the other arm around his waist. He smelled of dew and sleeping bags. As her sleeve brushed his armpit she wondered vaguely if she would have time to wash the dress before she packed.

Andy abruptly beached the motorbike at the far end of the bridge over Ronda Gorge, the vast fault in the plateau on which the town was spread like assorted crockery on a great white tabletop. He led her back across the bridge to one of its semicircular, railinged indentations. "Have you ever looked over?" "Once. It stinks." "Not at night." He suffered her to kneel on the paved seat and to look out through the bars into the deep stone valley. He stood behind her, very close. "It's eight hundred feet down. Lots of guys a year come here especially to kill themselves. I spoke to the old wreck whose job it is to hose them off the rocks. They always do it here, from the middle, climb over the railings, look around. Think of it." While Andy spoke Diana sensed a thickening presence at the top of her exposed thighs. At first she thought it was his hand and paid no attention. Then her knuckles whitened on the railings as she heard the discreet trickle of his fly zipper. "Then they look around," Andy continued huskily, "and they must wonder how they could hate anywhere so casual. So they look down. Look down." Diana leaned over further, listened to the sound of a stream, telephone crickets, saw water shine, fireflies winking at each other. "Then they just let go, and the earth soars up and—*AW, MY RIG!*" Andy backed off, half doubling over. "The zip . . . got it . . . aw, my fuckin' *snake!*" After Andy had disengaged himself and they had stopped laughing, Diana waited a few seconds and said, "I'm going back tomorrow"—but he made her take the ticket from her bag and he swung it out over the bridge wall. Diana watched the slip of red paper wing its way down through the dark air.

Whenever Diana thinks about those seconds now she re-experiences them simultaneously—discreet trickle, crickets telephoning, shine of water, winking fireflies—but it is with enduring consternation that she reviews the following month. "Come on," he said, checking her out of the hotel, "I'm going to make you nice." Halfway up Europe on that fucking bike. They spent the night with some unspeakable hippies in Granada, Andy conducting a sale of dud narcotics on whose proceeds the couple dined at the Ritornello club in Alicante, where he moreover made her dance. They spent two nights in a 100-peseta pension in Peniscola ("Cock-coke," Andy called it), slept on the beach at Sitges, and lived naked for a week on a Pyrenean ridge. They ate jumbo prawns and collected a mescaline consignment in the Marseilles docks, stayed at the George IV in Monte Carlo, contracted scabies in a Le Touquet youth hostel, and sat for thirty-six hours in the Orly waiting rooms. Apart from the squalor, the crappy people they encountered, the filthy macrobiotic food he occasionally bothered to make her eat, and that fucking motorbike, what appalled Diana most was the unforgivable *corniness* of her predicament. Tight little rich girl encounters working-class spunk. Seen from the outside everything he did was in trite inverted commas: he was uninhibited, zany, impulsive—"lyrical." And yet being with him was an utterly unreflecting activity; Diana never hesitated because nothing gave Andy pause. There was the sex, too, of course, and it was perhaps this that gave Diana most retrospective embarrassment. Unlike the delicate, artful sex technicians she had slept with in the past, Andy didn't seem to concern himself much with her own inclination or pleasure. For some reason this made her feel achingly passionate and (the word made her squirm) "tender," also. Once, in the Pyrenees, he encouraged her to drink too much wine and she was sick over her naked body. He held her shoulders. "Now you won't like me any more," she had said. Andy hurled her down in the long grass and made love to her with unprecedented ferocity. Ten minutes out of his presence and she began to feel confused, frightened, and intensely sad.

He dropped her off at the preliminary customs checkpoint in Boulogne harbor. Andy asked Diana what she was going to do when she got back. She told him she would be starting at London in October. Which college? She told him which college. Andy couldn't help it—he *had* to laugh. "Why are you laughing?" she asked. But Andy kicked the bike into gear and Diana kissed his lips quickly before he could zip off down the salty black road.

Diana was still crying three weeks later when she took her place in the check-in queue at Wolfson College, London, a huge post-modern matchbox which loomed starkly over Golders Green bus depot. Although her transparent silk trouser suit assumed a perfunctory sexiness, Diana stood in an unwonted slouch and her head hung, resigned and unalert. He recognized her anyway. "There you are at last—I've been here a year already." He kissed her condiment lips as the students threaded past. "Are you going to come and live with me, or what?" She started to cry again. "Yes, please," said Diana.

21: DOWN UNKNOWN PATHS

Oh, but it was not just from her that Miss Lucy Littlejohn got an uneasy reception when she flounced into Appleseed Rectory at seven o'clock that evening, chewing gum, smoking a cigarette, peeling a banana, carrying an empty bottle of wine, trying to mend a broken onyx necklace, and wanting a great deal of cash for the undersized mini-cab driver who had himself escorted her to the door. Andy greeted Lucy with exactly the kind of grisly animality that Diana had dreaded most. (As Andy kissed Lucy's mouth for the second time Diana remembered noticing that he really was a bit too fat, and noticing also that his being a bit too fat was one of her favorite things about him.) Quentin, on the other hand, popped his lips on Lucy's cheek with soldierly restraint, having preceded the gesture with the introduction of his wife. Distant twinges threatened Giles's normal equanimity when Lucy knelt by the side of his chair, whispered in his ear, and kissed his tightened lips; three ten-pound notes fluttered absentmindedly from his fingers. The Americans were then presented en masse by a fluent Villiers. Unintroduced, Whitehead observed these intercourses from the corner of the room, where he was perched on a baronial velvet armchair.

And Lucy. To little Keith's narrow blue eyes she was something of a disappointment. The tales he had heard about her were, by and large, dehumanizing in tendency. Lucy was a thing that fucked people for money, that would wank you off for a favor, that removed its clothes if you asked it to. But here she was—to all appearances spectacularly human. Further, while only slightly less pretty than Keith's much-thumbed mental photographs of her, Lucy's looks were so expressive of personality, so dispiritingly *unusual*. Surveying her crew-cut silver hair, sequinned eyelids, pendulous mouth, multipainted teeth, nonexistent chin, and quite extraordinarily baroque and bulky costume, one was at a loss to see why people hadn't thought of looking that way before. No. Lucy was palpably the holder of views, the entertainer of thoughts, the proprietress of some individuality. Just listen to her—

"Eye-eye-eye. I really made a friend of that dwarf taximan. When I got into the cab I said to myself, 'Kid, the man who's driving you—he's a dwarf. He's sitting on practically the *Encyclopaedia Britannica* just to get a hand to the steering wheel. Don't talk about dwarfs till he gets you there and goes away again.' I sat in the back trying to think of things not to do with dwarfs to say to him. Halfway through the park I got as far as telling him I'd just been to see *Snow White and the Seven* . . . and then sort of trailed off. It wasn't *my* fault—that's what I saw this morning. So what I want to make clear is, before we go on, I don't mean *any* offense, no matter what things come out of my mouth. So are there any dwarfs or queers or Jews here or anything like that, so I know?"

"Well, I'm a Jew," said Marvell.

"I'm a queer," said Skip.

". . . And I'm a dwarf," said Keith (before anyone else could), to vast applause.

"See? See? Hey, whose shoes do you have to walk a mile in to get a drink around here?"

As Quentin self-reprovingly poured Lucy a whiskey from the flagon that Giles had recently sauntered down the stairs with, Marvell asked, impatiently, "What do you want a drink for, Lucy, anyhow?"

The Americans, you see, had received Lucy with snotty reserve, with ostentatious cool. They had spent the past half hour in a more or less successful attempt to establish an atmosphere of gravity and devotional calm. Marvell had brought down from his room a large cuboid case, laying it carefully on the table in the grotto-like dining alcove of the larger sitting room, from which he fussily produced and then arranged various bottles, vials, syringes, nostril spoons. Skip had loped round the house marshaling its inhabitants, laconically instructing them to take their seats in the living room. There they were met by Roxeanne, who in the intervals of trying to restore Giles to life gathered chairs and incidentally cemented her alienation of Diana by sexily persuading Andy not to put a record on. The household had entered into the spirit of things with a kind of ironic docility, but the clamor of Lucy's entrance quite broke their mood.

"Is this a seance or something?" asked Lucy.

"What do you want a drink for, Lucy," Marvell asked again, less edgily. "I have much better gimmicks right here."

"Far out. I don't want a gimmick, I want a drink."

Since "far out" had come to carry roughly the same force as "oh really?," Marvell's asperity returned. "Look, explain it to her, Quent, willya? I reiterate, I don't want to get too straight about this but we'll be all out of whack if we do it unscientifically. Okay?"

The denseness of the sitting-room furnishings, together with its chocolate brown wallpaper and deep-blue fitted carpet, gave it a premature receptivity to the advancing dusk. Although, at 7:30, it was obvious that there was plenty of light left on the other side of its two tall windows, the texture of the room closed stealthily in on itself. When Marvell spoke his voice wandered out plaintively into the incipient evening.

"Have any of you . . . have any of you decided which way you want to go yet?"

"I have," said Andy, getting to his feet. He brushed his hair out of his eyes and clapped his hands together. "I want to feel sexed-up, big rigged, violent and strong."

"I imagine," said Marvell, his hands already busy inside his box, "I imagine you feel most of those things most of the time, don't you, Andy?"

"Check. But I want to feel all of them all of the time— all of tonight anyway."

Marvell took a multicolored capsule and split it with an unsettlingly long thumbnail onto a blank sheet of paper. To the pyramid of powder he added sections of two other pills. Andy was now instructed to fold the paper double, forming a channel down which the brew could be poured into his mouth. He asked if he was allowed to wash it down with whiskey and was told that he might. Marvell held up what could have been an eardrop syringe. "Take two drops of this on your tongue."

"What was it?" asked Andy, having done so.

"Adrenalin concentrate."

"Casual."

"You got about a half hour, forty-five minutes. Right . . . Uh, Celia?"

Celia frowned. "Well, it rather depends on what we're going to do tonight."

"Don't tell me," said Diana drearily, eyes half closed, "another club crawl."

"C'mon, Diana," said Andy, "what in the fuck's wrong with that? I'm feeling pretty . . . pretty loose already."

"Actually, Diana," Quentin joined in, "I *had* planned to give our friends a very oblique glimpse of our London night-life."

"Sounds okay to us," said Marvell, briefly consulting Skip and Roxeanne. "Celia? . . . How about it?"

Celia sat upright. "Well. Obviously I want to feel a bit speedy—in case we dance. And I wouldn't mind some mescaline, or perhaps . . ."

"Try to be more specific, Celia, please. Don't talk drugs. Talk feelings, moods."

"Well, I . . . I just want to have a good time." Celia turned again to Quentin, who warmly met her eye. "And to feel full of love," she said.

The room blushed. Raising his quiff-like eyebrows, Marvell rummaged boredly inside the case, eventually bringing out a single pink pill which he lobbed across the room. "Just a straight High extract," he sighed. "Okay, how about Keith there?"

Whitehead waved a hand negligently in the air. Bootless, he had no intention of performing a miniature waddle across the room, and the request he was steeling himself to make would in any case be for Marvell's ears only. "Haven't quite decided yet. Mind if I sit on it?"

"So what else do you do with it?" drawled Skip, smirking sleepily.

Keith did not see the relevance of that remark. "All right with you, Marvell?" he asked.

Marvell was smiling at Skip, but quickly returned his gaze to little Keith. "Sure—but not too long now, okay? Lucy," said Marvell, some sternness returning to his voice, "how about you."

"Ooh, *what* a treat," said Lucy. "Isn't Captain Marvell clever to be able to—"

"Can I have my turn now please."

"Pardon me?"

"Can I have my turn now please."

Giles had spoken with such robotic clarity that everyone turned to him in surprise. He was sitting erectly on the edge of his chair, palms open upward in the air. His face was tenser than it had been all day and his expression changed with unusual rapidity, like a blind man moving down unknown paths.

"Sure," said Marvell.

"Can I have my turn now please."

"Sure, Giles."

"Please . . . Just stop me . . . Can't you make my . . . Only stop me *worrying* all the time."

"About what?"

"Actually *little* things."

"About what things, man? I have to know about what?"

Giles relaxed, drunk and battered, into the sofa. His right hand was covered by Lucy's as his left fluttered like a damaged bird. A delta of tears formed slowly on his cheeks.

"Yawn," said Andy. "A crying jag."

"Well," said Marvell grimly, "I can give him a wide-spectrum anxiety calmant, but I . . . ."

Giles's head sank back on his shoulders and his slipped mouth readjusted itself, less sulky in sleep.

"A blackout," said Andy.

"I'd say it would be unwise to give him anything at this moment in time," said Marvell. "I'll lay it on him later. However, Lucy, you were . . . ?"

"Okay, Marv, okay. Here we go. I don't want any sadness tonight. Cast off, skipper, I'm on board. I don't want to worry about anyone but me."

"Autonomous? Self-determinant? Solipsist?"

"That ought to do nicely."

"I got it." Marvell unscrewed the cap of a tube of lozenges, one of which he cautiously immersed in a saucer of crimson ointment. "Great. Now, Diana. What do you want?"

"Nothing," said Diana.

"The fuck, Diana," yawned Andy, "you've got to have something. Why are you so fuckin' defiant all the time?"

"I didn't say it defiantly, just in complete boredom. I want a drug, but I want a drug to stop me feeling anything. And to kill the past. That is, if tonight's going to be as stupid and nasty as it looks like being."

Amused comment rippled through the room. Marvell stirred himself. "That'll be no sweat to fix," he said.

Roxeanne and Skip obligingly opted for the "usual" (sense intensifiers and heartbeat accelerators respectively), while, with considerable pomp, Marvell prepared his own stimulant, setting a match to a combustible powder whose sooty residue he lollipopped onto his forefinger and dipped into his mouth. "It's called a Prospero," he said. "Makes me feel in control. Mm—hey—I forgot: Quent."

Folding his arms, Quentin sat back, his choice muscula-ture extending itself adorably over the sofa. The residual unease that had slowed the atmosphere of the room was in-stantly chased away by the creamy mellifluousness of his voice.

"A hypothesis," he said. "It occurs to me that one's man-nerisms, one's behavioral ticks, are neither quite innate nor quite fortuitous. We project them as mechanisms of defense and appeal, of withdrawal and capitulation; they are means of stylizing our attitude to others and to the world. Forgive me—intolerably ill-put. At any rate, as a profoundly cultivated and therefore profoundly unspontaneous creature I thought it might be interesting if I were shorn of these—my reflexes, my stock responses—so as to become, as it were, socially unclothed. My fetching manner must at times be excessively irritating so I hereby give you the chance to banish it and refurnish me. I *throw* the matter open: make of me what you will."

"Isn't this all somewhat unspecific?" complained Marvell.

"Not for long," said Quentin.

"To begin with," said Diana, "you could give him a stutter. That at least might make him talk less."

"Bravo, Diana!" roared Quentin. "You've got the idea. Marvell, make me inarticulate."

"Make him gauche and gawky," said Lucy.

"Why not make him rather shy," said Celia perplexedly.

"Make him as horny as a dog," said Roxeanne.

"And make him terrified," said Andy.

Quentin spread his hands and smiled. "Marvell: you have your instructions."

Ten minutes later, after Quentin had inhaled, sucked, and sniffed various occult compounds, Marvell brushed himself down and regained the dining table alcove. He looked around the room. "That about does it," he said.

Whitehead sat tight in his chair until the very last moment. Couples were dispersing in the direction of the bedrooms. Giles, once revived, had gaggingly swallowed his calmant and was being led by Lucy from the room. Diana had gone up, muscularly alone; Roxeanne had followed Andy, Quentin, and Celia from the room. Skip remained in his seat, his features fossilized in a blocked daze, then sloped off.

"Hey. Marvell."

"Oh yeah. Keith."

Keith left his chair, hoisted himself into the room and went nearer to Marvell, nearer and nearer until he could lift himself up onto the bench opposite him.

"Hey there," said Marvell, looking over the lid of his box. "What can I do for you?"

"Make me tall," said Keith. "Make me tall, make me tall."

22: WHO'S HᏋ?

Andy unbuckled his belt and lowered his jeans. "Worrr, that's better. Christ, some scene with that cow. That mad fucker really whopped it, didn't he?"

"He really *is* mad," said Diana, leaving her pantie suit in a white puddle on the carpet as she stepped out of it and, naked, took up her hairbrush.

"Yeah. Those dead, undersea eyes," Andy said dreamily, untying his jockey pants.

"Mm."

Diana continued to look into the mirror, continued to brush her hair.

"You're skinnier, you know. You've lost weight," said Andy experimentally. She ignored him. Encouraged, Andy leaned a hand on the lower curve of her waist, where a trace of her bikini line was still visible. "Yes, I really think you've lost weight."

"Don't touch me."

"What for?"

"Just advice." Diana turned around. "It's just advice. I mean there's Lucy to consider, and that fat Yank. You've got stiff work to do tonight, big boy."

"No, I haven't. . . . And what if I have?"

"I don't care what you do. Look, fats, I don't care *what* you do so long as you're not going to come in here afterwards just kinda jogging your shoulders and just kinda talking about it and just kinda showing how casual and liberated you—"

"Liberated . . . ?"

"As if it's really quite attractive of you to do these things. I don't mind as long as it doesn't suddenly turn into something nice about you. Okay?"

At the beginning of the first speech Andy had compressed his neck, allowing his shiny fringe to fall over his forehead. Through it he reproachfully glanced at Diana's taut symmetrical face. She looked like a granite-hard hockey player recalling, for his consideration, a bad injury. "Diana, I really don't know what's the matter with you." Andy straightened up. He smiled suddenly. "No! I don't believe it! Come on, you're— you're *jealous*, aren't you?"

"Like fuck."

"*Christ.* You are! Well well well."

"I'm not jealous, just . . ."

"But we've discussed this," said Andy in disbelief. "Jesus. Did I grouse when you fucked that actor while I was in Amsterdam? When you fucked Bruce Howard after that party —did I beef?"

"So who's got the perfect memory—I didn't even fuck him!"

"So you *blew* him then. I mean, what the fuck *difference* does it make."

"What about you? You fuck girls you don't even *want* to fuck."

"How the fuck do I know I want to fuck them till I fuck them? Be reasonable, woman. And anyway, so fucking what? Diana, it makes me sick to hear this sort of talk in this house. Christ, you think you're living with civilized people and then someone springs this sort of crap on you." His tone had become confidently indignant, regretful. "You think you know someone—you respect them as decent, genuine human beings —then you find they've still got these sick anxieties about something as trivial as— Now, Diana, you just, you just hear me out here. Nobody's getting away with that kind of dead babies when I'm living in this house. I'm fucked if I'm going to get leant on with this trashy talk—"

Diana sat on her bed with her back to him as Andy lectured cheerfully on. Her form grew preoccupied. She spoke softly, without turning around. "Andy. Did you write this?"

"—and that's real dead babies. What?"

"Did you write this?"

"Write what?"

Diana turned and held up a sheet of foolscap paper. Her face was pale and very cold.

"What is it, man?" said Andy, with concern.

The letter was written in erect black capitals, justified at either margin, and so uniform that at first it seemed to have been typewritten or typeset. Andy frowned.

DIANA. YOU DON'T NEED ME TO TELL YOU WHAT'S GOING ON. OR DO YOU? HAVE YOU EVER THOUGHT, TURNING TO THE MIRROR OR CATCHING YOUR EYE IN A SHOP-WINDOW, WHAT YOUR FEATURES SAY? GOOD LOOKS, SEX, AFFLUENCE, SELF-PRESERVATION? OH NO. I SEE WHAT'S IN YOUR MIND, THE DISGUST IN YOUR MOUTH, YOUR EYES FULL OF BURNING PUS. CAN'T YOU SENSE THE LOATHING THAT PULSES AROUND YOU IN THE AIR? DON'T YOU KNOW HOW WE ALL FEEL? WE'D LIKE TO CARVE YOUR FAT THIGHS, CHOP OFF YOUR SPROUTING LITTLE TITS, GRIND SABRES UP YOUR ANUS, CHEW AT YOUR PERINEUM UNTIL YOU DIE,
AND GET THE DEVILS OUT.
JOHNNY

While Andy read, Diana folded her arms across her naked breasts and started to cry with childish volume, making no attempt to conceal her snot and tears.

"Christ," said Andy. It was only the second time she had cried in his presence. "Take it easy, baby. I'm looking after you. Nothing's going to happen." Andy patted her shoulder. "Hang on, baby, nothing's going to happen."

Andy belted a towel round his waist and walked out onto

the landing. "JOHNNY!" he yelled. "*Johnny*." Appleseed Rectory again recessed into silence. "Who's he?" he heard Quentin say somewhere. A few seconds later Roxeanne came out of the sitting-room door.

"What's going on, man?"

On an impulse Andy skipped down the stairs and seized Roxeanne's shoulders. Tigerishly he slammed her up against the door and kissed her mouth with incurious violence; Roxeanne pumped her middle against his, whispered, "I want to drain you empty," pushed him against the banister, and walked regally upstairs.

Andy staggered off to find Lucy. One way or another he thought it was going to be quite an interesting weekend.

23: DrunK SpaCe

Giles stands swimming in the center of his room. It is clear from his stalled face and dead posture that he is operating at drunk speed, a castaway in drunk space. His hands take interminably long to curl round the gin bottle and to train it on his mouth. While he swallows his eyes recede, as if only ten per cent of him were there. His face is a corpse's face, numb and luminous with a year of slow drunk hours.

Giles tilted away into his bathroom and steadied himself against the washbasin. The room was a real study. On a table by the basin stood two electric toothbrushes and seven manual ones of various rakes and texture, a waterpick, an economy tub of Selto, three sorts of toothpaste, four packets of Interdens, a serried rank of mouthwashes, a dentician's impression of Giles's teeth (which resembled a miniature mockup of a building site—pulleys, ladders, cranes)—and a white enamel tray of surgical instruments. Every sharp surface in the room, including the doorknob and toilet flush handle, was padded with sponge.

He bared his teeth at the mirror and jactitated feebly as a heifer ran toward him. On automatic, his hand crept out toward the gin decanter shelved to his left. He gazed with more intentness at his face, leaning forward *gradatim*. He watched himself for a full minute in puzzled accusation, and said, "You've got to stop *crying*." He closed his eyes and his mind dropped back through a penny arcade of dental afternoons.

"Giles? Giles! It's me. Lucy."

". . . Lucy who?"

"*Lucy.*"

"Oh, yes, sorry, Lucy, actually," said Giles, unbolting the door.

Lucy bustled into the room. Giles hugged the wall, like a spy, as if he were banking on Lucy passing him by unobserved. She had never been in Giles's room before but her far-flung senses quickly catalogued its contents. She opened the drinks cupboard and removed a liter of whiskey from it. To Giles's clogged nerves she was merely a spectral truss of clothes and color, and yet he felt also, more obscurely, that it stood for something he knew and could depend on. His mouth widened friendly as he tried to focus with more rigor on her loosening shape.

"Oh, hello, Lucy. Cheers, actually."

"What?"

"Actually. I mean . . . oh, God."

"Giles, honestly."

"I know."

She drew him to the bed and sat down beside him. She drank from the bottle, a rivulet of whiskey coursing down through the patchwork cosmetics on her cheek. Between them the air was motionless with a sense of dislocation, as if neither of them could believe what they had once meant to each other.

"Giles, why are we—"

But Lucy noticed a minute facial gesture, something instantly checking out in Giles's eyes. More cautiously, she said, "Why are we here with those baddies? Those awful Americans?"

"Yes," said Giles with abrupt animation, "they *are* awful, aren't they?"

"Awful. Real baddies. The worst people I've met for a very long time—for ages. Scum of the earth. That little Trog with the drugs."

"Mm, Skip."

"No, Skip's the streak of piss who never says anything.

The bossy one. Marvell. Fucking stupid name. And that girl!"
Lucy tensed her breasts and folded a hand sultrily over her
mouth. " 'Oooh, Indy, kin I bite yrr cack aff?' She looks like a
horse. It's just not on to have a body like that. It's just not on."

Giles's expression grew wistful. "I think she's got—I've
never seen ones like that before—I think she's got absolutely
the most beautiful . . ."

"Forget it," said Lucy. "They can't be real. She *has* to be
on two silicon boosts a day."

Giles had been going to say that Roxeanne had the most
beautiful *teeth* he had ever seen, actually, but he brought
his gaze down to the pillow and seemed to fall into a muse.

Her eyes absently quartering the room, Lucy lit a long
cigarette. "Where am I supposed to be sleeping tonight? Any
idea?"

Giles cast his mind torpidly through the house, filling rooms,
allotting bed partners. "In . . . At . . . With . . ." Realizing
that his was the only obviously eligible room, Giles turned
to Lucy in dawning trepidation. For a moment his eyes became guarded and quiescent, like those of a weak animal in
the presence of another species.

"Giles, whatever's the matter with you these days." It was
not a question.

"I don't know either, really." He blinked and sighed. "Lucy,
would you very kindly mix me a . . ."

Lucy stood up. "And tonic?"

"Yes, please, actually."

"Big one?"

"Yes please."

She quickly took his hand. "Don't worry, baby, I'll catch
a sofa or something."

Folding up on the bed, Giles wedged a pillow between his
face and the wall. His tongue patrolled the inner ridges of his
gums as Lucy's shape deliquesced before him. Almost weight-
less now, his mind backed off into random, punctured sleep.

24: Heavy Water

Look!

Here comes Whitehead, toppling out of his room, stilted on
heelless boots which he has stuffed with toilet paper up to the

calves and in which his crushed, unsocked feet now groan and rot. The resultant blockage of his sweat pores will soon give Keith the impression that a rubber plunger has been attached to his scalp, initiating a corpuscle-dash to his head. In fact, little Keith's face is worryingly white, like morning snow, and his legs are big with blood pools, putting extra strain on the sawn-off Whitehead Senior bags that he has hurriedly tapered with a stapling machine. Further sartorial attractions include a paisley nylon scarf with which he conceals the rope of fat encircling his neck and a blue cheesecloth shirt so coarse in texture that it has already reduced his nipples to blood puddings. Vilely, Keith pauses by the garage exit, his hand scouting his crown for bald patches. "What are you doing?" he asks himself out loud. "What makes you think you can pull this off?" But the drug prods him somewhere in the spine and he feels a surge not so much of confidence as of fuddled resignation. Wobbling queasily on his tight-packed shoes, Whitehead spills out into Brobdingnag.

Upstairs, in agreeable contrast, The Hon. Quentin Villiers leaned backward stiffly in order that Celia might clip up the collar of his frilled taffeta blouse.

"How do I look?"

In his violet suede suit, the half-length trousers tucked into alligator-skin thigh boots, and with his silver-blond flyaway hair curled playfully up from his forehead, Quentin looked blindingly beautiful, rather Chattertonian, and definitively upper class. It gave Celia a sweet toothache pang just to be near him.

"You look absolutely extraordinary. Like a sex cubicle. God, how I wish I had your complexion," said Celia, reclaiming her own with a palmful of thick brown paste. "My loathsome spots are bound to start *gleaming* through."

"Drivel, my sweet. It distresses me to hear you talk in that vein." Quentin leaned forward, no less stiffly, and smoothed his lips over Celia's half-open mouth.

She looked up at him, heavy water gathering in her eyes. The wave of sick disbelief passed as Quentin placed his dry hands on her cheeks.

"I love you," he said gravely.

"Thank you," she said. "I love you."

Quentin cruised away to stand before the full-length wardrobe mirror, teasing his hair with long fingers.

"Darling," said Celia, "can you feel any of those strange drugs you chose? You're not getting a sadness or anything, are you?"

"Nothing whatever. Not a murmur. And you?"

"Yes, my hands are in gear already." Celia stood up, her square face uncertain and amused. "Do I look not too bad?"

"You look *very touching*."

Celia smiled gummily—and for a moment she did indeed look just that. "Darling, have you decided on the itinerary yet?"

"I've given the matter some thought, yes. To begin with we could do much worse than look in at—"

25: THE PSYCHOLOGIC revue

The Psychologic Revue was held fortnightly at a semiderelict 1920s cinema in what used to be Kilburn High Road, now a jangling caravan grouped here and there beween the northern motorway access routes. The Chevrolet and the Jaguar swung together off the flyover and moaned down through the darkness toward the Universal, a sooty Gothic structure which hovered massively over the secondhand car showrooms and ramshackle eateries that littered its surroundings. The shadowy caves nestling between the motorway caissons, route-indicator stanchions, and overpass columns held a companionable gloom, secret and unmenacing. Overhead, the beams of a million streetlamps joined in a shaft of neutral, watery sodium which filtered off into the sky like an abandoned gateway to the night.

"Some set," murmured Marvell, as the Chevrolet approached.

"I tell you," said Andy from the back seat, "if any of those fuckin' little tramps gives anybody any trouble just let me know and he's going to be one sick junkie, is all."

Twenty yards away, scattered about the dim foyer steps, a score of down-and-outs looked on fearfully as the Appleseeders poured from the cars and moved toward them. "Ah, the vanity of travel," said Quentin. Andy raced on ahead to kick a gangway through the crowd—saying "Get out of here" and "Get some cash," occasionally boxing a protuberant head or stomping on a tardy hand. The tramps crawled away without protest or comment. "LEAVE HER ALONE, YOU FUCKIN' BUM!" bellowed Andy as a coughing hobo was slow to roll out of Diana's queenly path. Andy's heavy-duty boot eased his transit across the steps.

"Christ," summed up Andy, straightening his combat jacket when they had gained the foyer. "Try and take in a show around here and what you got to do? Beat your way through a mess of bums. Giles—pay the gentleman and let's get inside."

The interior decor of the Universal was not so much pretentious as straightforwardly apocalyptic: a distant channeled ceiling which receded in a succession of *trompe l'oeil* false summits, hundredweights of dank purple curtain, 3-D brass frescoes, deep-ribbed walls and stucco cornices. The building had been condemned, most emphatically and categorically, in the late 1960s—thereby vastly increasing its popularity as a decadent venue—but in the tinged red light it seemed to possess a certain monolithic solidity. The Appleseeders made their way down the aisle on the sticky carpet, appraising the small and opulent audience concentrated in the first few rows before the semicircular stage.

"Is it always this empty?" asked Marvell.

"Only cool people know about it—that's how come the cash," said Andy, referring thus elliptically to the dozen tenpound notes Giles had earlier offered the damson-suited commissionaire.

Although Whitehead had done a fair bit of equivocal hanging back and a certain amount of hesitant trotting forward in a bid to sit next to Lucy as they filed into the third row, he found himself wedged between Skip and Marvell—both of whom, even in Keith's estimation, seemed to be taking an unhealthily close interest in him. The patrons already seated made no attempt to retract their legs for the newcomers and had to be reminded by Andy of the need for this courtesy before obliging. The atmosphere was at once twitchy and slothful. A haze of terminal apathy hung in the gaunt auditorium.

"My God," said Quentin, brushing the plastic seatcover with a velvet glove. "It's like a dotard matinée in here. Open as my heart shall always be to persons of fashion, I wish they'd occasionally show some *sign* of real animation."

"What are the gimmicks?"

"Now just you wait and see, Skip. I promise you one thing —it's never quite like it was the last time."

As the girls chatted contrapuntally, as Quentin outlined his thinking on "counteralternative" theater, as Skip failed once again to engage Giles in conversation, as Whitehead wondered what to do when his legs exploded—as the whiskey flasks were snapped open and the marijuana showboats lit— signs, at least, of real animation gathered in the hall. It had now struck ten o'clock, and foot stamps, obscene catcalls, and seat rattling began a lazy crescendo. In particular, two tall youngsters dressed up as businessmen in the front row were exerting themselves to some effect, pitching an empty tequila bottle onto the stage, producing an anguished whine from a subsonic whistle, urinating without standing up into the orchestra pit.

Adorno was about to lean forward and invite them to shut the fuck up—when he appeared to notice something. "Hold it," he said. "They're Conceptualists."

"Who are they?" asked Marvell.

"Conceptualists." Andy had started to peer apprehensively around the auditorium.

"Oh, right, I've heard about them. Something between old-style Hell's Angels and Chuck Manson."

"Nothing like that," said Andy, in such disgust that for a moment he seemed to be looking at Marvell through his nostrils rather than his eyes. "Nothing like that at all. They're new, different. I think they're the only people who've made creative sense of what's happening to the world now. For me, they're the only ones to have really made something out of what technology has done to sex and violence. They'll last, too."

"Yeah?"

"Fuckin' better believe it, boy."

"How come?"

Precision and arbitrariness were the twin hallmarks of Conceptualist activity. On the morning that inaugurated their "Gestures," as they called them, fifteen lowly civil servants were found scalped in their beds. They were all sewage-disposal civil servants. A political organization? Fifteen days later a random selection of doctors, health inspectors, social workers, charity secretaries, and Salvation Army officials had their Achilles' tendons severed in a lightning wave of synchronized attacks. On the first day of the following month the newspapers reported that thirty hardware shop owners, in various parts of the country, had had their left eyes spooned out. Four weeks later stolen helicopters showered over key cities a bizarre confetti of pornographic postcards, atrocity photographs, suppressed medical reproductions, vetoed X-ray plates, and blacklisted urinalyses. (The police were not so much worried, by this time, as utterly hysterical.) The remains of perverse sexual scenarios periodically came to light—they weren't publicized, but it was assumed that the same organization was responsible: a stylized car crash, the impacted instrument panels of either vehicle stained with semen; an operating theater, broken into at night and made the scene of a bloody debauch; aircraft hangars, chemistry laboratories, racetrack pits, drug-experimentation plants, and electrical appliance showrooms similarly abused; the crippled and insane looted from various asylums and returned dumbstruck; a kidnapped surgeon required at gunpoint to perform strange anal surgery on a masked patient; an eighteen-month-old girl found in a ditch with severe genital injuries.

Andy's spirited championship of the Conceptualists was not entirely disinterested. He had known several, one or two intimately, and had long been impressed by their calm and ruthlessness, their eerie anonymity, the almost erotic yearning with which they talked of their Gestures, and above all by their icy efficiency. As a youth, Adorno had had a dream of establishing his own Conceptualist chapter in London's Earl's Court, marshaling his men with invisible dexterity, submitting his own projects to Conceptualist HQ, attracting the attention of the team's most hardened operatives, rising within the organization as an indispensable executive figure, being at last petitioned to mastermind all future Gestures. . . . Although Andy had already gained one of the two qualifications for Conceptualist membership (he was over six feet tall) and would shortly acquire the second (a humanities degree), that prayer had long ago begun to fade. Waking early, perhaps, or beached on a slow afternoon, Andy was often unable to lose the suspicion that he was too wavering a figure rightly to deserve membership of such a movement, that he lacked the coldness, cunning, and cruelty that so dignified its true representatives. The suspicion, and more recently the near certainty, of these failings in himself had given rise to some of Andy's blackest moments.

"I didn't know the Conceptualists were into all that," said Marvell in a tone of respectful apology. "How can you tell those guys belong?"

"The suits, sharp narcissistic look, cropped hair, tall, hard, very fit . . ." Andy shrugged limply.

"Yeah."

"And they're . . . they're *outside*. Do you know what I mean?" Andy seemed to want an answer.

"Yeah. I know what you mean." Marvell chuckled and said, "They're off duty now, right?"

"Not sure." For the first time concern showed in Andy's voice. Everyone fell silent. "It isn't standard, the way they're fucking about. They're not supposed to be flash like this. . . . Unless they've got some kind of Gesture going."

"Oh, let's leave. Please."

"Relax, Celia," said Andy, with a mixture of impatience and serenity, making it clear that he was more worried about a possible breach of Conceptualist decorum than about their own safety.

"Will it be all right, darling?"

Quentin Villiers lay back in his seat, exhaling huge rings of resinous smoke. He nodded slowly as the Universal lights began to go down.

Out onto the stage sidled a spectacularly deformed old man, a hand wrapped like a flannel over his dented forehead. Squaring up to the mike, he thanked all those who had been kind enough to look in at the Psychologic Revue that night and was sorry to have to inform them that the anticipated artistes, Neural Lobe, had regrettably been unable to keep their booking and that he hoped he would not be letting everyone down when he said that he had persuaded Acey-Deecey and his band to stand in for them tonight. He rolled his eyes haggardly at the audience and reversed through the velvet curtains, which swept grandly open.

Twenty minutes later the Universal was getting heavy. Acey-Deecey, a pensionable cabaret performer, had proved to be fat, ill-rehearsed, drunk, and entirely lacking in all the attributes of showmanship. As he told long, unfunny jokes, thrummed on the piano, and danced with wonky corpulence, he had become aware that his audience was by no means a captive one, and so began to simulate an even more toe-curling pathos, recounting his long history of failure, telling of previous flops with a forgiving smile, simpering into the microphone about his obesity, lack of rehearsing time, alcoholism, etc. The auditorium wheezed and bawled.

"But here's perhaps one song I *can* sing," Acey was saying, prune-eyed. "A song that perhaps I've got the *right* to sing. It was made famous by a very wonderful lady who was dead before any of you were born. It's called 'Nobody Knows You,' and it's the blues, and it goes something like this. . . ."

("They're trying to do the embarrassment routine again," drawled Quentin. "It's meant to be this bad, but no one *gets* embarrassed any more—embarrassment has gone. Surely they know that.")

"Once I lived the life of a millionaire," sang the old man, nodding his head raptly at his paunch. "Spent all my money, didn't have a care. Takin' all my friends out for a—"

And his voice was a horrible, dislocating thing, without body, shape, or feeling, a nerveless skirl that seemed to empty the air around it. The audience shrank back in appalled silence.

". . . bootleg liquor, champagne and wine. Till I began to fall so low, didn't have a penny, had—"

Then it happened. The two tall men from the front row had leaped the orchestra pit and were on the stage. Almost before his last words were out, Acey was on his knees with his hair pulled back—and the man had smacked him in the throat with the iron glove. A rope of blood jumped from his mouth. Then he eye-forked him with a popping sound and dug his boot into Acey's groin, making his legs spring up and flutter. The man wrenched his head from behind until a long sick crack folded out onto the stunned air.

The audience was motionless with italic terror.

"But Concep— They don't—" gibbered Andy, as the man ground his boot into Acey's face and it split like a waterlogged pumpkin. They stood panting over his broken body.

It wasn't until Acey had got to his feet, peeled back the sopping mask, and, flanked by the two "Conceptualists," given a deep bow that the audience made any reaction at all. Some whimpered, some emitted quiet, retrospective screams, some cried with relief, everyone gasped, and a few applauded. Slow with adrenalin, the audience shuffled toward the exit doors.

"Not bad. Not bad," said Marvell.

"Yeah," said Skip.

"I'm glad it amused you," said Quentin.

"A drag it wasn't for real," said Roxeanne.

"How did they *do* it," said Celia.

"Quite simple," said Diana.

"Thought I was going to be sick, actually. But then it all seemed a long way away," said Giles.

"Did you enjoy it, Lucy?" said Keith.

"Sorry, I can't hear you," said Lucy.

"Christ. To think that was supposed to be a gesture! That! They really had me worried for a moment—I thought they really *were* Conceptualists!" said Andy.

26: THE LUGUBRIOUS BOOGIE

"You a pig," wept the lugubrious boogie. "You all pigs."

Round the sackcloth table at the far end of a scotch-room alcove in the bowls of an alcoholic concourse beneath the bistro mezzanines of an eat-and-drink complex of an amenity estate north of Euston Station, the Appleseeders sat nursing half a dozen cork flasks of para-natural whiskey. ("And now some low life," Quentin had said, coughing into his perfumed handkerchief.) Incapacitated Irishmen, morose Mediterraneans, taciturn blacks, bronchitic prostitutes, and vomiting immigrant workers lined the scotch-room benches, being served whiskeys of varying sizes by unsmiling young men in pre-faded denim jumpsuits.

The lugubrious boogie placed his neck against the low bare-brick wall. "Pigs," he gasped.

Roxeanne moved closer to him and took his curled hand. "Why, man? Tell me why. Tell me why we're pigs."

"You all pigs."

"Forget it, Rox," called Andy from the other side of the table. "He's a mess. Drunk and all fucked up. No use talking to them when they're—what the hell do you know, you dumb boogie."

Roxeanne was not discouraged. Skip leaned over and droned quietly into Andy's ear, "Roxeanne has a thing for coons."

"What kind of thing?"

"A fuck-thing."

"With him? With that? He has to be thirty-five."

"Don't matter," said Skip.

"Pigs."

"Look—hey—boogie," shouted Andy, "better get the fuck out of here, boy, okay? You're all fucked up and got nothing to say."

"We're not like that," said Roxeanne; "he doesn't mean it," she told the lugubrious boogie, pressing his hand against her hard breasts.

"Oh yes I do," said Andy. "Beat it, boogie, and I mean now."

" 'Boogie'?" queried Marvell. "Jesus, this guy talks more American than I do. Haven't heard 'boogie' for a time. Say that in New York, Andy, and you'll get your head kicked off."

"I don't give a rat's arse. Because I *wouldn't* say it in New York. I respect and admire the American black. They fight. But over here they're just boogies far as I'm concerned."

A rank of nearby blacks straightened their heads, as if they might take issue with Andy on this point. Andy glared happily at them.

"You know," mused Giles to nobody in particular, "I thought I wasn't going to enjoy tonight, but I quite am, actually. Not *once* have I thought about my . . ." (Villiers extended a hand to refill Giles's beaker.)

Whitehead sat close to Lucy, achingly, illegally close. He noticed, with what he felt to be some impertinence, that her breasts were rather long and tubular beneath her virile white shirt— nothing like the trim conclavities of Diana's breasts nor the global fury of Roxeanne's. Nicer than Celia's, though; more touching somehow. He noticed too that her face was a bit colorless, for all its sequins and cosmetic murals, and her mouth somewhat puckered, but not testily so. Little Keith felt a kind of spurious intimacy with her. If only she wouldn't dislike him—never mind anything else yet.

"Have you ever been in here before, Lucy?"

(Did one bother with that sort of thing these days? Whitehead assembled and compressed his buttocks, thus increasing his sitting height by a couple of inches.)

"No. Have you . . . ? Sorry, what's your name?"

(Her face was blank—but Keith could scarcely credit the solicitude of her manner.)

"Keith."

"Keith? You're the one who . . . ? Oh, *Andy.*"

(And she smiled at him! At Whitehead! Without a whisper of ridicule in her face.)

"No, Lucy, I haven't either. It's interesting—all these different views. I think Roxeanne's on the right track really with . . . that man. Though you can see Andy's point of view. What do you make of it?"

Lucy leaned over and said in her relaxed London accent, "If I was a goner spade like that I'd rather have his talk than her finger up my bum."

(Her voice buzzed in his ear. Keith's pecker leaped.)

A sympathetic, empirical Whitehead followed Lucy's eyes across the table. With his arms at his sides the lugubrious boogie was watching Roxeanne massage his lower lap with the flat of her strong hand. Quentin and Celia exchanged fastidious grimaces and Andy snorted in disbelief. Marvell and Skip, however, looked on smiling, their faces full of pleasant expectation. Diana's, too.

"Let me be, pig. . . . Take . . . Don't . . ."

But Roxeanne murmured closer, urging him back against the wall with her powerful thorax. Her left hand joined her right on the lugubrious boogie's groin, and her fingers closed on something.

"Ah, no, don't," said Lucy. "Don't do this to him."

By now all Appleseed eyes were on Roxeanne and a tingling silence had gathered over the table, enclosing the alcove from the rest of the bay. She bit her lip ticklishly as she unsnapped the lugubrious boogie's thin brown belt and sought for the catch of his zipper with bent forefinger and sharp thumb. She straightened the toggle and pulled it downward, evenly unmeshing the silver treads to disclose a widening triangle of grayish rayon. The lugubrious boogie sighed in a baffled, plaintive way and made to paw at Roxeanne's wrists. She didn't seem to need to take any notice. Her right-hand fingertips dipped into the moist area of his perineal divide while she introduced her left down the loose front band under his navel. Roxeanne wettened her mouth as the light-brown prepuce was hoisted clear of the gauzy underpants. He contemplated his slack organ with a curiosity no less dazed and intent than that of his tablemates. Then, like a jerking second hand, the penis craned abruptly and the lugubrious boogie leaned forward into painful, heaving, tubercular tears.

Roxeanne stood up. She smiled. And they left him there with his elbows on the table, his face held in damp hands.

27: THE OLD COPS

In the concrete avenue Marvell looked around the semicircle of faces. "What now, Quent?"

Twenty feet away a cruising drophead MGE slowed in the narrow vehicle lane. It contained two swarthy persons in the front buckets and another perched up on the rumble seat; the third passenger wasn't good-looking enough to do that kind of thing, and he knew it. After a few seconds the car accelerated away.

"Hey, Quentin. What now?"

For the first time in the year Celia had known him, Quentin Villiers was showing less than his normally perfect serenity. He pinched the base of his nose with gloved fingers and blinked.

"Darling?" said his wife.

"I just want to . . . find the cars," he muttered.

"What about—what was it?—the Gerry Show, place you mentioned," said Marvell. "Where those freaks and oldsters strip and fuck and stuff like that?"

"Really . . . I somehow . . ."

"Or the Blow-Shop, get your . . . Or the Hetero-Club, dump where queers can't get fucked. Or the—"

"Marvell, I don't think . . ."

"Darling?"

"One moment." Quentin folded his arms and stared down at his crossed wrists. When he looked up his features had recovered their poise. "Roxeanne," he said, "why on *earth* did you do that?"

"Do what? Look, what is this," Roxeanne demanded. "What's with you people anyway?"

"Christ," said Lucy.

"Roxeanne: understand that I'm not asking you in accusation but in simple wonderment. What *was* the—"

"To show him who the pigs are."

"I'm sorry, I . . ."

"Roxeanne," began Celia, "you really don't—"

"Don't *what*?"

"I told her to stop it, didn't I," said Andy. "I tipped the boogie to deep six."

"You enjoyed it as much as I did," said Diana, which was broadly true.

"And what is all this shit anyway?" asked Marvell.

"Children children children—this will get us nowhere." Quentin consulted his spangled wristwatch. "It's past two. I don't think there's much point in going on anywhere now. Clash of cultural norms, no? Why don't we—?"

As if he were operating on a different oral threshold from the others, Giles's voice heaved clear of his strained throat. "I'm getting street sadness!" he cried, mouth open, hands over ears, neck bent. "I'm getting the street sadness!"

Lucy held his shoulders.

"Street sadness . . ." whispered Quentin to a frowning Marvell.

"I'm getting the street sadness!"

"The fuck, Giles," said Andy, still flappable, "sometimes you're like a fuckin' chick. Like a fuckin' *chick*."

"Make the gray go away!" said Giles. "Make it, make it!"

"Give him something. Quickly," said Lucy.

"Here," said Marvell. "Try this."

When the Appleseeders entered the underground carpark the old cops were leaning on the Chevrolet's heavy hood.

"Popeye," said Skip, hanging back.

"Take it easy," said Quentin, guiding him on.

As the youngsters approached and took up awkward formation around their cars, the old cops regarded them amicably. Their faces looked creased and shadowy in the expanse of the overlit vault.

"Good evening to you, officers—Sergeant, Constable," sang Quentin.

"Good evening, sirs, ladies," said the Sergeant. "Is this your car, sir, may I ask?"

"Certainly you may. No, it's my friends'. This is, however," said Quentin, nodding at the Jaguar.

"What is the Chevy, sir. '79?"

" '78," said Skip.

"How'd you get it over here?"

"One of the airlift cargoes."

"Must've cost you."

"Yeah, it cost us."

"Very nice. Very nice." The Constable took a tobacco pouch from his breast pocket and began to assemble a cigarette. "Very nice. You young people had a good time?"

"An excellent time, thank you awfully, Constable," replied Quentin dismissively.

The old cops' eyes conferred as Villiers unlocked the Jaguar and as Celia, Diana, Lucy—and Whitehead—milled round its four doors.

"Yours too. Well, well." The Sergeant placed a boot on the Chevrolet fender, straightened his hat and rested an elbow conspiritorially on the hood. "Where'd you go tonight, kids?" he asked Roxeanne and the remaining boys. His tone was not hostile or interrogative. On the contrary, he seemed if anything to be on the point of falling asleep.

The moment Quentin closed the Jaguar door behind him he saw his mistake. Andy was looking morose, Giles annihilated utterly, but Marvell, Skip, and Roxeanne were staring at one another in candid alarm. The old cops' slothful, obsequious patter, Quentin realized, would be indistinguishable from the gloating sarcasm of their American counterparts. Furthermore, everyone was carrying drugs.

Quentin lowered his window. "Gentlemen," he said in his most princely tone, "I'm well aware that you've got nothing better to do than lounge about improving your public image, but if you'll excuse us we ought to be making our way home."

The old cops' eyes conferred again. The Sergeant strolled over to the Jaguar and began to bounce his nightstick on the wheel mounting. "Know how long I'd have to work to get a car like this?"

"No. Nor do I care. A very long time indeed, I should imagine. Sergeant, I don't think this is . . ."

"You young people make me sick sometimes," he said in a hurt and angry voice, as if he would far sooner think highly of them. "Literally sick." He spun round and wiggled the nightstick under Giles's nose. "How long do you expect—"

Giles wheeled away from him, his whole body swimming. The Sergeant seized his shoulder.

"*Look* at me when I'm talking to you, you little bastard!
You're not home yet. You think we can't touch you—scum
like you." He held the club up to Giles's mouth as if it were
a microphone. "We still do it, you know, oh yes, but you
just—" Giles retched loudly into the Sergeant's face. "Christ, for
nothing I'd put you up against that wall and smash your
bloody tee—"

Before the jet of vomit struck the man's chest, Quentin
was out of the car—had stayed the old cop's raised right
hand, had directed Giles's collapse into the arms of Skip and
Marvell, had prodded a £20 note into the Sergeant's breast
pocket, was brushing his jacket down with a silk handkerchief
—and it was over, the untenable moment had opened and
closed like a vent in another time.

The cars sighed up the diagonal ramp. In the Chevrolet, Giles
had been laid out on the back seat. Skip drove fast through
the exhausted precincts. In the Jaguar, the leather seats
shone nervously under the silver motorway lights. A mile
from home, Lucy fell asleep and her head dropped carelessly
onto Keith's waiting shoulder. As Appleseed Rectory surged
up at them through the night, tiny tears were glistening beneath the lids of his closed eyes.

28: YANKED

There was—inevitably, we suppose—a certain amount of
coming and going that night.

As soon as Diana's breathing had steadied and she had
completed her repertoire of quiet, subliminal shrugs, the
wakeful Andy said her name out loud, got no reply, slid
out from between the sheets, furled a towel round his waist
and crept downstairs.

"What do you want?" said Lucy.

Kneeling at the head of the sitting-room sofa, Andy
lowered his head and kissed Lucy judiciously on her mouth,
which remained slack.

"What do you want?"

Tracing soft patterns on her ear with his left hand, Andy's
right felt for the familiar knot of Lucy's nightdress, which,
when tweaked, would render her naked to the waist.

"What do you want?"

Dipping his wettened lips to her breasts, Andy introduced cool fingers beneath the blankets, which burrowed surely through the warm folds.

"Look, stop it. Get off. What do you want?"

"Yawn!" said Andy. "Stop talking. How can you talk at a moment like this?"

"A moment like what?"

"Jesus—at a moment that starts getting fuckin' embarrassing when you start *talking* about it."

"But why?"

Andy untwisted the loop of his towel. It fell away to the floor. "Some snake," he said simply.

"Enormous deal. What's that supposed to do—get me going?"

"Yawn," he said.

"Well then, tell me—get *off*—what you *want*."

Andy persevered.

Down the kitchen passage Keith Whitehead fried on his hot mattress. He was burping terribly every few seconds. They were the very worst sort of burps to which he was subject, like hardboiled eggs imploding at the back of his throat. "Mouth farts" was what Keith had once called them.

Whitehead's legs still throbbed, in a way remote from himself, like—Christ—like glutted anacondas; he moved them about as if they were sections of another body. His stomach was gurgling to such effect that Keith punched it repeatedly with his fists; he kept shouting at it too, of course, with the impotent exasperation with which one shouts at hairtrigger alarm clocks, fizzy radios, banging shutters, some baby crying in a distant place. His frightened penis had retracted to the point of invisibility. The room itself was a 180-cubic-foot pool of wicked and unbelievable smells.

Little Keith was crying a good deal while he thought about his recent attempts to slim down for the Lucy weekend. Whitehead's program: twelve fluid ounces of water per day, jogging two hours a night round the garden, ear-bending aperients, two thousand shin-touching exercises every morning, no food whatever. His body's reply: nitric indigestion (what, Keith would ask himself, was he failing to digest?), paint-bubbling halitosis, 100 per cent constipation, a negligible increase in weight, and mouth farts.

"Thanks a *lot*," he said out loud.

What, then, were Whitehead's sex plans? They were as follows. A harrowing session in the upstairs bathroom—third-degree shower, industrial scrub, gargle with . . . Saniflush? Then Lucy. Kneeling on the bed, he established through his box window that the bathroom light had been extinguished. All was quiet inside the house. Ponderous with insincerity, little Keith stood up and dragged his dressing gown from the hook.

Whitehead was just deciding that he wouldn't, after all, knock on the sitting-room door when it whipped open and the half-naked majesty of Adorno was glowering above him. Andy stepped back in startled amusement.

"What the fuck do you think you're doing?"

"Just . . . I . . ."

Andy crouched. "Yeah, well, go easy on her, kid, okay?" he said, before straightening up and walking quickly up the stairs.

This, in any event, was more than enough for Keith. He was about to scurry quietly back to his box when a light came on inside the room and Lucy said, "Who's that?"

"Keith," he said weakly. "Sorry to disturb you, Lucy—just going to the bathroom."

"That's okay."

The light stayed on. Whitehead found himself peering round the door. Instead of the replete, engorged, spreadeagled figure he had expected, Lucy was sitting up on the sofa, evidently in some disarray, dabbing her cheeks with an old paper tissue.

"Anything the matter, Lucy?"

"Just Andy." She blew her nose. "He always makes me cry."

Andy swung round the corner of the stairs and halted abruptly. Dressed in a thin white T-dress, spreading her hennaed hair with firm hands, Roxeanne sat facing him on the landing.

Andy snapped his fingers, jabbed one of them at her, and spun around. "Right," he said, starting down the stairs again, "let's fuck."

Did Andy ever bother to check whether Roxeanne was

following him as he strode to the kitchen passage garden door? No way. But when he had slid the bolt and she was halfway past him, he snatched at her hair and yanked her face back toward his own. "I'm going to fuck your brains out," he then told her.

They hardly noticed the premonitory sheen over the horizon, the soft moisture in the air, the bluish grass that ran away from them to the garden wall, the low moon.

"I'm going to fuck you," Andy pursued, making for the gate to the neighboring field, "and, kid, I'm talking about really *fucking* you, till you think you're gonna fall apart right down the middle. Baby," he said, "I'm gonna fuck you till you die. You're never gonna be fucked like you're gonna be fucked tonight. *Christ*, am I gonna fuck you. Kid, I tell you, you're in big trouble, cos the way I'm gonna lay it on you's gonna be . . ."

Andy slowed in a gentle hollow on the far side of the field, perhaps two hundred yards from the house. He turned around and sneered sexily at Roxeanne, whose hair lay undisturbed by the warm wind. Our excellent Adorno was wondering whether to slap her about a bit first, or rip her T-dress off, or kick her legs out from underneath her—something casual like that—but suddenly Roxeanne skipped backward and in one double-armed action had pulled off her nightdress and was naked.

"Yawn. No—c'mon—no, nothing lyrical, nothing like that. Come the fuck over here before I really beat up on you."

"Just look at me first."

Andy sighingly reviewed her meaty, impossible body. "Yeah yeah yeah. Incredible, too much. Now lie down, girl. One more word and I'll break your arm."

"I want to see *you* first."

"Slow, baby, slow," Andy facetiously assured her. "You'll be feeling it up your gut." He stepped forward.

"No hard-on?" she asked lightly.

Andy's foot was suspended in midair as he saw the peculiar relevance of Roxeanne's question. He didn't have one. Throughout his interview with Lucy it had been plugged into his navel and he had naturally assumed that it was still there. His sense agents flooded to his groin, whence they returned despondent messages. No hard-on.

Now how's this gonna look? Andy asked himself.

Squaring blankly up to a long S/M session, a rugged humiliation session, a bestiality session, a session of haughty pretense that his failure to tumesce was yet another means of asserting himself, Andy flexed his shoulders.

But then Roxeanne dropped to the earth. She lay down, placed her hands behind her knees and guided her legs up until her ankles were hooked on either side of her neck. "See red?" she asked

Blinking, Andy stumbled toward her.

"Oh yes, baby. Ah, God, you were—you really meant it. Toward the end I was . . . God, you were beautiful."

"Shut up," said Andy.

Andy felt like crying. He rolled onto his back to face the lightening sky. "Leave me alone. Get out of here."

"So that's how it is to have your brains fucked out. Now—now I really know."

"Shut up. Get out of here. Get out of the house. And take those queers, too. It was that pill fuckin' Marvell gave me."

"Yeah."

"Well, maybe it's just that I don't like you. I don't like you. Maybe it's that."

"What's that got to do with fucking? You'd like me fine if you could've gotten a jack."

"Shut up. Get out of here."

"Yes, ma'm. Couldn't take *that* twice in a night."

She picked up her T-dress, waving it in the air as she walked naked across the field.

He looked on as she glided down through the windy grass. He sniffed. "Bitch," he said. Andy lay back and watched the stars begin to go out, his body sunk deep in the first dew.

29: SILENCE AND DAY

". . . and I still saw him but then it was all really over by then, or at least I don't think it was for him any more than it really was for me, but he seemed to want to pretend to think that if we went on not doing what we pretended to think were the most important things for us not to not do, then things wouldn't sort of . . ."

Etc., etc., thought Whitehead.

Keith could scarcely keep his little red eyes open. It was 5:30, and he had long relinquished any intention of—you had to laugh—"making a pass" at the white-haired girl in the bed over which he leaned. Unversed though he was in these matters, little Keith supposed he was right in thinking that a two-hour analysis of a past affair would not have been the gambit of a woman keen to go to bed with him. In addition, only her pillow-propped head was visible and she hadn't taken her eyes off the ceiling for better than ninety minutes.

". . . so we decided that if we just took it easy for a while and didn't try and hide the things that weren't mattering anyway, and so guess what, we—"

Whitehead started. "What?"

"Oh, Keith, I'm sorry. I'm speeding, and I always go on when I speed."

"Not at all."

"Maybe we'd better go to sleep now."

Perfunctorily Whitehead fluttered his eyelashes.

"Thanks for letting me bore you."

Perfunctorily Whitehead leaned forward, pursing chapped lips.

"Good night." She turned over away from him, pulling the sheet up above her ears. "Could you put the light out as you go?"

"Of course. Good night. Lucy."

He put the light out and walked toward the door. On the way be stubbed his toe viciously on the metal-based coffee table, but he was half in tears anyway, tears of tiredness and contrition and self-disgust, and didn't bother to register the pain.

Diana waited and waited in the kitchen, her fingers stitched tight in front of her. The invigorating coldness she had felt all evening had not dissipated into sleep, and when Andy had showed no sign of wanting to make love to her and every sign of wanting to make love to someone else, Diana had decided to let him get on with it, to let it happen. She had allowed half an hour to pass before coming downstairs, listened at the door and heard Lucy's voice, entered the kitchen, made coffee, smoked, and sat where she could see the drawing-room door. She looked at her watch and realized that not once all night had she thought about *Johnny*.

More or less simultaneously, Keith stepped out into the hall and Roxeanne emerged from the direction of the back door passage. Whitehead wiped his sore eyes and began to smile. Roxeanne folded her arms and looked away. Diana put down her cigarette and said, "Well, well. Aren't we a lot of night-owls? What have you been up to in there, Keith?"

"Merely chatting to Lucy."

"Oh—you mean to say you haven't been fucking her?"

"Oh no. Nothing like that. She was feeling a bit low so I thought I'd . . . chat to her."

"Really?"

"Just tried to cheer her up, that's all."

"How about you, 'Roxeanne'? Done anything good?"

"Nothing too great." Roxeanne folded her arms tighter. "And take that I-smell-shit look off your face."

"Haven't seen Andy by any chance?"

"Yeah."

Diana resisted it, but sadness entered her voice. "What happened."

"He—he . . ." Roxeanne unfolded her arms and sank down loosely on a chair. "Andy couldn't get a hard-on."

They were still laughing when Andy came in.

He beheld the kitchen with some diffidence. "What's up?" he asked.

"No—no hard-on!" shrieked Diana breathlessly, pointing at him as she rocked to and fro in her seat. "No hard-on!"

Andy blushed, frowned, traversed the room and hit a convulsed Whitehead as hard as he possibly could on the ear, and stalked into the hall.

One by one they followed.

Seven o'clock. Silence and day fall on Appleseed Rectory.

Marvell and Skip grunt and fart contentedly as Roxeanne slips in between them.

Diana joins an Andy fetal and taciturn.

His ear thudding like an earphone, Whitehead slaps a cache of glistening nude magazines onto his winded bunk.

Quentin smokes at the ceiling, Celia clinging to him tightly in sleep.

And, out across the landing, the padded alarm buzzer sounds for Giles.

part two
saturday

XXX: GILES

Giles awoke with a short bark of displeasure. The Risen-shine buzzer faded, the radio hissed, and the machine clankingly set about preparing the crude Baby Bullshot—which Giles never drank anyway.

Out of bed seemed no place to be these days. It came on him sideways when he hit the floor, unraveled past him diagonally when he rushed the fridge, as if the whole house were on slipped land. Giles undulated against the refrigerator door. He was normally convinced that he would vomit before he could swallow so much as a half liter of vodka and tomato juice, but this morning, Saturday morning, his stomach felt scoured. Why? Friday night waved round his head like a fan of old curling photographs.

Both his hands closed on the wet glass and bore it deliberately to his lips. He drank it in one swallow, retched appallingly, and leaned to refill it.

"Glug glug," said Giles. "Glug glug glug."

Giles had recently fallen into the habit of sleeping in his clothes—or "ready-dressed," as he liked to think of it. All that needed to be done, then, in the half hour before his maxi-cab arrived, was to lower himself below the Plimsoll line of sobriety.

"Luigi, Luigi," mumbled Giles as the alcohol lapped at his smudged brain.

(Luigi was Giles's chauffeur. After three months of complete idleness in his lodgings at the Gladmoor public house, Luigi had motored the Daimler back to London and started a small car-hire concern with it, his overheads defrayed by Giles's continuing monthly checks. The chauffeur's name still came to Giles's lips whenever he had to get somewhere, but he no longer had any settled idea of what Luigi was supposed to be for.)

He moved to the window. Moistly he peered out at the shining lawn. He sipped. He thought about cleaning his teeth, shaking his head dubiously. He sipped. He retched, without changing his expression. He sipped.

"Old mother," he said. "Old mother, what do you want to see *me* for?"

He sat at his desk and ran his fingers up and down the skiddy red glass.

"Too early to cry yet," he said. "Too early now."

He reached for his shoes, placed side by side on the floor. His left sock, he now noticed, had a hole in it, revealing one white, quivering toe. He leaned forward and gently rearranged the frayed material.

"Baby Giles," he said. "Baby Giles."

Giles's mother's mouth comprised, from left to right, a tapering upper eyetooth which eroded a millimeter a year into the black pool of her gum socket, two long wedge-shaped frontals which overlapped like tightly crossed fingers, a retreating bead of crushed molars, a lower incisor as yellow as sunshine off dusty glass, an El that resembled a squat, burnt-out matchstick, and a lonely lopsided masticator which jutted out between her lips even when they were closed. Maria Coldstream would argue that her teeth had got that way during Giles's gestation and slightly premature birth; before that, she would argue, they had been clean and strong.

In any event, the young Giles felt bad whenever they came near him—bright and various among the strong colors of the greenhouse, monochrome cogs down the dark hall, wet shadows at his bedside. They came on him interminably, the bits and pieces behind some recrimination or entreaty or kiss. At night they creaked down the long corridor to his room and ushered through the door as expectant as saddening dreams.

Mrs. Coldstream had no idea that she frightened her only son in this way and would have been greatly distressed to learn as much. Even when her behavior had become, by almost anybody's standards, very frightening indeed, Maria never imagined that she favored Giles with any attentions which he did not warmly reciprocate. This was because her frontal brain had taken to being inoperative whenever—for example—she joined Giles in the downstairs shower closet after his Thursday cricket matches on the village green, whenever she offered to undress him prior to his Sunday afternoon naps, whenever she kissed him gorily on the mouth last thing at night.

On three occasions Giles woke up—to the usual sun, to the usual bluster of radiator pipes—and stretched marriageably in his broad four-poster, half opened his eyes, and found his mother pinned out on the bed beside him. The first two times this happened Mrs. Coldstream regained a sort of consciousness at once and slipped unseeingly from the room. On the third morning, the morning they took her away, Giles had lain there for ninety minutes, statuesque with terror, gaping at his mother's mouth; it rested sullenly ajar on a pillow heavy with blood.

Some observations on Giles's sex life.

For a start, the village girls liked him. They would gather in the sweetshop as Giles, shy hander-out of bubblegum and gobstoppers, blushed under the encouragingly avuncular eyes of the gardener's son. When the fair arrived in the village, and it came to sitting next to Giles on the Dodgems and Whirligigs—the girls took it in turns. At fetes, bazaars, and other functions at which entertainment and goods could be exchanged for cash—Giles forked up. He got to kiss them after cricket matches. Giles was much in demand down the alley during youth-club dances at church. On half-day holidays he played Nervous all afternoon up in the back hills.

They called him Little Lord Fauntleroy. This pleased Giles and he always tried to look smart, got Mrs. Baden to press his elephant cords, tiptoed down the drive straightening his gray school shirt, glanced gingerly back at the house, Victorian and insane in the early gloom, was joined at the gate and led up the long path above the lake by a posse of the pungent, frizzy-haired daughters of the village, and would be drawn giggling into the hillside copse, there to be tickled, pinched, and affectionately reviled. Next, in ghostly periods, all but one of them disappear. She crosses her arms in front of her chest and slides the crackling pink jersey over her head and turns to unzip her dress, which tends to be navy-blue and very creased. Giles bides his time, panting quietly with gratitude and disbelief. Her underthings seldom match. Giles lends circumspect assistance with the removal of her dimming bra, for all the world as if he hasn't got an erection, keeps noticing the weather and the scary trees as she debarks her pants and helps him off with his. A tensed Coldstream might shinny on top of her for ten seconds before she goes away, flushed and ironical.

Then he sits and gasps the air, gets to his feet, races down the open hill with arms like spindly cartwheels, pees at the

wind, shouts into the dark swell of the land, attempts to vault
the gate, falls over, climbs it vibrating like a tuning fork,
and sprints across the lawn to the gardener's son.

The gardener's son. "What happened?" "She just let
me do it!" "Which of them, Giles?" "Ellen." "Want to watch
her. Boys from Dowley have her." "Still, she was very nice.
No, she was." "What was it like then?" "Oh, I wasn't any good
again." "Oh, well. Still." "I enjoyed it."

So they go down to the lake and sit on the log and smoke
fags and talk into the night. There they kiss tremulously, walking home over the lawn in one another's arms.

Outside the Dowley Kinema, a Wednesday night, the gardener's son disappeared into the pub for two packets of crisps.
The local boys approached, faded jeans folded up over the
ankles, collarless striped shirts, bright braces, and cropped
crowns, their breath smoky in the autumn air. Giles turned
around; for the last time in his life his face was candid and
unperplexed. Suddenly the wet pavement slid up and hit him
on the shoulder. With all the time in the world Giles folded
his arms across his face. When the first boot caved into his
mouth, Giles thought of his mother, aware that a lastingly
terrible thing was happening to him.

But the teeth were on him now and they wouldn't go away.
They kept saying, "We'll get Mrs. Baden back, because she
was your favorite cook, baby, wasn't she? She was, I know.
And your room, of course, shall have to be entirely gutted and
redone. It's entirely ridiculous to think you bore it for so long.
We should only have to get the man who plated the little
greenhouse along so he could do it, your room—could he?
Can they? People who do greenhouses? Little ones?"

Giles stood at the high window, staring down at the tiny
mad dolls in the street below. "Yes, mother," he murmured.

"See? Oh, baby, I *knew* you'd love it!"

Mrs. Coldstream was a manic-depressive. As a child, Giles
had quite liked her being manic, but nowadays he always
tried to catch her when she was depressive. *That* wasn't so
bad. Sometimes she was so depressive that you could just sit
it out, watching light move while she obviously stared and
wept. Once or twice, Giles had simply crept from the room
after a quarter of an hour.

But today she was manic and Giles's face swam in the windowpane.

"Giles—darling—come and hold me."

Giles turned to her with stolen eyes. "Mother," he said, "is there anything good on television?"

"Giles—I don't want to gogglebox! I just want you to hold me—baby, baby, please. I can't bear it. A moment, a moment."

"Gosh, mother, you really can't—you're not allowed to, someone like me, actually."

"Oh, my baby—please please please. Come *here*, my *dar*ling. I've got so much, so much. Hold me tight before I die. . . . Baby? Yes, yes. Ah, yes. That's a sweet darling. Thank you, my baby, *thank* you."

Gauzy skin and dying pillows, old smell of chloroform and hot baby powder, stiff webbed hands in his hair, that bad mouth drinking up his tears.

"For you can never leave me, Giles, can you?"

The tears eddied down his cheeks. "No, mother. I can never leave you."

"Baby Giles," she whispered. "Baby Giles."

31: PICKING UP SPEED

He gave the fat-necked cab driver an unspecified number of five-pound notes and began to apologize, firstly for seeming to have no idea at all where Appleseed Rectory was, and secondly for having repeatedly addressed him as Luigi. The chauffeur counted the money, allowed his face to fall into an uncontrollable gloat, and accelerated stridently away. "Oh, and—keep the change, actually," Giles told the spinning dust.

Giles milled round to face the house, slowly finding his footing on the ripped gravel. He drank from his liter hip-flask and looked meltingly up at Appleseed Rectory. He looked up at its bleached walls, the flaking sills and drainpipes, the wasted concrete and dark windows, with a familiar jarred relief. He had no feeling for the house, nothing whatever beyond provisional recognition, but he was fairly sure of there being good things in it—drink, friends, a known room. Perhaps the most attractive feature of the house, Giles moreover mused, was that he wouldn't have to leave it until his mother called again. Through the air came the sound of distant

wings. Sudden foreboding discovered him. He was all teeth
once more. Giles swayed before the neutral building, the
clouds picking up speed above his head.

Which, of course, is precisely what everything else has
started to do—*pick up speed*. Friday was slow: it sailed gaily
by in commodious chunks, like a procession of battered river-
boats heading for the jeweled estuary of night. See? But Saturday is fast and rough; adrift, it rushes along in snatches,
sideways, at an angle, never head on, and is finished, really,
before any of them know it.

32: THE COOL DOVES

Twice a day, at midmorning and just before dusk, the brood
of doves which nested in the roof of the nearby church sailed
down the rise of the village, treading air in the thick thermals
above Appleseed Rectory, and swam across the garden to
land in the friendly branches of the oak in the neighboring
field, where they would ululate and moan at the changing
light, compose themselves once again and lift off, swerving in
line over the roadside stream to regain their mossy tiles. They
came with ritual calm and regularity to Appleseed Rectory, as
if in decorous salute to a former home. Time always seemed
to pause and take a breath when the cool doves approached,
and their lessening wings never failed to hold the eye.

"I swear, Quentin," said Andy yearningly, "unless some
normal birds start coming here again, I'm going to get going
on those fuckin' doves."

"Ah, but Andy—they're doves," said Quentin.

"They're still fuckin' *birds*, aren't they? What difference
does that make?"

"But they're holy birds."

"Yeah, and I bet they read the Bible and do quid-a-jobs
and never say 'fuck.' "

"Now, now, Andrew. Now, now."

For Quentin and Andy were out killing birds in the
garden. This recreation had recently come to carry a sense
of strain, particularly as regards Adorno. In the golden age of
their first few weeks at the house, Andy would rise before
six, gulp down some Irish coffee, and prowl into the garden

with the Webley rifle for stealthy two-hour sessions, often claiming to have dispatched between twenty and thirty of the pests in a single morning. Two months of this and aerial word got round that birds were *non grata* at Appleseed Rectory, and soon the little visitors ceased to wake Adorno with their song. Spiritedly, Andy got into the habit of emptying large bags of Swoop, Airies, and Wingmix on the lawn last thing at night, a wheeze initially so successful that he would sometimes find it unnecessary even to leave his room, picking the massed creatures off from his window. (If reproached by an Appleseed female about this policy Andy would counter, depending on his mood, that birds weren't cosmic and were therefore expendable, or alternatively that such crusades restored the precious bond of blood reciprocity between animal and man, or alternatively that it taught the greedy little fuckers a lesson.) Later still, of course, the most famished robins in England would give the Rectory lawn a mile-wide berth—despite the cream, dripping, paté, and freshly exhumed worms that Andy would array to tempt them to his green preserve. More recently still, in the early mornings, Andy could be glimpsed, a solitary and enigmatic figure, pacing the garden with his gun, forever gazing up in mute appeal at the indifferent skies.

"Well, they do live in the church," pursued Quentin gently, "and they are virtually the property of the village. Best to leave the doves alone, Andy."

"Yeah, well. And I suppose if I did get to work on them the fuckin' locals would only start to bitch about it. I just don't like the way they come down here every day so flash. As if they owned the fuckin' place . . . Well, I'll leave them alone for now but they'd just better not push their luck, is all."

"That's a sagacious Andy. Must maintain good relations with the pez. Have Lucy last night?"

"Nah— Just let her mouth-fuck me."

"I see. Was Diana pleased."

"She didn't get to know about it. I outsmarted her again."

"And tell me," Quentin asked him, "did you have Roxeanne too?"

"Course."

"How do you mean, 'course'?"

"Well—anyone could tell she was going to make a play for me. For a start she was eye-fucking me all night—at that booze bar and stuff." Andy gestured across the garden. "A field-fuck," he said.

"Really, Andy. You and your fucks. What was it like— tolerably enjoyable?"

"Nah. Nothing special. Okay. Nothing special. You've fucked her, surely?" asked Andy, slightly taken aback.

"No; now you come to mention it, I don't believe I have. You see, Andy, when I ran into these people I was, shall we say, the houseguest of a certain screen actress, and so Roxeanne seemed, well, a tiny bit superfluous."

"Which one?"

Quentin shrugged and turned away. "Margot Make-piece . . ."

Andy's lemur eyes bulged. "Bull*shit*," he said. "No!"

"Oh yes."

"The one that— Can she? Right up the—?"

"Oh yes."

"Jesus."

"Anyway, we digress. With Roxeanne— I trust you acquitted yourself well?"

"I hit colossal form," said Andy.

"And Marvell and Skip? Did they try to get in on what I'm sure was a splendid act?"

"What, those fags? You're kidding. They're smarter than that."

"Don't underestimate them. They're peculiarly persistent. And persistently peculiar."

"Mm?"

"In a way, I'm beginning to regret having asked them. It doesn't seem to be going markedly well up to now. They've changed since I knew them. And they're generally so . . . so different, don't you feel?"

"The fuck, they're just American, that's all. Look, there's one!"

Andy was referring to an airborne speck well into the middle distance. Even as he spoke he lifted the gun and fired. They watched the little slug of metal die in a slow, plaintive arc; three hundred yards beyond, the dot winged its way purposefully on. Lear-like imprecations fled from Andy's mouth.

On Quentin's suggestion, Andy sought solace in peppering the Tuckle drainpipes and windowpanes for a quarter of an hour. But he soon grew bored and pitched the gun bitterly onto the grass. There was a dejected silence.

"It's going to be a hot mother today," said Quentin, resting a thin hand on Andy's shoulder and wincing at the sky.

"Yeah." Overhead, a DC 70 strained upward through the blue air. "Take me to America," Andy murmured.

"Come on, kid," said Quentin. "Let's go in."

33: BUT WHAT'S PERFECT

The Whitehead had beguiled the early morning in a sweaty fight with the garage toolbox, restoring and partly refashioning a pair of old platforms, platforms which he had worn every day between the ages of seventeen and twenty-one until —lined with asbestos and bakelite though the boots were— they had gone critical on him practically in the course of an afternoon . . . emptying lecture halls, toppling freshmen, razing flowerboxes, and asphyxiating charladies in his wake. Keith had had no choice but to seal the footwear hermetically that night and swathe them in dead towels at the bottom of his trunk. He was meanwhile required to go to college in Clark's sandals for a month, as he saved the necessary money —by going without such things as transport, warmth, food and drink—for some new supports.

Little Keith had nailed fist-thick, roughly-hewn wooden slabs to the soles of the rescued boots, chipped them flush with hammer and chisel and blackened them with polish. It was a painstaking and in many respects an imaginative piece of work; but it was his most daring reconstruction job to date—and Keith was no cobbler.

In his room, Whitehead placed a two-pence piece between his teeth and drained his legs into the hot holes. He levered himself—ever so cautiously—from the bed, in order to exert his full weight on the palpitating platforms. Gradually, gradually . . .

A tenth of a second later Keith was an invertebrate puddle on the floor of his room. "So far, so good," he croaked. Whitehead was, after all, fairly experienced in these matters and, even as he lay on the rug, twitching to the black anguish that coursed through his body, he was reasonably sanguine. He had a shrewd idea—thanks—of the sort of state his feet were in these days; he knew, at any rate, that they opened up whole new worlds of semantic reach to the epithet *raw*. (A drunken dietary consultant had once advised him, unofficially but with real concern, simply to have them off—and quickly.) And yet little Keith knew also what they, and he, could master and endure. Presently, he was confident, a soothing elixir of sweat and blood would begin to soften the chips of ruptured cardboard, would begin to lubricate the craters of the scored heel, would begin to deliquesce the stiffened creases of the biting vinyl. True, it would not compromise the bent nail ends which had already eased themselves a quarter of an inch into his hooves, but—

"But what's perfect," Keith asked out loud of his floor rug, "in this life of ours? As long as they don't squelch," he continued, reaching for a pillow to scream into, "just so long as they don't squelch, then I'm a happy man. Then I'm walking on air."

Ten minutes later Keith was on his feet, tears of pain running unhindered down his cheeks. He took an exploratory step, allowed his chest to billow, growled mightily deep in his throat, and willed on his body a species of control. Through his wall slit he espied Quentin and Andy ambling back toward the house. Stripped to the waist, Andy was gesticulating stylishly at the wholesome garden. Tugged at by Keith's tears his brown body swam beautifully through the knobbled windowpane.

"You can get used to anything, really, I suppose," Whitehead muttered.

Corrosion seeped up his ankles like rising water. It then occurred to Keith that if he had to wear these foot engines for as long as (say) a week, the loss of ectoplasm would more than discount the artificial gain in inches: with his gory shin stumps wedged into six-inch lifts, he'd be four-foot-eleven all over again. But it was unlikely that he would have to wear anything that long. How fortunate. For this small blessing Whitehead gave laconic thanks.

34: BREAKFAST

"Giles! What are you doing up? Have you been *out*?"

The Mandarin on his lap, Giles was sitting at the kitchen

table, a cup of coffee cooling in front of him. Without curiosity he returned Andy's stare.

"Seeing my mother in London, actually."

"Yeah? How's she?"

Giles reached for the coffee cup. It got as far as his chin before he lurched forward violently and replaced it with a lingering, wristless hand. Frowning at the room, he took out his hip flask. "Who? My mother? Oh, she's mad. Gosh, she's so mad now."

"What she want?"

"She wants to come to the special Institute in Potter's Bar. So I can see her more often."

"The Blishner place?" said Andy. "What's she going in there for?"

"So I can see her more often."

"No, you little . . . What are they going to *do* to her there?"

"Actually, I don't know. But, gosh, she's jolly mad now."

"Do you get more cash?"

When Giles showed no loss of attention but no obvious interest in replying, Andy waltzed over to the dresser (on which numerous mugs were hooked and against which Diana leaned), taking an apple from the oriental bowl there. He placed the fruit in his mouth whole, chewed vigorously and swallowed—a habit of his.

(Giles averted his appalled gaze.)

"You've been out shooting birds in the garden, I suppose," said Diana unaffectionately.

"Oh, you haven't, have you, darling?" appealed Celia to her husband.

"The fuck we have," said Andy. "The little bastards won't come anywhere near here any more."

(Quentin crossed the kitchen and took Celia lightly in his arms.)

"I put," Andy went on, "I put stuff out for them—worms and stuff—but that's not good enough for them. Dripping, stuff like that. But do they come anywhere near the place? Not them, *oh* no."

(Diana lit a cigarette and sighingly exhaled.)

"I mean, how's a guy supposed to see any decent action around here if the flash little shits won't come near the place? Those doves . . . coming down here every day so casual."

Andy's face darkened. "They'd just better watch themselves is all I'm saying."

Quentin was about to assure Celia that, nonsense, he was sure Andy had no intention of doing any such thing, when little Keith merged slowly through the doorway, his eyelids dark with pain.

"Good morning, campers," said Whitehead.

Keith's voicebox had been under orders to say this with volume and gusto. But the words had evaporated dryly from his mouth. "Good morning, campers," he said again. No improvement.

"Why, it's little Keith," said Andy. "Keith, good Christ, are you dying?"

"Good Lord, Keith," said Quentin with unfeigned alarm. "Here, quick, you'd better sit down."

Keith knew this to be excellent advice, and he took it as soon as his unstable form could get him into the room, thawing on to the nearest chair. Giles gazed up at him with expressionless eyes.

Diana disapproved of Keith on account of the horrible way he looked, and surveyed him now with fatigued contempt. Celia disliked him too, but was insatiably compassionate when it came to physical suffering and actually asked Whitehead whether he would like a cup of coffee. Andy, also, half remembering that he had struck Keith the night before—and quarter remembering that he had struck him very hard indeed—solicitously observed that Keith never looked up to much anyway and that perhaps he was just a bit under the weather.

All this made Keith want to cry again. He normally counted himself a lucky man if he could get into a room without exciting open derision: being totally ignored was, for him, an imperial entrance. However formal or perfunctory, actual concern always made him wistful for the status he knew he would never enjoy. With what was in fact his very least attractive smile, Whitehead explained that he had slept poorly and was suffering from acute migraine.

(Giles was watching carefully as Keith spoke. He, for one, had never been able to understand the point of all the fuss about little Keith. Whitehead's teeth looked okay to him.)

"Well, what about it?" asked Celia, exuding personal as well as general wariness. "Breakfast?"

"Don't *call* it that," said Andy sharply. "Just call it *food*. Food. All right," he said, relenting, "we might as well give it a try."

35: Lagging Time

Although the Appleseed Rectory kitchen was a large, square, farmerly apartment, its lowness of ceiling and its habit of containing a lot of vivid sunlight tended to make the room seem oppressively populous when more than four or five persons were gathered between its walls. It began to seem so now. The shuffling Appleseeders—all of whom, except Giles and Whitehead, were engaged in the cautious preparation of orange juice, coffee, and thin toast—were joined by Skip (in very filthy underpants), Marvell (in filthy underpants), Roxeanne (in underpants), and by Lucy, dressed, lard-skinned, small-eyed, and coughing into the hot light. Between permutations of legs The Mandarin erectly strolled.

"Christ, that cat's bum," said Andy in a critical, almost painterly tone, his eyes on the pink anus revealed by the Persian's high tail. "Can't we do something . . . ? *I* know. I'm going to get a gray magic marker and color its arse over. Aw *my* HEAD!"

No one was thinking about it, no one was thinking much about anything, when the room suddenly became a miasma of hangovers. Alcohol crapulence clogs perception, but drug crapulence flays it, and by now the kitchen was a noisome feast for peeled senses. The room appeared to change its shape. Voices scattered into piano mumbles. The cigarette smoke formed a shelf at shoulder height, above which sunbright faces wafted like mad masks. They plugged in kettles, hawked, ran water, retched; the Americans swung open the fridge, picked with dirty fingernails at a staling loaf, scratched, burped, farted, snorted into the dregs of yesterday's liquor bottles . . . "This butter's like off chick . . . *Just sugar's safest* . . . My eyes, my eyes . . . *Eggs! The fuck* . . . Gangway! I'm gonna be sick . . . *Water—fight the dehydration* . . . Stop *breathing* like that . . . *Gag gag gag* . . . I'm flashing! I'm flashing! . . . *What's—the sizes are all wrong* . . . Strange heat, strange heat . . . *Don't be there, just don't BE there!*"

Then came the lagging time. It came abruptly, flopped down like an immense and invisible jelly from the ceiling, swamping the air with marine languor and insect speeds— lagging time, with its numbness and disjunction, its inertia and automatism, its lost past and dead future. It was as if they were wandering through an endless, swarming, rotten, ter- minal marketplace after a year of unsleeping nights.

Now they were all moving to no effect—just moving, just switching things off and switching things on, just picking things up and putting things down and picking things up and stroking the cat and counting the mugs and fighting for air. It seemed that everything they did had already been done and done, and that everything they thought had already been thought and thought, and that this would never end. *Excuse me,* said panic to each of them in turn. They had no mouth and they had to scream.

Quentin forced his way across the room and gripped Giles by the shoulder. Giles looked up, apparently quite unaffected. His face cleared as if emerging from shadow into day. He stood up and opened the door. Time flooded in from the passage. The room stopped, and clicked back. They turned toward him.

"I think that, I think that what we all need is a drink."

They crowded into the corridor. They were out.

"Jesus!" said Andy on the way to the sitting room. "What in the fuck was *that*?"

"Lagging time," said Quentin.

"Yeah," said Marvell, dabbing his cheeks with a red bandana. "Fuckin' lagging time."

"*Jesus.* Never had that cocksucker before." Andy halted and turned toward them. "You know, my theory is that it was the food that did it." He started walking again. "To hell with this food gimmick. It's just not on any more, food. Fuck *food*."

36: THE real THING again

Under Giles's sleepy but telling supervision, champagne cocktails went into production—"After all, it's practically eleven o'clock," Andy had said. One-and-a-half-liter bottles of

1979 Moët & Chandon were removed by Quentin and Andy from the semi-deepfreeze in the washroom while crates of re-inforcements were shipped in by Skip from the garage. Giles then entrusted Quentin with his doorkeys and commissioned him to go up and enter his room, locate and gain admittance to his drinks cupboard, and detach from it five, perhaps six, liters of Napoleon brandy. By this time people had revisited the bedrooms and had started to appear in less advanced stages of undress; in particular, Marvell and Skip were in their usual jean suits, and Roxeanne was wearing a black midriff stole and a fishnet body stocking.

"Beat me, beat me," enthused Andy as the record player emitted sounds of what might have been a burning menagerie superimposed over a Sunday school choir practice. Windows were thrown open. Quentin marshaled the hash kits and amyl-nitrate poppers. Skip toured the room, his large hands cupping a pyramid of wide-spectrum amphetamines. Marvell issued depressants from the dinette-feature alcove. They were all talking.

"The thing is, actually," broke in Giles, keeping a sensible distance between himself and the waiting rank of champagne bottles, "I've always found that the thing is, actually, is to put *a hell of a lot* of brandy in them. About four or five times as much as anyone else ever puts in them—ever. At least half and half. At least. If in doubt, make believe the brandy is the champagne and the champagne is the brandy."

"Check," said Andy. "Check."

Celia accepted a tablet from Skip. She held it in the air between finger and thumb and said quizzically, "I don't know, darling, but shouldn't we be taking it a bit easy?"

"Relax, darling," purred Villiers.

"We can't feel any worse," said Diana, to Lucy's pale agreement.

"Hell, it's only a weekend," said Marvell. "The fuck."

"Keith! Get the liquor over here," bawled Andy, "—and I'm talking about now! I mean, what's a court dwarf *for* if he can't even . . . Christ, this is more like it, eh? The real thing again."

"*Wait!*" Giles held up his hands. "Wait a minute. Tell me before you start opening the champagne, okay? All those corks flying about, might catch me one right in the . . ."

"Is everyone . . . Look," said Andy, "go and lie down or

something, will you, Keith, okay? I can't cope with you in here looking like that. Right, is everyone ready? Then let's go!"

Within a quarter of an hour, things were pretty well back to normal.

37: THOSE CONVERSATIONS

Those conversations.

"That's what they did. In the seventies. That's what they achieved. They separated emotion and sex."

"Nonsense, Marvell," said Quentin. "They merely showed that they could be separable. In the last analysis, of course, they aren't separable at all."

Marvell looked in appeal toward Roxeanne and Skip, who were abstractedly stroking one another on the floor, then back again. "Let's—let's try seeing it historically." Marvell swallowed his drink. "Things happen faster in the States so perhaps the situation's not clear yet for you people. Sure, there was a kind of reaction to the Other Way in the States a few years ago, but—"

"Shut up," said Andy tonelessly, to no one in particular.

". . . but—but it was a reaction really to the *spinoffs* of the Way, not to its thinking as such—the beaver displays, the fuck shows, the sex emporia, stuff like the experimental prostitution thing in LA. Then all last year there's been a whole reaffirmation of the whole thing, of the fundamental thing. And I don't just mean the sex conventions and the fuck-ins. Everywhere you go now, you can see that it's happened. People're quiet about it. No need to shout. They just know."

"Yes," said Quentin, "and in another few years there'll be another reaction and eventually we'll be the way we were."

"The fuck, after a million years of denying your needs, you can't expect the change to come in a week. But it's here now." Marvell laughed. "Kids over there, they're fucking in the first grade. We thought we were smart getting laid when we were twelve. They're blowing each other in the fuckin' playpens over there. No, it's here now and it won't go away and it won't turn into anything else."

Andy came alive. "I think that's disgusting," he said.

"Little bastards. *I* didn't get fucked till I was nearly thirteen!"

"More importantly," Villiers resumed, "when are these promiscuous tots going to put in time on growing up? When will their sexual emotions have time to develop? When will their natures have time to absorb frustration, yearning, joy, surprise—?"

"Christ, Quentin," said Marvell, "you trying to reinstitute sex angst, or what? Know who you sound like? Fuckin' D. H. Lawrence! 'Sexual emotions'—fuck them. Sex is something your body does, like eating or shitting. Yeah, like shitting. Just something your body does."

An expression of weary decisiveness overcame Quentin's superb features. "Well, it's not something *my* body does for me. Nor Celia's, I should imagine. Nothing so brisk and heartless, thank God. Why do you suppose we got married?"

Marvell looked up at Quentin shyly, sneakily. "Come on, Quent, come on." He winked. "You did that, that was just some sort of gimmick, Quent, wasn't it?"

"No, it was marriage. And we got married to keep sex emotional."

"Christ. You're too much, Quent, truly. But look—it can't be done, man. Forget it. The iconography of desire's too pervasive now. The minute you're . . . the minute that you're fucking Celia here and you start to think about something else—some model or screen actress that's on every billboard and magazine you look at"—he snapped his fingers—"you'll know that's true. You'll know it."

"What you appear to be forgetting, Marvell," said Quentin, "is that Celia and I happen to be in love."

"Ugh," said Roxeanne.

Skip let out a low whistle.

"You know, Quentin," said Marvell seriously, "you can really be quite upsetting at times. I thought I might be able to get through my life without hearing that fuckin' word again, and now you come along, now here's a good friend of mine comes along and . . . Two years ago you wouldn't have—" Marvell looked up. An intense solar warning flashed in Quentin's green eyes. Marvell quickly dropped his head.

"Check," said Andy.

"You agree on this thing, Andy?" asked Roxeanne.

"Check. Not all of it. But love *can't* mean anything any

more. That's hippie talk. Love's through. Love's all fucked up."

"Yeah, it's had it."

"Well, it hasn't had me," said Quentin with finality as Celia's hand crept toward his. "I know what love is, I know when I'm in love, and I'm in love. Is that clear?"

Marvell hung his head again. "Babies," he muttered. "Dead, dead babies."

38: Placements

The room reshuffled from time to time and people began to break away from the main group. Skip was probing, methodically but without success, for signs of conversational life in the couchant Giles. Andy talked to Lucy on the unmade divan that had served as her bed. Diana, accordingly, remained alone on the club armchair wondering up whom to sex: Quentin was engrossed in a new critical appreciation of Rimbaud, however, and Giles, the only other male she could conceivably approach, had roamed to a distant windowseat. With a picturebook on her lap, Celia sat on one of the ogre's cushions in the L of the larger drawing room. These last placements did not evade Marvell's notice. He caught Roxeanne's eye. They exchanged glances.

Giles was, actually, sitting in two places: in the windowseat alcove and in his own brown study. But this was one of his very favorite nooks, comfortable, cushioned, contained. He especially enjoyed it when, as now, the sun spanned him with its warmth, lulling his shoulders and hair. Sometimes his mind would go quite blank and Giles would briefly escape, returning with a soft sigh of gratitude.

"Hi. Want another cocktail, Giles?" It was Roxeanne.

"No, I . . . the actually gin," he mumbled.

"Okay. Okay if I sit here, Giles?"

"No, I, in fact."

Partly of necessity, the windowseat being the size of most windowseats, Roxeanne sat close to Giles. She sat so close, indeed, that Giles felt as if proximity were a concept to which he had hitherto been a stranger. Surely, Giles thought, I've never in my life been this close to *anyone*. She smelled, for a start, really tremendously strongly—a smell he identified dimly, and with reluctance, as a mixture of fresh sweat and of vaginal fluid of no less recent provenance. By way of corroboration he noticed that glistening red hair coiled both from her exposed armpits and from the eventful crotch of her pants. Within her transparent body stocking her breasts lapped and teemed. Giles gulped.

"Have a good time last light?"

"Gosh. Well I— It wasn't—"

"I can't hear you, Giles."

Is she on my lap, thought Giles, or am I on hers? The all-inclusiveness of her presence seemed to mantle them from the others and the rest of the room talked in a faraway rumble.

"*It was jolly good fun, yes.*" He readjusted. "I didn't think it was going to be."

"How come you didn't think so, Giles?"

Her eyes were half closed and her voice, while intense and fully awake, appeared to be constantly on the point of slipping away. Her treasure cave of teeth was inches from his tightened stripe. With difficulty Giles said, "Just worries, worries. Just little things."

"That what you wanted the drug for, Giles? Why worry? Why worry? Why do you have to worry?"

Roxeanne's face was now completely glazed, her body irreducibly, suffocatingly close. The odor of her body, not unpleasant in itself, had become overpoweringly rank; it didn't remind Giles of anything now.

"Can I fuck you, Giles?"

". . . Well, d'you know, I'm not very keen on all that. . . ."

Circling her wet tongue round her lips, she had trailed her hand up Giles's taut thigh.

"Then can I blow you, Giles?"

"I don't like *that*, either, much, actually."

"Do you want to come upstairs with me for a little time, Giles?" her voice moaned distantly at him. "For a little time, so I can kiss you. See my tongue?" It slipped like new meat from her mouth and looped to wetten the tip of her nose. "Kiss you, kiss you, wrap it right round your teeth—"

"No!" Giles sat up straight and burped into her face.

Roxeanne's expression did not change. Drowsily, moonily,

she leaned close to his ear and said in a voice just as gentle and caressing as before,

"Eat shit. You ugly little fuck."

"Hi. Want another cocktail, Celia?" It was Marvell.

"No; honestly. Two would make me feel funny so early."

"Okay. Okay if I sit here, Celia?"

"I don't mind."

"Hey, what have you got there?"

"My picture book."

"Hey!"

"Oops! I'll move up."

Celia had what's known as two sides to her character—her docility would become girlish ingenuousness, her lack of imagination would phase into blinking naïveté—and it was the smaller, more junior side that she was now letting out to play. Although the disparity between these personae was considerable, at times even grotesque, Celia seemed to be aware of no incongruity, slipping friskily between them with as little fuss as a child changing her toys. Marvell sensed her mood and for five minutes they discussed in equable undertones the adventures of Olly the Sailor, of Harry Hare, of Pig the Whistle and Small Stanley, of Water-Rat Reginald and Trap the Goat. Then Marvell wiped away the jewel of yellow-flecked blood that hung from his left nostril and said, "See Giles? Looks like he's doing just great with Rox."

Celia looked up.

"Yeah. Rox knows what the hell it's all about."

Celia did not answer.

"Knows how to get it all—from her body, her sensations. Knows how to make her senses *work* for her. She uses her senses like—like you'd use colors to make a pretty picture, Celia. Or like you'd do a jigsaw or dress a little doll. She knows what the brush is for, what all the colors do, how the surface likes it. That's how she regards her senses—as tools to make something full of joy and wonder. Would you like to express your body like that, Celia? See her with Giles? Know what she'd like to make with him?"

Celia shook her dipped head.

"No? D'you know what I'd like to make with you?"

Marvell cupped her far cheek with his fibrous right hand.

He whispered moltenly in her ear. Beneath flickering lids Celia's eyes raced.

She stood up and said evenly, the woman again, "And to think my husband knows someone like *you*."

Marvell laughed drunkenly as she stumbled toward the door.

Quentin swept into the room. Celia was sitting on the bed. He knelt before her. "Dearest, dearest, don't," he honed tenderly.

"Oh, darling, I don't want them to be here."

"My poor bunny. What on earth did he say?"

"I couldn't ever tell you. It was . . . I couldn't tell you. *Ever*."

Obscure relief showed in Quentin's eyes. "Oh, some silly sex thing. Darling, you must . . . that's just the way they *are*."

Celia struggled. "I won't have people here like that. I *won't*. Make them go away now—why won't you make them go *away* now."

He held her. "Tomorrow. They'll be gone tomorrow."

"Too late then."

"There there."

She looked up and sniffed. "Tomorrow? It'll all be over by tomorrow? Promise?"

"I promise," promised Quentin.

39: CUNNING STUNTS

"How many bloody times do I have to tell you, Mrs. Tuckle, I don't take sugar in my tea."

"So sorry, sir, I'll—"

"Don't bother." Whitehead placed a heavy damp slipper on a nearby poof. "And I suppose you've drunk all that gin I brought you," he said, looking at the unopened bottle on the sideboard.

"No, sir. I don't think we've even—"

"I can see that. Well, I think I'll have some now. You wouldn't have any ice or tonic, of course, would you."

"I'm afraid the electricity's not—"

"Well, put some water in it then, for Christ's sake."

"Yes, sir, of course. You will remember to thank Mr. Coldstream for us, sir, won't you?"

"As I said before," Keith reiterated, "I will if I remember to."

"Thank you, sir. If you don't mind me asking, sir . . ."

Keith waved a hand.

"If you don't mind me asking, who are your houseguests this weekend, sir?"

Whitehead reached out and accepted the glass of gin that was being waved cautiously around in front of his face. "About time," he said. "Well, I've asked just the four friends along. There's Lucy Littlejohn, an old . . . an old 'friend' of mine from my London days. And three Americans I met when I toured the States last year."

"I see, sir. Very interesting. Tell me, sir, what was the purpose of your visit to America? Was it your commercial concerns took you there, sir, or was it a purely pleasurable trip?"

Keith sipped his gin. "Mind your own bloody business," he said.

Whitehead walked back across the lawn with something less than his customary vim. The novelty of the Tuckles was palling. It wasn't the timbre of their remarks which bored him so much as the crude monotony of his own. Well, he would just have to think up more ways of being disagreeable to them, that's all.

Narrowing his eyes at the bay-windowed rear of Appleseed Rectory, little Keith established that activity was still centered in the drawing room. On all fours, he crawled behind the derelict well, waited, then snaked quickly into the garage.

Keith squirmed past his door, wedged it shut behind him, and stopped *dead*. Protruding from the thin brown top blanket of his bunk was the face of a girl. Keith recognized the face at once: it belonged to Miss See-See della Gore, the wonderful showgirl who had posed with her legs open on the centerfold of *Cunning Stunts*, a recent specialist purchase of his. What was she doing there? The effect was curiously disturbing. The color photograph, with its luminescent, undersized face, rested on his pillow, disappearing into the bed, which bulged as if some amorphous body were actually shrouded there. Keith approached the bunk. The rabid eyes glared up at him. He twitched back the top blanket a few inches, disclosing See-See's starfished body. He pulled the blanket off. Her spread legs seemed symbolically to enclose the debris of the rest of his pornographic library, torn to streamers, stained with what looked like semen and other obscure liquids—in his bed.

With agitated but determined movements Keith gathered the remains into a large pile. He turned, deciding to get a sack from the garage. He hardly registered the crude poster bearing the legend JOHNNY tacked to his door. He wondered how the photographs could most unobtrusively be destroyed. He started to cry. A whole way of life was coming to an end for Keith Whitehead.

XL: WHITEHEAD

The Whiteheads have several claims to being the fattest family alive. At the time of writing you could just go along to Parky Street, Wimbledon, any Sunday, one o'clock in the afternoon —and you'd see them, taking their seats in the Morris for the weekly Whitehead jaunt to Brighton.

"Get your huge fat arse out of the way"—"Whose horrible great leg is this?"—"Is this bit your bum, Keith, or Aggie's?"—"I don't care whose guts these are, they've got to be moved"—"That's not Dad's arm, you stupid great bitch, it's my leg!"

"It's no good," says Whitehead, Sr., eventually, slapping his trotters on the steering wheel. "The Morris can't be expected to cope with this. You can take it in turns staying behind from now on."

And indeed, as each toothpaste Whitehead squeezes into the Morris, the chassis drops two inches on its flattened tires, and when Frank himself gets in behind the wheel, the whole car seems to sink imploringly to its knees.

"Flora, close that sodding door," Frank tells his wife.

"I can't, Frank. Some of my leg is still out there."

A crowd has gathered on the pavement. Neighbors lean with folded arms on half-washed cars. Curtains part along the terraced street.

"Oh, God," says Whitehead, Sr., "they're all watching now. Keith! Give your mother a hand with her leg."

Keith squats forward and fights his mother's thigh up into the car, while Frank leans sideways and tugs at the far door strap with one hand and a fistful of Mrs. Whitehead's hip with the other. Aggie, Keith's sister, sits crying with shame in the back seat; she sees her family conflate into one pulsing balloon of flesh.

"Come on—nearly home."

"No!" shrieks Flora. "There's still a bit of arm hanging out!"

"Got it," pants Keith.

The door closes noiselessly and to ironic cheers from the crowd the four grumpy pigs chug out into the street.

"Get your arse off the gear lever, woman," Frank demands as they pull up at the lights. "How'm I expected to drive with arse all over the gear lever? Keith! Move over, can't you, you fat little sod. You're weighing down the right rear wheel. I can feel her listing to the right."

"Ah, shut up, you fat old turd. How can I move with Aggie all over the place back here? It's *you* who's weighing it down, you great fat old fool."

"I happen to have reduced considerably of late. And there's no cause for *you* to be so heavy—you're only four foot and a fart."

"Ah, shut up. You fat old bugger. You fat old cunt."

"Keith," said his mother, "don't talk to your father like that."

"Ah, shut up. You fat old bitch. You fat old slag."

"Keith," said Aggie.

"Ah, shut up."

"This can't go on," says Mr. Whitehead as the car wobbles down through the motorway heat haze. "Starvation diet, all of us, all next week. You too, Keith. All next week. Starvation diet. This can't go on."

One hour later they sit in silence round a sea-front coffee shop table, paw-like hands dipping occasionally into a dome of cream, jam, and custard slices. Warm sugary tea runs down their chins.

The four Whiteheads are ninety stone, heavier than the average rugby pack, a crazily overglanded brood, their house a billowing cartoon world of sunken sofas, hammock-like beds, and winded armchairs. They shuffle about it snarling and swearing at one another with the sheer thyrotoxic strain of keeping their bodies afloat.

Whitehead, Sr., for instance, is a fabulously obese human being, better than thirty-five stone. As he trundles down the street school parties are floored by his myriad stray fists of flab; bus platforms snap off should he climb on board; lifts whinny, shudder, and stay where they are when he presses the UP button and plummet terrifyingly whether or not he is so foolish as to depress the DOWN; chairs splinter beneath him; tables somersault at a touch from his elbow; joists crack and floorboards powder. Frank's weight problem endangered, too, his position as cook at the bus terminus cafeteria: he would bend down in front of the cooker and—why—his behind had swiped a shelf of pans off the opposite wall; he would turn round from the sink to find that his paunch had cleared the table; loaves, half-dozen cartons of margarine, even sides of beef would get lost for days in the fleshly gowns of his stomach. (Old Whitehead had been known also to eat the cafeteria bare while the manager went to the lavatory.) When it became quite impossible for Frank to enter the kitchen without some of him being automatically—by definition—either on the hot plate, under the grill, in the oven, or down the toaster, he was invited to pick up his cards. Frank had been a worthless cook anyway, hardly able to prepare an egg.

To make up the loss in income Mr. Whitehead decided to expand the ailing family sweetshop. By compelling his wife to model eighteen hours a day at the Hornsey, Wimbledon, and Baron's Court Art Polytechnics, he saved enough money to gut the sitting room and have installed some bright steel ovens, a fablon-decked counter, and a sign saying *Whitehead's Takaway Fish and Chips*. The concern prospered, and eventually the sweetshop was phased out.

The turning point was the turning point also of little Keith's life.

He well remembered the transition. Keith would come home from school, a crimson-faced four-foot box in his sixth-form blazer, be refused a chocolate bar, snap at his father, then change into his white overalls. (He hated changing into these because they made him look appreciably more horrible than his school clothes did.) In hostile silence he and his father would serve the remaining children from the adjacent primary school—there would be more of them than usual because of the many white-stocks-last bargains featured in the closing-down sale. At 5:15 or so Frank's knuckleless fingers were curling round a Mars Bar or a Turkish Delight. Keith would wait a few seconds, then remove a few peppermint creams from the high glass case. With slightly more hurried movements Frank might reach for a sachet of Poppets and Keith for a box of Maltesers. Now Frank whips his thumbnail down a carton of Savoy Truffles and upends it into his mouth; Keith's head fizzes with imploding sherbert lemons. Bubbles of Caramac pop on Mr. Whitehead's lips; his son is lockjawed with fudge and Newberry Fruits. Frank skillfully flips a tray of violet creams onto the counter and laps them up like a dog. A runaway train of Toblerone shunts down the tunnel of little Keith's throat. By six-thirty they are engaged in a lurching, slow-motion alligator race to the downstairs lavatory-vomitorium. By seven, their batter-moist mouths gape beneath the fish-shop chip chutes.

The family gained a hundredweight in five weeks.

Shortly afterward, Keith went mad for a time.

Nothing seemed to precipitate it. One moment he was toddling out of the Mod. Lit. Library in Milton Avenue, London NW20; the next moment he was toddling into the Gregory Blishner Institute, Potter's Bar, London NW36. What had happened in the interim was a rush of terror and confusion as solidly chemical as adrenalin, a telephone call, and a bus ride.

Not that the preceding week had been entirely uneventful. For one thing it had included his inaugural few days at Wolfson College, London—days that had opened up whole new eras of ostracism, mortification, and self-loathing. But Keith had been banking on that, and by and large he was agreeably surprised by the cordiality of his reception. On top of this, though, he had been independently menaced on the Monday by a traffic warden, an old man on the underground and a floor sweeper in a local pub. Keith had offered them no provocation and had accepted their threats and denunciations with respectful apologies. On the Tuesday he was denied service in a cafeteria —no reason given—and badly stoned by little boys in the park. The next day he crouched in his bedsitter drinking quarts of instant coffee. On the Thursday an entire Woolworth's shop counter went into hysterics when he tried to buy a comb, a poker-faced conductor barred his entry onto an uncrowded bus, he found and removed a sheet on the lodge notice board which read KEITH WHITEHEAD IS A HORROR-SHOW, his tutor advised him—for personal reasons which he would as soon not disclose—to change subjects, and his father rang to say that he spoke for the whole family in asking Keith never to contact them again. A more or less average week, you'd have thought. But on the Friday White-head started to be insane.

For an hour he sat waiting in the Institute's arc-lit vesti-bule. He beguiled it in an examination of the back of his hand, trying hard not to look down the endless yellow corridor where mad persons now groped and slunk along the walls as wraith-like male nurses swept past them with throbbing steel cylinders. "Whitehead? This way."

"How are you feeling?" the doctor asked.

"Sad and frightened."

The doctor knitted his fingers together over the desk and leaned forward. "How long, would you say, you have felt this way?"

Keith looked at his watch. "An hour and twenty minutes."

The doctor, a slow-talking Ceylonese, went on to ask Keith about his background, in a patient but unimaginative attempt to reveal traumas, blocks, repressions, and so forth. Although Keith answered all the doctor's questions with grim candor it soon became clear that his life had been quite devoid of emotional incident.

"Look," said Keith after a while, "you don't have to do all this. I know what the trouble is. It's quite straightforward."

The doctor sighed. "Okay. What is it?"

"No. I'm not telling you. You'll just think I've got para-noia."

"No, I won't."

"Yes, you will."

"No, I won't."

The doctor had already seen twenty-one male university students that morning. Six had complained of impotence, five of canceled sex, four of bedwetting, three of false memory, two of insomnia, and one of somnolence. The doctor had pre-scribed Contentules to every student except the one complain-ing of somnolence, whom he had instructed to go away.

"All right then," said Keith. "Well, as I told you, it's quite straightforward. No one likes me—actually most people dislike me instinctively, including my family—I'm not much good at my work, I've never had a girlfriend or a friend of any kind, I've got very little imagination, nothing makes me laugh, I'm fat, poor, bald, I've got a horrible spotty face, constipation, BO, bad breath, no prick, and I'm one inch tall. That's why I'm mad now. Fair enough?"

"Yes," said the doctor.

Every life has its holiday, and Keith's month in the Institute was assuredly his. To begin with, he didn't go any madder. The panic and confusion receded at once, becoming a faint accusatory gibber at the nape of his neck. He found too that within a suspended community his sense of isolation could be turned to good account. He grew to think more coldly and shrewdly about his personal shortcomings. He found out what the average weight was for a five-foot man; he worked his way through the reading-room magazines, appreciatively noting down all instances of deformity and privation more acute than his own; a study of "The Human Body" section of the *Guinness Book of Records* assured him how puny his problems really were. In time, the feeling he had carried round with him since the age of six or seven, the feeling that he ought to be dead, gradually began to fade.

And with every day that passed little Keith took solace and grateful encouragement from his fellow inmates, watching the old teddyboys who yawned and sniveled in front of the common-room television, the fat forty-year-old infants who lay staked out with depressants in the wards, the mumbling bitches who leaned slumped like rubbish bags along the corridors, the sparrow-like girls kneeling nervously on the lawn. Airy with barbiturates, Keith would rove the Institute grounds, every now and then his face folding into a sneer or lightening with a thrill of relish as his colleagues made their twitching way past him. He had overheard it said that you always went madder at the Institute because "there was nothing to relate to." But Keith didn't want to relate to anything; he felt only hatred and contempt for the mutants around him, and if ever he wished to remind himself of the true direction of his life he simply gazed at the high Institute walls, visualized the road that went to London, and listened with pleasant detachment to the sounds of buses and high

heels in the street outside. The month did wonders for his
confidence. Heck, he even got a girl.

Whitehead's sex life?

Eighteen years old, with £25 in the pocket of his tightest
trousers, Keith had paced the clotted streets of Soho one mid-
August evening, to cries of "Having a night out, Shorty?"
"Isn't it past your bedtime, darling?" and "Hope it's bigger
than you are, baby," until a frowning Negro beckoned him
down the steps of a cafe basement. The Negro spread out his
arms to introduce Keith to three sirens who perched on stools
round a dirty hot-drinks machine.

"Well, well," said the center blonde. "Come on, then, big
boy. How much you got?"

"Fifteen," said Keith.

The whore turned to the Negro. "Look, Mr. Boogie-Woogie,
who the fuck do you think we are? You bring two-foot
wonders down here with fifteen bloody—"

"Mary, I'm sorry," began the Negro brokenly.

"Why should I take it, Lester? Why, Lester, please tell
me?"

"Oh, Mary," Lester implored. "I did not—"

"Twenty-five," Keith seemed to say. There was a silence.

"What was it you wanted, sonny jim?"

"Eh? Oh, just a fuck."

"Yeah? Nothing flash?"

"Honestly."

Mary wagged her head at the girl on her right, who clicked
her tongue.

Half an hour later Keith stood drowning in Piccadilly
Underground. Melissa had taken his money, led him to a
smelly cubicle, undressed on the bed and lay there like a
section of plaster of Paris while Keith bounced and wriggled
on top of her trying to purchase an erection. Then Melissa
dragged out her cardboard box full of stimulator gadgets, elec-
trode triggers, and prostate gimmicks, and sighingly applied vi-
brators, fur gloves, calipers.

"Look, you've had your twenty minutes."

"Oh, God," said Keith. "Look, couldn't you just try it with
your hand?"

"*Hey.* C'mon now, sonny, you said no flash stuff."

"That's not flash! What's flash about that? What could be *less* flash?"

"Go on. Bugger off. Go on, bugger off, you dirty little sod."

Keith demanded his money back. Melissa refused. Keith asked for half his money back. Melissa refused. Keith begged for his tube fare home. Melissa advised him to get going before she kicked the shit out of him. Whitehead got going.

Things had been different with Lizzie.

When Keith first laid eyes on Lizzie Bardwell, in the Institute cafeteria, he naturally assumed that she was blind. She wore dark spectacles, kept her arms outstretched before her at all times, and had to be slotted into her seat by the two fat male orderlies. Keith watched closely as she ate. Lizzie was a thin, asymmetrically jointed figure with sparse carrot-colored hair and a triangular, freckle-dense face—but there was something about her Whitehead liked. Egged on by his Valium, and deciding that in the Institute no one knew what the hell was going on and that all the mad cunts wouldn't notice him getting shooed away, little Keith idled over to her table as she was eating her semolina and curds.

"Hi," he said. "Keith's the name. Mind if I sit here and talk?"

Lizzie shook down the bench a few inches and Whitehead vaulted in beside her.

"I am Lizzie Bardwell. Why are you in this place?"

"Hell—free meals, free bed, free drugs. Kind of restful. You?"

In a fast, highly inflected voice Lizzie said, "I've always had a sort of a squint, you know, which I'm very paranoid about. And it's got like I can't see because they're right on the side looking at the inside of my head." She placed her forefingers on either temple. "Like a kind of whale," she said, beginning to laugh, very loudly.

Keith began to laugh too, far, far louder.

Whitehead's dream girl. For the following week Keith was gallant and deferential, parading with Lizzie over the grounds, escorting her to therapy, sitting next to her at meals, waiting outside the shock-treatment booths, listening to incredibly boring self-analyses, and only every now and then going noiselessly down on his knees to look up her skirt, or peering down her blouse when he rose to take his leave, or making faces and V-signs at her while she chirruped on in sightless self-regard.

It happened on the eve of Whitehead's discharge, among the trees at the end of the front lawn.

"Although The Lunch have more native talent than One Times Two," said Keith, putting an arm round her narrow shoulders, "they haven't the professionalism."

"No?" said Lizzy. It was the first time they had touched.

"Or so it seems to me," he replied, pressing his free hand against one or other of her breasts. "Do you not feel this?"

"I always thought The Lunch lead guitarist, Gary Tyler, was too technical to ever really let go."

"Tyler, certainly," assented Keith as he guided a hot palm between her thighs. "But only in composition. In performance" —he hooked her dress over her waist and began to force down her tights—"he's as limited as the rest of them."

"Even in the *Dark Tunnel* album?"

"Not so much there, I grant you," little Keith conceded, tugging her bunched underthings over her shoes, "but you'll agree that his predictability is seldom, if ever, accompanied," he continued, rolling effortlessly on top of her, "by what might be called a satisfactorily fulfilled expectation. For example . . ."

It was quick, as he remembered—quick, pleasureless and very mad.

Five days later Keith was enjoying a glass of water in the college bar when Quentin, Andy, Diana, and Giles came in.

"Nowhere to sit."

"By that little fattie over there," said Diana.

"What, the dwarf?" said Andy.

"I dislike dwarfs. They depress me," murmured Quentin, examining his rings.

"I'll handle it," said Andy.

Keith looked up in furtive terror as they crossed the bar toward his table. Andy stepped forward, compressed his nostrils with thumb and index finger, and nasally inquired, "There can't be anyone sitting here, now can there?"

"Highly unlikely," said Diana as the four sat.

"Bust out the fuckin' brandy, whyncha," said Andy.

Keith sat stretched with horror. He didn't dare leave because they'd see just how short he really was.

"My mother's got manic depression again," said Giles through his laterally placed fingers, "and's got to go to the bin. She actually wants to know about some Institute near her, in Potter's Bar, actually. I don't want her to though, cos she'll make me see her more."

"That Blishner dump?" said Andy. "Yeah, I go there for drugs."

"Tell me things about it," said Giles. "Where is it, for instance, actually?"

Nobody seemed interested in replying.

"I can tell you," Keith found himself saying. "I can tell you, if you like."

"Really?" asked Giles. "Thanks, that would be . . . that would be . . . Have you got a pen or anything?"

"Yes," said Keith, producing one.

"Howda fuck do you know?" said Andy.

"I was there last month. I was in there."

"Yawn. A maddie. Let's make a run for it."

"No, I was in there, but I'm all right now."

"Good. Look, who the fuck are you anyway?" Andy asked, quite friendly now.

"Keith."

"Who?"

"Keith."

"Keith *what*, you little prick."

"Oh. It's an awful name. Whitehead."

"Whitehead's not such a bad name," said Giles. "Whitehead," he repeated experimentally.

"It is if you've got them all over your face," said Whitehead.

They all laughed.

"Hey," said Andy. "I like this dwarf. This dwarf, he's all right, you know? This dwarf's . . . *okay*."

41: HIS LUCENT GIRLFRIENDS

He watched the last of his lucent girlfriends curl in on herself, rise yearningly on the stirred embers, erase in black smoke, and shrink to a charred and wizened ball. He poked the scattering fire with a stick. They were all dead now, his girlfriends . . . the one with the tenderly veined breasts, the one that looked like a woman he had sometimes seen in the village, the one with the impossibly concave pants, the one with the deep and pleading eyes, the one whose lips had seemed to say . . . No, they were all dead, dead, and their ashes strewn upon the wind. What will my nights be now? he thought.

The question of who had done this thing to him interested Whitehead not at all. He had expressionlessly removed the JOHNNY poster and burnt it along with everything else, without considering the matter further. It made no difference anyway. All the shame was his. He looked at Appleseed Rectory, half a mile away, hiding behind a nylon curtain of misty sunlight. "Get your staring done with," he said, beginning the long haul down the field.

"Open up, open *up*," shouted Keith wearily at the Tuckle door. "It's *me*, it's *White*head."

The slat opened and the bolts were thrown back. Mr. Tuckle emerged. He stood there stonily.

"Out of the bloody way then," said Keith. "I want some more of that gin I brought you. That's if you haven't already bloody—"

Mr. Tuckle stood there stonily. Keith fell silent. He was in slippers, and now even Mr. Tuckle towered above him.

"What's the matter?" asked Keith.

"Go away, Mr. Whitehead," said Mr. Tuckle. "I'm sorry, sir, but we've decided that we don't want you here any more. Go away, Mr. Whitehead, please."

Keith limped in tears across the lawn. Once in his room he got to his knees and prayed for a few minutes. He then sat on his bed, sniffing richly. On the bunkside table, a piece of cheap writing paper and a ballpoint pen awaited the caress of his pudgy fingers. *Dear Lucy*, he began. As he wrote, his boots beckoned from the corner of the room.

42: PLUS WHICH

"Why, I'd restore a feudal society, of course," pronounced Quentin.

"Casual," said Andy, nodding.

"Casual?" said Roxeanne. "You mean you people aren't

revolutionaries? Marvell, what the hell are we doing here with these people? What in fuck are you then?"

"We're ecstatic materialists," said Andy as he crawled across the floor, holding spent brandy bottles up to the light. "Meaning, we grab whatever the fuck's going." He drank deeply from an unattended glass. "Plus which, we grab it from people who haven't got much anyway. Check?"

Those conversations.

"Quentin," said Marvell. "In this feudal society, what if you were—what the hell are they?—serfs, yeah. What if you were a serf?"

"Bliss," Quentin replied. "The point eludes you. A hier-archical society is inversely reciprocal. The satisfactions of the higher echelons lie in command, protection, responsibility, in giving orders; the satisfactions of the lower echelons lie in docility, security, myopia, in obeying orders. It's a quasi-ritualistic enactment of one's role."

"What if you had a dumb lord and a smart serf?"

Andy pounced: "Then it's tough shit on the serf!"

"Precisely," Villiers affectionately agreed.

With conviction Roxeanne said, "You people have to be kidding. What do you feel—hey, Giles."

Giles looked up, smiling palely.

"Don't ask him," said Andy. "He's one too—practically a millionaire."

"Hey, Keith?"

Whitehead's boots were hurting him so much that he could hardly breathe, let alone speak.

"Don't ask him," said Andy. "He's not anything. He's just a wreck."

Roxeanne shook her head. "But you *can't* regress. There's no way. It's too late for that now. All you can do is smash everything, raze the entire planet, and then start over, make it new."

"In which event," crooned Quentin, "a feudal society would soon re-establish itself. It sounds very arduous. Why bother?"

"Not if you smashed *everything*. Culture, books, buildings, all the way back, every kind of institution, all the foci of—"

"All the what?" said Andy.

"Foci."

"Fuck you too," he said, shrugging.

"All the foci of human memory. Obliterate it all. Entirely. Then we could really start over."

Throughout the morning Giles's anesthetized ears had fastened on and absorbed only the odd word or phrase— "bridge . . . gumboot . . . I'd give my eyeteeth . . . to crown it all . . . cap in hand . . . that's the drill . . . wisdom . . ." At Roxeanne's last words, however, he decided he could no longer remain silent. He sat up straight and said, "But what would happen— But what would happen to modern—"

Before Giles could stutter out the word *dentistry*, Andy was saying, "What's going on here? Hey! What's going on— there's no more lush! Come *on*, what's going *on* around here."

At length, Giles held out his cupboard keys.

"Christ, Giles," Andy said earnestly, "what kind of stunt was that to try and pull."

"Gin for me, Andy, actually," said Giles.

As Andy dashed from the room, Roxeanne turned to Quentin. Her voice was drained and plaintive. "What's the *time?*" she asked achingly.

"How much more *day* is there," Lucy said.

Quentin looked at his watch, a guilty host. It had stopped. "Not long," he said. "Not long."

Alcoholic inebriation had well passed the stage at which it might responsibly be explained away as extreme drunkenness. Even the relatively teetotal Celia had consumed well over a liter of brandy-orientated champagne cocktail. And yet the Appleseeders still seemed quite opinionatedly game. Their blood pressures and body temperatures were dropping, finding the time for various drugs to catch up to their stretched metabolisms. Whitehead, for example, felt that his torso might be a shipment of jumping beans, Diana and Celia alike believed that they were on the brink of grave hormonal upsets, Marvell burped with unusual volume and candor, and Lucy was under the impression that she was a ghost or a dead body. All about them, cellular and glandular negotiations raged.

Marvell gazed at his watch. "Oh-kay," he said. "Everybody all right? We should be out the other side of this thing pretty soon. Just wander around a bit and do what feels best to do. Any more of that cocktail . . . ?"

The air in the room rolled. People began to fall through doorways.

43: Cruel BODY

All morning there had been talk between Andy and Skip of a game of badminton. Noticing that Skip's mouth was white-crumbed with dehydration, Andy malevolently challenged him to an immediate match.

"Now it's not a fuckin' American game," Andy briefed Skip as they extracted net and posts from the hall trunk. "So don't try kicking it or heading it or running around with it or any crap like that. You just"—he motioned with his racket—"whap it over the net with this, is all. Okay? And watch it, cos I'm fucking good."

Diana went upstairs to view the game from her bedroom window. She did this partly because she felt too ill to tolerate company, and partly because the confusion of her feelings for Andy had not yet abated the pleasure of watching him move about when he thought her eyes weren't on him. She lit a cigarette, resting her elbows on the wooden windowsill. The game began.

Andy won a few quick points by variously fair and foul means, penalizing Skip for "technical" misdemeanors, mis-positioning him to receive serve, capriciously amending the rules; but Skip had caught on fast and was moreover proving stubborn about the more audacious contradictions in Andy's scoring system. At 6–6, Andy was no longer master of his good temper, and when little Keith staggered out to admire the contest, Andy suggested that he fuck off again, menacing the craven Whitehead with his raised racket.

To Diana, Andy and Skip seemed equally strong and skilless, equally powerful and uncoordinated. Stripped to the waist, Andy looked marginally the more impressive, with his thick hair flapping and the glisten of sweat on his tanned back and glossy shoulders. Further, he had a habit of shouting *Yeah!* whenever he made a good shot and hooting sarcastically whenever Skip coerced him into a bad one. For all his clamorous bulk, though, Andy looked about seventeen. Skip, bespectacled, in T-shirt and khaki shorts, was far more composed, his mouth set resolutely throughout. And his body was hard and metallic by comparison, as if operated on tight cords—a sharp and unfriendly body, a cruel body.

"Johnny," said Diana.

After a long, noisy rally, in which several reverses appeared to take place, Andy snapped his racket over his knee and stalked back toward the house, watched by a blankfaced Skip. Diana peered down as Andy's head bobbed out of sight. She smiled unpleasantly, until her eyes returned to the center of the lawn, where they were met by the American's.

44: wars and SHIT

"I can't believe I'm hearing this babies," said Marvell. "What are you, a fuckin' flower child?"

Giles did not reply.

"Listen," said Andy. "Listen," he said, flexing his shoulders as if about to lift some formidably heavy object. "Man has *always* been violent. It's only for a few years that we ever thought he might not be—and he was still having fuckin' wars and shit, Vietnam and that. Violence is innate, so it's sort of felt selfhood, realized livingness, it's expressing life in its full creative force—it's sort of creative to do it."

Giles frowned. "But what if you just went up to some poor old lady in the street and knocked out her, got her right in the . . ."

"Christ, hippie," said Andy, "what a crappy example. That's more like torture or something."

Giles frowned. "But isn't what you want . . . anarchy? I mean, what would become of law and policemen and fire engines and denti—"

"Yeah, well, you need all that too," said Andy, folding his arms. "But if I took you outside now and smacked the shit out of you, don't tell me you'd go running to the village pig, now, would you?" Andy leaned forward warningly.

Giles swallowed. "No, I promise, Andy."

"Well, then."

Those conversations.

"Hey . . . uh, Trip or Flap or whatever the fuck your name is—"

"Skip," said Skip.

"Skip. Check. *You* like fighting and fucking up animals and smashing things up and stuff, don't you?"

"Sure. Makes you feel good."

"Check. Marvell, am I wrong?"

"No, you're not wrong," said Marvell.

"Check. Fuckin' check." Andy sat back and turned haughtily to Giles. "Okay?"

Giles was a worried man. This sort of talk was all very much in accord with his occasional anxieties about the house, with the air of unreason and casual menace that struck him at odd moments of sobriety: he didn't know—unpredictable shadows on the stairs, pockets of sourceless, murmured conversation, the feeling you got that no one was really alive there, the sense it gave of being *suspended*. Giles remembered his terrified awe when he had overheard a speed-racked Andy soliloquize one night about how he was going to slay Mr. and Mrs. Tuckle . . . "Then I'm going to get this fuckin' great meat cleaver," Andy had droned to himself, "and stuff all these ants and stuff up her snatch. And pull out her teeth with pliers. And staple up her lips. 'Ain't no use you beefing about it Mr. Tuckle. Take a seat, sir, please, whilst I make with the meathooks.'" Shudder shudder shudder. Giles had crept back to his room and hadn't come out of it again for five days.

"Andy," he said. "If you do decide to hit me, don't hit me in the face, please. All right? Anywhere, but not in the face. I'll pay you not to . . ."

Andy leaned forward and tousled Giles's hair. "Don't worry, chickenshit," he said. "It's not your turn yet."

"Thank you, Andy," said Giles, getting up to leave.

"Hey. Andy."

"Yeah, what do you want, Rip?"

"Skip," said Skip.

"Check," said Andy.

"Why—how come you didn't want me to go kick that heifer?"

"What heifer?"

"The heifer yesterday."

"Oh, the cow. Cos . . . it was all fucked up—and it had attacked *us*, so you ought to treat it with respeck."

"I wanted to go fuck it up some more."

"Well, I didn't want you to, see?"

"I wanted to kill it."

Andy gave Skip a hard look. "Well, you'd expect that from someone whose dad killed his mum."

"Pardon me?"

In the same tone Andy said, "You'd expect that from someone whose father killed his mother."

The scene changed like a film cut. Andy was carpeted on his back and Skip straddled his chest, hands white on Andy's throat.

"*Aw—get him—!*"

Providentially Quentin was mulling over some Rousseau in the smaller sitting room when he heard the struggle. He raced through the dividing doors. With Marvell's aid he peeled Skip from Andy's thrashing figure and flattened him on the sofa.

"What'd he *say!* What'd he *say!*" bawled Skip as Marvell ran to the dining alcove. He returned, fumbling with a hypodermic.

"Jesus," said Marvell. He eased the needle into Skip's flapping arm. "The *fuck,* Andy."

"What'd he say," moaned Skip, tears welling from his closed eyes, "what'd he *say.*"

"I'd better lay an amnesiac on him too," said Marvell through his teeth. Skip's consciousness died from the room.

"What on earth happened?" asked Quentin.

Marvell explained while Andy climbed to his feet. He saw with relief that no one else was present. Moodily he dusted himself down.

"Now all we fuckin' need," Marvell was saying, "is for him to find the letter."

"The letter?"

"The one from his fuckin' father. It's in our room. I told you about it. It'd wreck his head to see it now."

"Ah yes, I remember. Give it to me," said Quentin, "for safekeeping. I'll return it before you leave. How fascinating. Tell me—"

As they conferred Andy moved over to the sofa, his back to the others. He leaned a palm on Skip's forehead, in the manner of one feeling its temperature. "Hope he's okay," he muttered. Andy's voice shook slightly when he said this because he was pinching Skip's damaged ear with all his might. "He'll pull through," said Andy, wiping a bloody thumbnail on Skip's khaki shirt. "I think he'll pull through okay."

45: THE BILLET-DOUX

Meanwhile, little Keith was sobbing loudly in the joyful soli-
tude of the back passage. Following this treat, his legs now
shooting out in all directions, Whitehead regained his cubicle
where, with tweezers, chisel, and light hammer, he prised and
chipped the blazing shoes from his feet. He sat back against
the wall and let out a quiet roar of suppressed pain. Black
blood ran down his shins.

Next to Whitehead on the floor lay the sex letter, the
billet-doux, that he had composed for the delight of Lucy
Littlejohn. Keith picked it up and surveyed it without embarrassment. It had, after all, none of the flaws common to
such missives; it was not heated, rarefied, florid, or imprecise.
On the contrary, it was a pedestrian—indeed, in style almost
bureaucratic—synopsis of his present plight, with the rider
that he would kill himself if Lucy did not alleviate it by sleeping with him. It began *Dear Lucy* and it ended *Yours sincerely*.

" '. . . the sum of nineteen pounds and seventy pence. It
is imperative,' " Keith read out loud, " 'that you notify me of
your decision within the next twenty-four hours. Thank you.
Yours sincerely, Keith (Whitehead).'

"That'll get her going," he said, hobbling to his knees. "Oh
yes, those brackets will get her going." He knelt against the
bed and joined his hands in an informal attitude of prayer.
"It's confidence wins today's girls," he snuffled.

"Please, God," he said to himself, "don't let *all* of this
happen to me. It won't do to let it all happen to one person—
to anyone, not just me. I still can't believe that it all has,
really. I suppose it's that that keeps me going. Oh, great—
fabulous. Look, why doesn't someone just come off it, is what
I want to know." Keith looked around him. "I can't cope with
this." Keith looked at his feet; even he was shocked. "I'm
falling apart here. I can't cope with this. And who's doing it
all to me, eh? *Who?*"

Well, we're sorry about it, Keith, of course, but we're afraid
that you simply *had* to be that way. Nothing personal, please
understand—merely in order to serve the designs of this par-

ticular fiction. In fact, things get much, much worse for you later on, so appallingly bad that you'll yearn to be back at the Institute, or even in Parky Street, Wimbledon, with that family you so loathe. It's all too far advanced for us to intercede on your behalf. Tolerate it. You'll turn out all right in the end. Now go and lie on your bunk.

Keith lay spread on his bunk—spread like soft butter on warm toast, his body trickling gratefully into the folds of blankets and counterpane. He oozed nearer the wall as he heard female voices from outside. Next to the tobacco tin on his bedside table was a creased manila envelope. It contained an agitated reminder from the Advanced Dietary Research Commission. Whitehead replaced this with the *billet-doux*. "Ah, fuck it," he said, crossing out *Kenneth Whitehead* and putting, instead, *Lucy (Littlejohn)*.

46: WAN WINDOWS

Gazing about himself, Giles found that he was in his bedroom. This appeared to please him in a mild way. He strolled to the refrigerator. He started to hum. He removed from the frosted compartment a tall glass of gin and Southern Comfort, a drink he had not experimented with, nor indeed heard of, before. He even started to whistle. Shadows wandered in from the corners of the room.

He sipped, and held up the glass to examine it against the light. "Hey. This stuff . . ." He sipped, and held up the glass. "This stuff . . . isn't bad." He sipped.

Halfway across the room Giles remembered his daily letter to Mrs. Coldstream. He came to a halt and his knees wobbled. An expression of delirious puzzlement overtook his features.

What did she want him to write, what could have happened today, how could things change still, how could you make it new any more, what was there left to tell her now?

"Dear Mother," said Giles. "I nearly tripped down the stairs on the way out. Good job I didn't! Dear Mother, Luigi wasn't sure of the way back and we had to ask a man in the street. A bit of luck *he* did! Dear Mother, Everyone was up by the time I got back. High time, too! Dear Mother, I got drunk all day. Why? Dear Mother, I'm dying here fast. Dear Teeth, I'm gum the crown drill."

Giles sat down at his desk. Languidly he synchronized the jar of 15B pencils, the deck of A4 writing paper, the eager glass. Fifteen minutes later he had completed a letter full of such typically filial charms as sullenness, torpor, complete want of understanding or sympathy, plainly sarcastic affection, explosive false amusement, and clueless self-pity—spread like giant's graph readings over eleven airy sides. Giles forced the scroll into an envelope, well pleased with his work. Outside, the afternoon backed off across the hills, causing light to glow on the wan windows of some underwater warehouse or distant farm.

Gazing about himself, Giles found that he was in his bathroom. This appeared to displease him in a mild way. He felt intimidated by the white porcelain and hard steel. He stared sleepily into the mirror. He didn't notice that something had been written in shaving cream across the glass. "Heal me, heal me," he whispered. Then he noticed. It read *Johnny*. And then he saw the thing on his basin sidetable, the smashed mockup of his mouth, wet with someone's snot, saliva, and blood. Giles fainted half sideways into the deep carpet.

47: a BIT permanent

"You can get used to anything in time, I suppose," said Lucy, descending like collapsed taffeta onto the lawn. "But I'd better start feeling better soon."

"Me too," said Diana. "I feel like a fiend."

"That's an awfully nice blouse, Lucy," said Celia. "Is it Thai silk?"

"Mm. Got it from La Soeur."

"Christ," said Diana. "How'd you manage that?"

"Whoring."

"Whoring," echoed Roxeanne. "I used to whore out on the Strip. Throat jobs. The guys used to get really phased because I wouldn't take any cash."

"Why wouldn't you?" asked Lucy.

"Had plenty cash of my own."

"What sort of men?" asked Celia.

"You know, just men. It was part of some project of Marvell's, I think."

"That's smart," said Diana. "Why did you?"

"Fun."

Celia frowned. "I think I'd find it terribly difficult to do anything with someone I didn't fancy a *bit*." She stopped frowning. "Do you know, I don't think I've ever been to bed with someone I didn't quite like," she lied.

"Me neither," lied Diana.

"Well, you're required to do that in my line of work," said Lucy. "The men you don't like require it. *Fun*? It's a nightmare. Sometimes I'm lying on my back counting wallpaper patterns and thinking about . . . pork pies or something, and there's some little Chink wriggling around like a maggot on top of me—and I know, I know: this is hell. This is hell. Think you wouldn't mind so long as his hair was different, his eyes were another color, his toes weren't like that. You would, though. It's a bloody good job I've got a heart of gold. Still, it beats typing."

"Right. And I don't think it makes that much difference," said Diana. "Say some man takes you out to a forty-pound dinner and everything. I mean, you'd feel a real slag if you didn't. It makes sense. Most people hate what they do. They spend all their lives hating it. It makes sense to finance what you like doing even if you get a bad fuck at the end of it. And with this protobiotic stuff . . . nothing too bad can happen."

"Nothing too bad," said Lucy. "You get to want a little bit more than nothing too bad."

"It's not that difficult," said Celia mildly. "I've done it— at a time I thought I never could again. It can be done still."

"No one I know can still do it," said Lucy. "And I'm fucked if I can."

Those conversations.

"Me too," said Diana. "If only women got sexual boredom too. But they just don't seem to get it the way men do. And you can't stay with someone who doesn't want you."

"Doesn't what?" asked a preoccupied Roxeanne, lifting her hands palm upward in a supplicant gesture in order to flex her breast muscles. "Give you a minute and you'll be saying women are basically monogamous."

"Well *I* am," said Celia. "Now."

"Pardon me, Celia," Roxeanne said, "but I think you're the one who's in real trouble. This marriage gimmick— I mean, just think of the children, think of—"

"That's not really what I mean. I think I mean just having something serious and, well, and a bit permanent."

"That's what I think I mean too," said Lucy.

Diana looked away down the lawn. A vague regret edged at her, but she shrugged it off. When she looked back, Lucy was smiling at her. Diana smiled too.

"I've fucked them big," sang Lucy Littlejohn, closing the lavatory door behind her, "I've fucked them small. I've fucked them fat, I've fucked them all! I've fucked them—"

Shrewdly Whitehead had positioned himself on the first rung of the hall stairs; one hand clutched the banister rail, while the other held up a creased manila envelope.

"Hi there, Keith. Wotcher doing?"

"Lucy. I've written you a letter," said Keith.

"Fancy," said Lucy.

"Will you read it, please."

"Okay."

Little Keith watched as Lucy did so. She ran her eyes over it quickly, releasing a snort of incompetently suppressed laughter. Then her expression sobered and she perused it with some care.

"Well?" said Keith.

Lucy moved closer to him. She took one of his fingerless hands in hers.

"No? You won't?" he asked evenly.

She shook her head.

"Fair enough. Why not, by the way, just out of interest? Not enough money, or is it just me?"

Lucy leaned forward. "No one else knows this," she whispered. "Heroin. A year. I'm dying now."

"But your . . . It isn't . . ." Keith stared at her bare forearm.

"No, but my bum's like the far side of the moon."

Keith experienced intense gratification. "Why? Can you stop it now?"

"Nope. So you see, you sort of go off sex. You lose sex. That's one of the good things."

"Ah, fuck it," said Keith. "My cock doesn't work any more anyway."

They laughed together.

"That's what I mean," said Lucy. "All this . . ." she gestured vaguely, "it's too many for me. Look at us now. Can you imagine us *old?*"

Keith seemed to consider this for a few seconds. "No way," he said.

"No way at all," said Lucy.

48: THESE DAYS

When she reached the end of the drive Diana turned to make sure Andy was following her. She heard the front door being yanked shut and Andy trotted into view. Diana looked beyond him at Appleseed Rectory. The dead texture of its bleached walls was even more pronounced in the summer-thunder afternoon. "All right, all right," he said.

Andy and Diana had spent so little time simultaneously alone and conscious in the past few weeks that they felt slightly adrift strolling together along the warm macadam of the village street. Her head bowed, Diana walked with arms folded across her chest. Andy's mind felt oppressively clear. The badminton had evaporated the champagne cocktails and the hash he smoked continuously did about as much for his jaded system these days as oxygen. Minutes passed. To forestall, or at least delay, boring things from Diana, Andy said, "Those Americans are getting me down. I'm going to beat one up if I get half a chance. And I mean really beat them up."

"Like you really fucked Roxeanne?"

This took Andy by surprise. He had forgotten Diana knew about that. He chose to ignore the remark. "Especially that tall fucker—the one with the crappy name. Rap. Yeah. Hey, I bet they sent you that note—the one on the bed. What you reckon? If I could just prove that I could really go to town. What you think?"

Andy shadowboxed unenthusiastically. Diana walked on.

"Fuck, Diana, *you* said you wanted to talk."

"I'm sorry. Andy, wait here a minute. Won't be long."

Andy stood grumbling to himself outside the mini-market.

He had been banned from its premises following an occasion two months earlier on which he had collapsed drunkenly into a six-foot display pyramid of BeanMeal tins and then slapped the elderly assistant manager round the shop for . . . for . . . Andy couldn't remember what for. He scanned the street for village down-and-outs—in particular Godfrey de Taunton, the legless hobo who had recently won Appleseed obloquy (and a skillful walloping from Adorno) for being found asleep in their coalshed. "De Taunton," Andy muttered, "you'd better not show yourself this afternoon." He looked the other way, shielding his eyes with his hand. "Is all."

Diana emerged from the mini-market. Andy noted with fresh boredom that she was still looking hunched and pre-occupied. They began to walk back. To walk back in that foot-dragging, tense, dilatory, pregnant style that comes when something is nearly being said. Andy wanted to run, do cartwheels, leap in the air, go to the pub, scream.

"Baby, can we sit here for a bit?" said Diana, turning her head to a wooden bench recessed a few yards from the road and partly canopied by the leaves of the dying elm on the loose-soiled verge. The bench, they now noticed, was patterned with the amorous graffiti of the local young . . . *Billy fks Jane, Susan Fs Emily, Tom fucks Cynthia, Chris F Peter.* Andy sighed with disgust as he made out a much more scored and faded etching, *Peter L Anne.*

"It takes you back, doesn't it?" said Diana.

"Mm? Takes you back to what? Doesn't take me anywhere."

"I don't know. Christ, to when you carved this sort of thing on benches."

Andy shrugged. "I never did."

"Well, to when you could be bothered to think about things like that. When you had time to be bothered."

Andy shrugged. He took out his large, multipronged penknife and began to chip absentmindedly at *Peter L Anne.* "I've never had the time. It seems like I've always been like I am now, always lived like I live now. That's how it seems, anyway."

"You don't care about me any more, do you, baby?"

Andy kept his back turned. At first he had enjoyed her calling him "baby." These days it made him shiver, as if in fear. He hesitated, then a listless determination came over him. He dug the knife harder. "A bit. Not much. I don't know. What you feel about me?"

"I don't know. Something. Something or other. I've never stayed with anyone as long as I've stayed with you."

"Me neither."

"Do you want to forget it?"

Andy shrugged. "Up to you."

"No it is *not* up to me."

Andy shrugged. "I don't mind going on. See how it goes."

"Christ, isn't there more than that? What's going to happen to us all?"

"You just go on," said Andy, hardly able to believe his luck. He had never known Diana to be so dejected and unaggressive, so unsure.

"Quentin and Celia have more."

"Yeah, well—hey, give me a, a . . ." he snapped a finger forgetfully, "fuck, a *cigarette*. Jesus. Quentin and Celia—it's just a question of going on till you get too pissed off to change. And you can't cope with being alone. And the street sadness and false memory get bad. When that happens you stick with whoever you're with then. I can't see that it matters a shit who."

"You don't fuck me any more. You don't even *hit* me."

Andy leaned harder on the knife. "Yeah, well, that's just what I mean about getting pissed off. You get pissed off with cunts."

"It's *my* cunt."

"Nothing personal, Diana. It's just cunts. I hardly want to fuck anyone these days. I've done all that now." He chipped the last of the wood away and sat up straight. "Maybe we'll end up together. Things are beginning to slow down for me now. I haven't got that far to go."

"I want more."

"More fucks?"

"No. Just more. Not much more, but more."

Andy shrugged.

Diana dropped her cigarette to the earth. Although she was crying a little her voice was firm. She looked at the fading graffiti. "Don't you think we must have made a mistake a long time ago to end up like this. That something went wrong and that's now why we're all so dead . . . Baby?"

Andy started.

"Can't we go back?"

"Go back? Oh, to the house. Oh, yeah. Check."

49: HELL OF a PLaCe

Andy returned just in time to break up a talk about bisexuality. Marvell had that minute asked Whitehead what his leanings were, but of course little Keith fell silent when he saw Andy swank out onto the lawn.

"All that camp and unisex and crap," said Andy: "dead babies now. When I was a kid they were doing all that. All a bluff set up by the queers. It's a pain in the arse."

Marvell laughed uproariously. "Would you—would you honestly claim to be a 'heterosexual'?"

"There are two sorts of bisexual," said Quentin. "Homosexuals and ugly heterosexuals."

"Yeah, well I'm a fuckin' heterosexual," said Andy.

"Andy: by saying that you realize you're limiting your relationships to a mere half of the human race?"

"Babies, babies. That's hippie talk, boy."

"You truly *want* to limit yourself in this way?"

"Yeah," said Andy.

"Don't you remember what you were saying about the Conceptualists? Think about it, Andy. We agree, don't we, that sex isn't erotic any more. It's carnal—conceptualized— to do just with geometrics and sensations?"

". . . Yeah."

"And that Other sex is to do with choice rather than urge?"

". . . Yeah."

"And that perversion is justified—no, *demanded*—by an environment that is now totally man-made, totally without a biology?"

". . . Yeah."

"Then why," concluded Marvell, "why negate yourself into a rationalist one-sex block?"

"I just don't like queers, is all," said Andy, deep in thought.

Marvell snorted a nostrilful of blood onto the grass, wiped his nose with the back of his hand, and laughed drunkenly.

"Heard about the Body Bar in Santa Barbara? No? Hell of

a fuckin' place. The waiters and waitresses are nude, natch—and you get fucked there for the cover charge. But you hear the gimmicks? You can have *cunt cubes* in your drinks. I mean it. And not just flavored with cunt. Real juice in the cubes. They got . . . yeah, they got tit soda, cock cocktails, pit popsicles . . . Oh yeah, and ice cream that tastes of ass. Hell of a place."

Marvell snorted a nostrilful of blood onto the grass. He wiped his nose with the back of his hand. He laughed drunkenly.

"It's arse, not ass," said Andy, rolling over. "Arse."

Those conversations.

Marvell stood swaying at the kitchen door. "Okay," he said, closing it noiselessly behind him and joining Skip by the cooker. Marvell handed Skip something small. At their feet The Mandarin purred stertorously as it worked its way through a large bowl of Kat.

"Right," said Marvell. "Dump it in its fuckin' food. Give it fuckin' all of it."

Skip crouched, chuckling.

"Is it eating it?"

"It . . . Sure," said Skip.

"Fuckin' cats. Kick the shit out of them one minute, feed them the next, they think you're fuckin' God. Okay?"

"Okay."

"Right. C'mon. Let's go watch the preview."

"Whose cat was it, Mar? D'you know?"

"Leave the door open. So it can get out. Celia's, I think. Yeah, it—I think it belonged to Celia."

L: CELIA

When Celia Evanston was seventeen her stepmother, Lady Aramintha Leitch, drew her into a frescoed alcove of her Roman apartment and offered her stepdaughter a new Jaguar, a flat in Cheyne Walk, Chelsea, and 10,000k. per annum on the condition that Celia didn't make a pass at the water-ski instructor Lady Leitch was currently drunkening on the patio sundeck. Spottily Celia blinked into her stepmother's over-tanned face, slipping both hands into her jean pockets.

"What makes you think I want him?"

"Darling, it's just that Giovanni and I should like to be alone together."

"What makes you think he wants me?"

"God knows, but I do think it." Lady Leitch poked a cigarette under her top lip; it wobbled as she asked why Celia didn't do something about her complexion, her poise, and above all her hair. "And why are you so fat?"

"I eat a lot. And what does it matter about Giovanni, if I'm so hideous?"

"You're sixteen. It's not that he wants to but that he knows he can."

"And what about you?"

"No. Come on. Off with you. Off. Off. Off."

For two years Celia threw in her lot with the decadent London young, gave parties for shits in satin plus-fours and bitches in neon camisoles, ate at Tastes and Casa Ari beside pricks with powder-puffed hair and tarts in three-piece pinstripe suits, went to Serena's and Poor on the arms of bastards in high-heeled gambados and slags in tapestry body stockings. She awoke at eleven, exhumed whatever ponce or pimp happened to be in her bed, dressed with the care of the not-quite-pretty, would be drinking Bloody Marys with fat hairdressers and scum-of-the-earth antique dealers in an underlit Chelsea restaurant by twelve-thirty, on to the conservatory cool of the chosen lunch venue with trashy photographers and one-hundred-word models, stupid middle-aged fashion designers and vicious pop-group managers. In the afternoons she cruised the Fulham Road for minors, the street markets and coffee shops, a sampler of public schoolboys in their first velvet suits, suburban tikes with bouffant hair-dos, incipient queers in see-through strides. She dined on the park or by the river with the same cast of crooks, fools, and whores, before submerging into the heavy, soundless, crypt-like opulence of a preselected nightclub, where vile aliens trade in old models for new and shrewd prostitutes keep a few inches between the toilet seat and their bodies. Cocaine until three, some kind of sex until four.

How foreign this was to her compliant and shockable nature Celia never realized until Quentin swept into her life. She had had no clue but her money, and this existence was launched and kept afloat by money, was described and identified by money, was all about what money could do.

Celia didn't know her stepmother was in town until she rang from the Connaught. Aramintha had flown in from Rome to finalize her divorce, having a month before surprised Giovanni in bed with the bellboy and screwed a broken Fanta bottle into his startled face. She was now going under the name of Lady Aramintha Gormez.

"Darling, come to lunch," were Lady Gormez's opening words, as if Celia had dined with her the night before. Celia said she would and replaced the telephone on the bedside table. She gazed at the wall of clothes in the fitted closet opposite, wondering what to wear and whether her stepmother had changed much in two years.

"I'm never going back to Rome. And it's Barces up your Arces too," said Lady Gormez, referring to her Barcelona penthouse. "I just can't stand those honking little dagos. Franz and I rather think Switzerland. I must say, darling," Lady Gormez told her grapefruit, "you have improved enormously." She looked up. "You're not as fat as you were . . . your skin's improved, and your hair is really, really quite lustrous. London life must suit you."

Celia turned away. She thought that she probably didn't want to see her stepmother again.

An oblique glimpse, then, at Celia's sex life.

The day before she met Quentin Celia threw a small soiree at her Cheyne Walk flat: two actresses (good friends of hers), a personable interior decorator, and the loutish, sidling bass guitarist of a successfully retrograde pop-group. And so Celia straightens clumsily from the cushions, declines a joint from the interior decorator, takes the bass guitarist's hand, and says, "Are you going to come to my room for a little while?"

Jeff gets up and stumbles after her.

It is clear that Celia is naked beneath her smock, so old Jeff simply folds her onto the bed, hitching the material up with his own body. Their lips joggle scummily. Then, with sharply flexed elbows, Celia pressures Jeff's head down over her breasts, stomach, until it lodges between her thighs. This is where she likes his head best to be.

Two minutes pass.

Downstairs, the interior decorator starts like a cat that has heard a distant meow in the night. Jeff rocks down the stairs, rubbing his mouth with his jean jacket sleeve.

"*Christ,* man, what am I *doing?*" He stops in the middle of the room and clamps his face between his hands. "Why'd you let me *do* it, man, plating a girl like that. My head must be really . . . really *scrambled.*"

"Wow, what went on, man?" asked an actress.

"Oh, fuck, I don't know. Here."

An actress holds up a brandy glass.

"Jesus. Let's get out."

"We can go to my place," said an actress.

"Right," said the interior decorator.

Rigid, legs still apart, The Mandarin sniffing at her thighs, Celia hears the door slam shut.

"You're spreading yourself too thin, lovey," said her stepfather when she gave him a minimally bowdlerized version of the incident the following morning. He was on the way to a heavy mistress on the Embankment and had called in for tequila and sympathy. "Perhaps you shouldn't be spread that far. Just a suggestion."

"How do you mean?"

"Well, if you leave a little bit of yourself with everyone, you might find one day that there isn't much left. See?"

Celia said, "Then you'd have been used up long ago."

He laughed painfully through his hangover. "No, don't misunderstand, lovey. I've always thought that fucking was a godsend for us oldsters and a bane for you youngsters who came up with the idea in the first place. Bloody marvelous! All these people suddenly willing to do it, and no guilt! That was the really new thing for us." He coughed horribly.

"Yes," said Celia.

"Well, *our* sexual natures were formed, so we could never suffer from anything worse than ennui. I think that's why we let you do this to yourselves. To liberate *us.* But your lot, lovey, you free libbers . . . you thought you'd get free. You didn't get free." He picked up his cigarette case. "I must be off. Suki awaits. Give my cordial regards to the old bitch should you tangle with her again while she's here. Who's she with now—nine-year-old Indonesians? Ta-ta, lovey. Take care."

Celia had not been intending to score that afternoon but the moment she saw Quentin she knew that she would have to have him. As he danced down Beauchamp Place, the breeze playing cheekily with the soft curls of his hair, the traffic seemed to wind to a halt and the very air to trail motionless in the sky. If necessary, she thought, she would simply present him with a blank check, waiving her more subtle last-ditch measures—the bland preludial offer of a tape recorder or silk robe, the ten-pound notes fanned on the hall table.

Oh, let him not be queer, she beseeched, bundling her shopping into the Jaguar and leaning negligently on its silver haunches.

"Hello," she said as he cruised past. "Didn't we meet at the Ormondes'?"

He paused and smiled lightly. "I have met a great many people at the Ormondes'," he said, "but I believe that you are not among that select band."

"Oh, dear. What a shame," said Celia.

"Yes. Isn't it," said Quentin.

She had wanted to roar back to her flat and beach him straightaway. As it was, she was led into beguiling the most adventurous and sensual few hours of her life: he took her for a walk. They promenaded via Kensington Gardens, along the Serpentine, to Speakers' Corner, and back through the park. For Celia it was a sweet, cocaine afternoon; she floated by his side, strummed by the resonant ease of his voice and the spectral beauty of his presence. At six o'clock, Quentin refused the offer of an introduction to The Mandarin and a Bellini at her Cheyne Walk flat, kissed her transiently on the forehead, and arranged to meet her for luncheon the following day. At Thor's she drank heavily to tame her sexual excitement. Quentin divined that it would not be hard for him to take advantage of Celia. He did so. As soon as she had finished a second Green Chartreuse, Quentin took Celia straight out and married her.

"I *do*," said Celia.

51: JUST CHECKED OUT

"Look!" she cried. "Here's my friend The Mandarin."

Celia turned and smiled into her husband's green eyes. Those present looked up blearily.

"*Isn't* she in a good mood!"

She did seem to be. The Mandarin came jumping in from the kitchen. It spun round. Its tail hairbrushed and its body went tense. It leapt hissing in the air. Its body flattened out like a hunter. It ran galvanically round the room, on sofas, chairs, walls. It cuffed a champagne cork along the carpet. It lay on its back and indolently feinted at the air. It chased its tail. It ground and flexed its claws on the skirting board. It went into a series of soft little springs. It nosed about the floor in impossible caution. Its eyes closed. It edged into the lap-like convexity of a cushion. It curled up and—

"It curled up and then we all like flashed that it was dead," Roxeanne explained.

Andy knelt over The Mandarin's body. He raised its kittenish head—the creased eyelids, the folded-back, lupine ears. When he let go it fell at once into its dead posture.

"It just freaked," said Marvell.

"Yeah."

Andy crossed the room and gripped Celia's trembling shoulder. Quentin, in whose arms her head was buried, looked up hushedly at his friend.

"It was very old," he said.

"Yeah."

Andy returned for the last time to The Mandarin's body. "I loved that cat," he said unsteadily. "I did."

"It just checked out, man," said Marvell.

"Yeah," said Andy, breathing in. "But Jesus I hate this no-good motherfuckin' chickenshit weekend."

52: TEAR-TRACKS

"Good evening, sir. What can I get you? It's been an absolutely glorious day, sir, hasn't it?"

Andy pitched two one-pound notes onto the bar. "Brandy," he said. "Two doubles."

"Right you are, sir. The Hine, sir . . . ? Or would you like to try the Martell?"

"Yeah."

"Would you prefer the three-star, sir, or the four?"

"I don't give a shit," said Andy.

Within half a minute Andy had two glasses of brandy in front of him. He emptied the first glass into the second and emptied the second into his mouth. He pitched two one-pound notes onto the bar. "Again," he said.

"Certainly, sir."

The landlord refilled both glasses. Sighing histrionically, Andy poured the one into the other. "Barkeep," he said as he moved off to the window with his drink, "you're a pain in the arse."

Andy felt bad. It wasn't the death of The Mandarin—it had been quite a casual kick bag, he supposed—but he had had no emotion for the cat other than mild irritation. No: it was false memory. He had sustained an attack of it that afternoon, his second in a week. For fifteen minutes he had lain on his bed thinking about his father—a gray-haired man who looked like a successful doctor, with an efficient, reserved manner and a charmingly defenseless smile—before realizing that he didn't have a father. He didn't have one. But, again, it wasn't this that depressed him; he wouldn't have been able to understand such a loss. The memory had come, as always, with none of the piecemeal haze of fantasy, but with all the settled and poignant soft clarity with which the past reconvenes. Only it was false memory. It wasn't his. Those images! They were like the displaced memories of someone else's mind, the photographs of another's past. Sadness washed through him. He felt secondhand.

"I feel secondhand," Andy muttered. "False memory. Bastard false memory."

"Sorry, sir? What was that. A refill, sir?"

Andy flipped a hand in the direction of the bar. "Ah, shut up," he said. "Just shut the fuck up."

Ignoring Skip's invitation to join the others in the sitting room, Andy rolled a ten-paper joint on the kitchen table and took it out to smoke in the garden, the air gun swinging loosely at his side. He sat down on the slope beneath the trees. It was evening and the cool doves filled the humming air.

The joint lit, Andy lay back and thought about a holiday he had had a few years ago, when he had taken a beaten-up Land-Rover to Italy. He had been hopelessly in love with a friend of his sister's at the time, a small, lithe Jewess called Anna whom he'd met only twice and kissed only once. He had written to her every day with youthful desperation, gushing more and more extravagant promises until . . .

Andy opened his eyes. The trees were suddenly loud with birds. "How long . . . ?"

Andy sat up straight. He had never had a sister and he had never been to Italy and he had never been in love with a Jewess called Anna. False memory again. He pressed his palms to his temples and exhaled breath. "False memory again," he said. "Sonofabitch false memory again . . . Fucking *hell*."

"Andy? It's me."

Andy opened his eyes. Giles hovered uncertainly above him. "Uh, hello, kid," said Andy.

"You've been crying too," said Giles, noticing the fresh tear-tracks on Andy's cheeks.

". . . Yeah."

"What was it, actually?"

"False memory."

"Oh. I don't get that. I get street sadness. Even when I'm nowhere near streets. Why's that?"

"It just keeps getting back to you."

"Mm. Funny, isn't it, about drugs," said Giles. "They always said it would be brain damage, something like that. It isn't, though. It's just sadness. Sadness." Giles sniffed. "Marvell sent me to get you. He wants us to go and take some more. Shall we?"

"Drugs got me into this," mumbled Andy, "and drugs are gonna have to get me out."

"By the way, Andy, is one of those American chaps called 'Johnny'?"

Andy half shook his head.

"I *thought* they weren't. Andy, what are you sort of doing, actually?" Giles asked, gazing up at the white doves in the branches overhead. "Killing the birds?"

"No. I . . . they don't . . ."

"May I have a go?"

Andy flapped a hand torpidly at the rifle.

"What I . . . you just . . . it won't . . . pull the . . . and it . . ."

A compressed thud ignited the tree and the threshing castle hurled the birds off into the sky. A wide dove swung down to the earth. It spun like a dislodged catherine wheel.

Andy stared up through the frightening leaves. "Giles! You stupid fuck! It's a *dove,* it's a *dove!*"

Giles reeled away from the wounded bird. *"Kill it, Andy,"* he wailed. *"Kill it."*

53: THE LUMBAR TRANSFER

Inside Appleseed Rectory, the first light came on. From their various corners they were all moving quietly and purposefully toward the main room. With the passing of day and the advent of evening their sicknesses and anxieties seemed to be momentarily neutralized, blent off into the changing air. Soon the windows would be dark and there would be nothing but Appleseed Rectory and themselves.

"The central nervous system is a coded time scale," began Marvell, "and each overlap of neurones and each spinal latitude marks a unit in neuronic time. The further down the CNS you go—through the hind brain, the medulla, into the spinal track—gene activity increases and concentrates and you descend into the neuronic gallery of your own past, like your whole metabiologic personality going by in stills. As the drug enters the amnionic corridor it will start to urge you back through spinal and archaeopsychic time, reactivating in your mind screen the changing landscapes of your subconscious past, each reflecting its own distinct emotional terrain. The releasing mechanisms in your cytoplasm will be awakened and you will phase into the entirely new zone of the neuronic psyche. This is the real you. This is total biopsychic recall. This is the lumbar transfer. Come over here one at a time, please."

. . .

Yes, it was seven o'clock and a pall of thunder hung above the Rectory rose gardens. The formerly active air was now so weighed down that it seeped like heavy water over the roof. Darkness flowed in the distance, and the dusk raked like a black searchlight across the hills toward them.

But pity the dead babies. Now, before it starts. They couldn't know what was behind them nor what was to come. The past? They had none. Like children after a long day's journey, their lives arranged themselves in a patchwork of vanished mornings, lost afternoons, and probable yesterdays.

54: TOO GOOD TO WASTE

"Keith!" shouted Andy as he wheeled the videotape into the center of the room. "Lie down and plug that bit in under there. You dumb fuck—not that bit! Christ. How long did Marvell say it'd take? An hour? Roxeanne—Diana—get me a brandy, willya. I'm practically blacking out here."

"This stuff should really be heavy," said Roxeanne eagerly. "We picked up the tapes in New York just before we came out—haven't seen all of them yet."

"Not really heavy," droned Skip. "Just with pigs, shit like that."

"It remains axiomatic," observed Villiers, "that sex films fatigue. If they're not sexy, they're sexy. Which is the more tiresome?"

"That's good coming from you," said Marvell.

"I've never seen a sex film before," whispered Giles over his glass.

"Keith! Will you—will you get the fuck out of there?"

Whitehead had been subject to crawl beneath the bottom shelf of the fitted bookcase in order to plug in the videotape. So very short were his arms, however, that he couldn't reach the socket. Andy kicked at and stomped on his tremblingly obtruded legs.

"Give me that." He snatched the plug from Keith's hand and knelt on the carpet. He sipped his drink. "You're too fuckin' fat anyway."

At length Andy slapped the cartridge into the tape console, turned on the power, and sat down, adjusting his groin and staring with hostility around the room.

"Right then. If I don't get a bonk," he said, "somebody pays."

Twenty minutes later the room was awheeze with boredom.

Various unspeakable acts had been variously portrayed. A porker had indeed made a young lady his, and there had been an additional coupling between a twelve-year-old boy and a representative of the monkey tribe. Large helpings of excrement had been consumed ("Oh, wretched evacuees!" Quentin cried), people had showered in urine, and they were shown a genuine sex death, in which an elderly actress was asphyxiated on a brace of craning phalloi. The remainder was a jangling bestiary, in whopping closeup, of gaping vaginas, rhubarb penises, and gouged behinds.

"Fuck you, Marvell," said Andy. "Fuck you. I wouldn't cross the street to *do* all this shit, let alone watch it. I don't know why the fuck I'm still sitting here. I don't know the fuck why I am."

"Why not put on something really sexy," said Lucy, "like *Dumbo*."

"What, what's the matter?" asked Skip. "Nothing wrong with this stuff."

"Change it. I don't like all the . . ." said Giles in a muffled voice. His head had been buried in a cushion ever since the first reel, when an actress had removed her false teeth the better to fellate a crippled Negro.

Marvell shifted in his seat. He appeared to be genuinely pained by the coolness of the Appleseed response. "Hey, Skip, get— put on the thing Archie gave us. The new one." He turned to Quentin as Skip broke the cassette seal. "Yeah, I know. But this one's different. Some Canadian sex outfit put it together. This should be new."

"Can anything be that any more?" breathed Quentin, crossing his legs and folding his arms.

The scene opened up onto a featureless suburban sitting room. Directly in front of camera stood a low-slung sofa. No other furniture was visible between it and the gray, picture-less far wall. Simultaneously, from either wing, a young man and woman entered and sat down next to each other. Dressed in white shirts and dark suits of conventional cut, they were of pleasant but unremarkable appearance. After a stylized pause, the young man put his right arm round the young woman's shoulders. She turned to him with an expression of cordial reserve. They kissed. The young man moved closer, by way of consolation, but the girl was not responding so much as lending her acquiescence, her hands remaining palm upward at her side. When, half a minute later, he began to kiss her throat and ear, something flickered remotely in her half-closed eyes. He cupped her far cheek with his left hand, allowing it to ski down her shoulder to the top button of her blouse. The girl shrugged the hand away. The action was repeated several times, the girl retaliating with less and less resolve. Then the man's palm descended quietly, contingently, on the bosom of the girl's blouse. Their kisses grew more arrowy.

"The fuck with this. That Archie's gonna—"

"Shut up," said Andy, erasing Marvell with a wave of his arm. "Shut up."

By now the top two buttons of the girl's shirt had been breached and the man had begun to pay studiedly oblique attention to her thighs. His long right arm was hooked round her shoulders, where it continued to mobilize her chest, as his left casually smoothed her neat charcoal skirt. The girl diverted her hands against this new threat. Another button popped open.

"Jesus," whispered Andy. "She's wearing a bra!"

The girl's ambiguous resistance was by this stage centered exclusively on her nethers, abandoning the quarter-naked billows of her breasts to the man's importunate palm. As he stepped up the tempo of his kisses, he endeavored to slide his left wrist between her kneecaps. They remained firmly clamped. Changing his tactic, the man raised his left hand to her breasts and began to circle his elbows on her loins. The skirt hitched up a few inches.

"Stockings," said Andy raptly. "Bloody *hell*."

Whether through arousal or agitation, their movements had become strained and aggressive. Bearing down on her breasts with his face, the man had introduced a stretched left leg which he attempted to steer between hers. The girl's legs gave. Now he seemed to be climbing on top of her, his mouth and both his hands congregating on her breasts while his forearms and torso hoisted up her skirt. As he did so the girl gave the impression of settling below him but abruptly began to slither out from underneath. Her skirt rode high up her thighs, shoving into camera view stockings, white suspender-belt, and taut pink panties—on whose strained mound the young man closed his fingers.

". . . YEAH!" roared Andy.

At once the girl lurched to her feet, struck the man forcefully across the cheek, and strode off the screen. The picture melted on a face all beaten up with lust.

Giles had frozen with a glass inches from his parted lips. Blood had suffused Whitehead's visage, momentarily banishing its dull cadaverous sheen. The Villierses had clutched each other, and Diana and Lucy were glancing confusedly around the room.

"She . . . she . . ." Andy writhed in his chair. "She didn't fuck him . . . she didn't fuck him," he croaked.

Only the Americans had showed no reaction. They consulted one another cluelessly; and then Roxeanne spoke. "If that's . . . Listen—" She raised her voice to pierce the jerky chatter. "*Listen*. If something like that gets you up, why don't we get something going right here."

". . . hit him—just cos he . . ."

". . . almost made it. Thought he was gonna . . ."

". . . laid it on that bra . . . those fuckin' stockings . . ."

Roxeanne looked threateningly at Marvell, who spread his hands and said, "Quent. Hey, Quentin! Listen, uh, we're . . . Is just that Rox is all pissed off cos nothing's happening?"

Quentin's exquisite brow puckered. "What species of thing isn't happening?"

"Doesn't anyone like to fuck around here?" asked Roxeanne.

Andy climbed to his feet and gazed down giddily at his groin. "My prong. I can hardly blink!"

"Hey, Andy," called Marvell, "why don't you start things rolling?"

"Yeah," said Roxeanne, "now that you've got one."

"Mm?" He looked up. "Nah. Nah, fuck all that. Do it yourself." He began to stagger toward the door. "I'm gonna have a wank. This is too good to waste. Awww, my *snake*," cried Andy brokenly as he tumbled from the room.

"I'm beginning to see what's the matter with you people," said Roxeanne. "You're so fucked up you can't even— What have I got to *do*. Any of you. Let's just get going. Let's *move*."

She looked at Quentin, at Giles, at Celia, at Diana, at Lucy, at Quentin again. "Any of you. Come on. Let's just start with *something*."

"With me?" asked Whitehead.

55: DON'T BE DISGUSTING

For the rest of his life Keith was to remember the divine comedy of that slow, andante ascent to the Rectory attic. One part of his mind, of course, was still anxiously trained on his immediate surrounds. The exit from the sitting room, for instance—with what eerie ease it had been conducted! Roxeanne had simply turned to him—had, then, actually, *smiled* —and walked coolly out of the door. Picking his way through a forest of embarrassment, Whitehead had followed, *encountering neither laughter, protest, nor spontaneous intervention from any member of the room.* As he now scaled the thinning stair carpet, a different area of his mind—though a no less self-conscious area—shook with hilarious awe. Another step. Watching Roxeanne's strong legs lift in front of him, he felt that whatever happened, however pathetic and grotesque the scene turned out to be, he would have captured something of real and lasting value. Another step. He would have swerved his life alongside something not entirely ridiculous, would have completed a raid on the inarticulate, would have transcended this bad body, would have touched good skin. Another step. Foreboding flashed against him as they passed Andy's creaking room. Another step. Safe. On the last flight he experienced a rush of sheer gratitude; he wanted to stop, to take her in his arms, to kiss her at length and with soft languor, and return in silence to his friends. Another step.

But things started speeding up.

She walk fast into room, turn, take off shirt, slip down she jeans, no pants, take she breast in she hand. On bed. "Come here." He go, he kneel, she mouth over he lip. She push he back on bed, climb up front of he to kneel across he shoulder, grip he ear to press to she pubis. Straddle he lap then. Undo he shirt, shinny down he trousers next. He sit up sudden take off he boot, she lick he back and she lick he under arm. He lie down she climb onto he again for tug he hair, drive sheself up he face. She swivel full circle, bend forward. She draw he genital into she mouth and gimmick she perineum to he face so good. She urinate some. She climb down he body so lick he thigh. She get she finger, grind it to it root up he anus. He defecate some. She press she nail into he hip, drag breast up he leg, feed on his penis. He head stretch back in long silent scream.

As Andy slipped down the stairs, Quentin loomed out of the passage shadows. Together they stole into the kitchen.

"A good one?"

"Fuckin' marvelous," said Andy, dusting his palms. "I don't know why people bother with anything else—I really don't. I was practically bent double."

"Guess what's happening?"

"Lemme see. Skip's fucking Mrs. Tuckle."

"Wrong. Roxeanne is fucking little Keith!"

"Quentin," said Andy, "call the police."

"To arrest Keith?"

"To arrest Roxeanne. What kind of pervert can we have up there? *Keith!*"

"No, it's true."

"Don't be disgusting, man. I mean, it's not that I'm shocked; I just don't happen to think it's particularly funny, is all."

"It's *true*, Andy. No one else would, so little Keith volunteered."

Andy threw his head back in a roar of dark, anarchical laughter. "Keith! That shape!"

"If shape it could be called that shape had none."

"Still, you know, you've got to give her credit. Come on, man, you have. Anyway, what difference does it make in the end? You get used to all kinds of shit." Andy wagged his head at the sitting-room door. "What gives in there?"

"Not a great deal, as it happens. Skip's trying to pull Lucy, who appears to be trying to pull, or at any rate solace, Giles. And—well—Marvell's trying to pull Diana. . . . I oughtn't to have mentioned it. He's having small success."

"I don't give a pig's rig. I talked to Diana this afternoon. We're forgetting it."

"No, really?"

"Yeah. I just fuckin' told her, was all. No *sweat*."

"How did she take it?"

"Well, it completely cracked her up. Course. But the fuck, you know? Hadda happen."

"I'm sorry to hear that, Andy."

"Relax."

"And tell me—what devilment are you planning now?"

"Nah . . ." Andy was about to shrug deprecatingly, but then his face cleared and became quizzical. "I . . ."

"You're feeling it, aren't you?"

"Yeah, I am, actually."

"It's quite impossible to describe, isn't it?"

"Yeah. It is."

56: IT STARTED STRANGELY

It started strangely. Not with a rush or a jolt, but as if it had always been there. The rosewood of the kitchen table seemed to have faded into a weak pastel brown. The blue and yellow tiles on the ceiling had receded and blurred so that its pattern was no longer distinct. Even the plain white of the walls appeared to have become something more washy, more neutral. Color had begun to drain from the house.

Andy had just sat himself down on the sofa and poured himself a sextuple Benedictine when Roxeanne came into the sitting room. He banged down his drink and hurried toward her. Marvell and Skip got to their feet.

"Well?"

"Well what?"

"Did it happen?"

"Did what happen?"

Andy's shoulders went slack. "Okay, I asked you nice. Now did you fuck him or didn't you fuck him?"

"I didn't fuck him." Roxeanne nodded to Marvell and Skip. They moved toward the door. Skip was rolling up his right sleeve. Marvell's fingers toyed with his belt buckle.

Andy wheeled round. "What's . . . ?"

Waving Skip and Marvell on, Roxeanne said to Andy, "He couldn't get a hard-on. And he threw up. It's not girls he likes."

"When we get in there," Marvell was telling Skip as they

left the room, "don't fuck around. Just get his fuckin' legs and—"

Andy gestured hesitantly at the closed door. He turned to Roxeanne. "What's going on?"

Roxeanne sat down. She looked hot and very angry indeed, but her voice remained calm, even rather piano. "I'm getting some theories about this house. There's no one in it knows how to fuck right." She sighed. "What they're going to do, Andy, is: Marvell's just going to screw him—okay—but Skip's gonna fist-fuck him first. Got it?"

"Fist-fu— You mean—right up the . . . ?"

Roxeanne placed her straight right hand on the inside crook of her left elbow. "Fist-fuck," she said.

"All that? Up the . . . right in his . . . ?" Andy placed his arm obliquely across his stomach. It went from his hip bone to his solar plexus. He stared at Lucy and Diana. "But it can't. He's only little. It'll go right up to his— It'll fuck him all up."

Roxeanne reached for the liquor bottle. "Skip told me that after the initial tightness it goes all sort of hollow," she said matter-of-factly. "It all sort of . . . gives, you know? It does no permanent damage. It's amazing what people can get away with these days."

Andy stared flinching at the door. A thin, insect scream had joined the sounds of violent struggle from above.

"That fat little fuck," said Roxeanne.

Marvell bent down to zip up his boot. "That bastard Archie," he said.

"Yeah," said Skip, pulling a T-shirt over his head. "What was he trying to pull?"

"Last time I go to that shiteater. He can't do that to me, he knows that. It'll finish him. Time to retire."

"Maybe," droned Skip as he buckled his belt, "maybe it was some kinda, like a joke. I mean, the other movies, they were okay."

"Maybe, fuck. It was a hundred, same as the rest. That cocksucker. Shirley Temple I want I go to the movie library."

Skip leaned in front of a suitcase. Suddenly he let out a roar of consternation and outrage. Marvell shivered. Then he remembered that the letter from Skip's father was safely in Quentin's keeping.

"What is it?"

"A motherfuckin'— Come here, Mar. Take a fuckin' look at that."

Marvell crossed the room, straightening the collar of his shirt. Skip motioned limply at the suitcase. Among a knot of tightly packed clothes was a spilt bottle of yellow nail varnish.

"At least it's colorless," said Marvell.

"How many, how many times? I fuckin' *told* her."

Marvell clicked his tongue. "Yeah, well don't tangle with her right now about it. I know Rox and I know when she's getting impatient."

Skip turned. "Yeah? Any ideas for next?"

"Some." Marvell drove his hands through his hair. "Some. How's the drug doing?"

"Kinda scary. I like it."

"C'mon. Let's go."

At the far end of the room, between the bed and the wardrobe, was a pile of blankets, sheets, and clothes. Inside it was a motionless lump. That was Whitehead.

57: OLD Dreads

During the Americans' twenty-minute absence from the sitting room Celia joined in her husband's wholly successful attempt to restore calm to the room, to moderate Roxeanne's rebarbativeness to the odd aside, to reduce Andy's climbing temper to a rubble of imprecation. Nor was it Villiers' superb diplomatic skills alone that softened the atmosphere. The mood of the room was one of growing introspection, of cold solipsism, and things were passing them by.

Celia herself was having a good time. In gradual, succulent stages, she was re-experiencing all the joy and security of her recent months with Quentin—the farcically beautiful Hamlet beside her—reliving each declension of the tender and exquisite deliverance his love had been. But it was also going, all this; she was falling away too—tumbling slowly from the present, the present that Quentin so notably adorned—falling away to the isolation and contingency of a life without him. Celia thought she saw something out of the corner of her eye. She swiveled to meet it but her mind kept slipping back to . . . to *I do beach him straightaway but didn't get free used up The Mandarin best to be good friends told her grapefruit*

what money could do and their bodies with bastards pricks
shits eat a lot be alone and you're Celia.

She turned to the man next to her on the sofa and he
could have been anyone; he had lost the lineaments of
Quentin Villiers. Even when he turned to her, meeting her
troubled eyes with a smile that completely defined her thoughts
and fears, she was unable to suppress a shiver.

Celia excused herself and climbed the stairs to her room,
confused but unterrified. She had found the old strengths
along with the old dreads. She closed the door behind her,
reassured that all was quiet now above. The solidity of the
familiar objects—her makeup, her shoes, his books, his hair-
dryer—steadied her further. The present was there all right,
then, even if it was leaving her for a short time. What were
those phrases she had heard? They weren't from her mind.

Celia shrugged, and smiled at the unmade bed, leaning
over to kiss the aromatic pillow where her husband's face
had recently lain. Then she noticed a slip of paper pinned to
the headboard. Thinking that it was one of Quentin's apho-
risms or epigrammatic love poems, she knelt on the bed to
examine it. There was a crudely drawn arrow directing her
under the blankets, and a caption reading: *Johnny's left it all*
down there. Intending to make the bed anyway, Celia pulled
off the quilt and exposed the bottom sheet. A wild noise
gushed from her hanging mouth.

Keith awoke from a shallow, hurtful sleep. Sensing the shag
of the blankets and the heat of the close darkness, he thought
at first that he was in his room. He was, he noticed, in
tears, and his nose was running freely, but then again he
quite often woke up like that. As he snuggled closer to himself, wondering how much night there was to go, a sick wave
of memory dragged over him.

Keith sat up, throwing off the sticking clothes. The light
jogged his eyes—he was naked suddenly. A shaft of hollow-
ness in his stomach burned the way to his numb backside.
He looked down and saw that he had at some point ejaculated.
This made him start crying again.

He hobbled and rocked round the room assembling his
clothes. His puffed skin, at once babyish and corpse-like,
dappled unhealthily in the swinging light. From time to time
he fell over, or gasped in breathless grief. His madras shirt

was torn; the staples on his trouser seat had been wrenched apart and there was an irreparable split down the inside thigh. He got into their remains and grafted on his boiling boots. He thought what to do.

Keith's first, and only, instinct was to *hide*. "Hide," he said. He felt no self-pity about what had happened, none at all. He felt shame merely. What he wanted now was not to be seen. He would forgive them anything but their talk and their eyes.

He knew where to go. There could be nowhere else now. Keith opened the door and stood tensed in his ragged clothes. With alarming speed he darted down into the shadowy stairs.

58: everyThing WILL Be mad

Andy had been wondering on and off how much of a storm to kick up when Marvell and Skip finally reappeared, but as their absence continued the possibility of a fertile, visionary brawl was getting more and more abstract. In a curiously gentle manner of which he was only half aware, his body seemed to be melting, rendering down to a weaker and less robust version of himself. He kept staring gravely at Diana and Lucy as they sat conversing on the divan. He thought how pleasantly asexual they were in appearance, how talkative and inconsequential. What he wanted to do, really, was to go over and lie down in between them both. He wouldn't disturb them. For once in his life he just wanted not to be minded.

The door welled open. Skip and Marvell came into the room.

Andy made as if to stand up. "Okay— What have you done with him—you fuckers?"

Skip eased himself into the dining alcove while Marvell sauntered across and sat on the arm of Roxeanne's chair.

"Hey, you fuckin' fags . . ." Andy's mind jolted. All along the room had been silent, expectant—but no one was hearing him. With an appalling effort Andy sat up straight. "Marvell," dragged his voice, "you fuckin' little . . ."

"Hey," said Marvell lightly. "What's with Andy?"

"Andy," called Quentin from the end of the world, "what's happening to you?"

"I . . ."

Andy fell from his seat. He was treading air in the middle of the room. He saw the french windows and moved numbly toward them. Hands jutted out to assist or prevent him, but he fought them away and burst through into the colorful night.

His mind was flashing with tremendous activity—not thought, not thought: the phrases in his brain had been there long before he had; they were ready made. For the last time he tried to shout but his mind kept slipping back, slipping back to . . . to *come after me and don't go mad you're born just in time her distant eyes a long-ago Andy with no far-flung canceled sex but to hear the choppy water of the city's sleep with sick junkies on the lookout for warmth in a dark mattress land of crying grass and* Andy.

Some minutes later Andy was picking himself off the lawn. Cold tears had evaporated from his cheeks. He had been back. And to what? To nothing and a tickling heart.

"Bastards," he said. "Deaf, dumb, blind fucking bastards." He turned and began to stride back toward the house.

"*Andy* . . ."

Andy spun toward the garage. It was an impossible sound, like an animal or a wounded baby.

"Andy."

It was inches away. Andy looked down suddenly—and saw him through the tiny window slot of his room, his face lit by a crack of wan upstairs light.

"Keith?"

"Andy. I've done it. I'm dying."

Celia stood outside the sitting-room door. She was trembling with almost theatrical violence. "Quentin!" she shouted. "Quentin!"

The door opened. "Darling . . . ?"

She seemed to collapse in his arms but then jarringly drew back. He reached out to her. "Darling, darling. Ah now, ah now."

She backed away. "Come here," she said, leading him up the stairs. "There's something you must see. There's something you must know. Something everyone must know. Now."

"Darling, what is this? My dearest, you're . . ."

She halted on the landing and held up her hands to silence

DEAD BABIES : 176

him. "Listen. There's— Someone's . . . There's *excrement* in our bed. In our *bed*."

"How unutterably squalid."

Celia shuddered and he moved closer. "Don't. Just listen. It is not human excrement. There are . . . it's got other things in it—the smell is quite foul—I don't know what they are. It's sort of *alive*."

He followed her into their room. Celia walked to the bed, turned toward him and lifted the top sheet. He gagged softly through his raised palm. "Like essense of human being," he said. They gathered the sheet by its corners, folding it double, double again, and double again.

"You see, darling, don't you," said Celia, "that it's all changed now. That we must do something. If we don't then nothing will mean anything any more. Everything will be mad if we don't. If we go downstairs now and pretend this hasn't happened—what'll we be then?"

"You're right, of course, darling."

"We'll just have to go down there and find out what's going on."

"Yes."

They embraced quickly. He picked up the folded sheet. They were about to move toward the door when sounds of clamor came from below. Then Andy's voice rattled cheerfully up the stairs: "*Hey, Quent!* Better get along, Mac. Little Keith's dying on us here!"

Dropping the sheet into the laundry basket he hurried from the room. Celia watched him go with a hard face. She knew that she had lost then.

59: SOMETHING TO DO

It was by no means the paradox it may at first appear that the news of Whitehead's forthcoming death saw an infusion of coltish high spirits into Appleseed Rectory. It signaled, for one thing, the end of what Dr. Marvell Buzhardt was later to call "the slipway factor," which invariably obtained when the retrodrug took hold, and the Appleseeders' vertiginous slide into their own insecurities was wonderfully lightened by the more graphic and spectacular sufferings of the dying boy, who now sat on the baronial sitting-room club armchair, with a full male audience gathered round his swilling dressing gown. And was Keith himself going to throw a dampener on their good cheer? Not a bit of it. Whitehead had never felt better in his life.

"Okay," said Andy, rubbing his hands together. "Now the way I see it is: we got to keep the little bastard from having a fit or blacking out or whatever. Check?"

"Obviously we can't involve the authorities," murmured Villiers.

"We could, we could make him throw up a lot," said Skip.

"Yeah," said Marvell. "Dump him in the fuckin' bath. Boiling water. Liter of gin. Make him drink fuckin' all of it."

"I've done that myself," said Giles. "It makes you feel *awful*."

"I'm not pregnant you know," said Keith huffily, folding his arms. "I mean, not one of you has even asked me what I took yet."

"Oh yeah," said Andy with a snort of laughter. "That's a point. Okay, Keith—wotcher take?"

"The eighty downers you gave me yesterday morning."

"Gave . . . downer—? But they didn't work."

"Oh yes they did. I tricked you."

Andy sat back. "Fuck me," he said.

"What were they, Andy?" asked Marvell in a forensic tone, reaching for a ballpoint and pad. Stumblingly Andy told him. Marvell listened, nodded, and said to Keith, "Boy, you're very nearly dead. In twenty minutes or so you're gonna want to go to sleep; if you do, you're fucked. We better get that stuff out of you. If we don't you're gonna be on your feet. All night. Rox, bring me the brandy— I'd better monkey with it. Cos we're gonna be too."

" 'It is imperative,' " Lucy read out, " 'that you notify me of your decision within the next twenty-four hours. Thank you. Yours sincerely, Keith (Whitehead).' "

"See what I mean?" said Celia.

"Mm. Pretty sexy stuff. Can really turn a phrase. Celia, it hardly compares with 'Johnny's' letter to Diana." She held up the second piece of paper. "What's a 'perineum,' by the way?"

"The bit between your cunt and your bum," said Diana.

"Ah."

"Listen," said Celia. "Keith's been to an asylum; we also know he's been very ill—something to do with his stomach, so he could have"—she gestured sideways at the laundry basket—"and now this. He's obviously in a desperate—"

"Come on, Celia," Lucy said jovially, "don't be so silly! If Keith was *Johnny* he wouldn't . . . Keith just wouldn't do things like that. Honestly! Poor little bugger— he was in my room half of last night wondering how to give me a good-night kiss. He may be a bit looney—I mean, wouldn't you be?—but he wouldn't— *you* know."

Lucy appealed to Diana. The three of them were sitting in Celia's room, Lucy and Celia on the stripped bed, while Diana draped the adjacent sofa. All three were drinking liberally from the double-liter of tequila which Lucy had recently fetched from Giles's (by now untended) alcoholic archives. As with the men, the new crisis seemed to have presented them with at least a handful of transient certainties, a focus for their loosening minds, something to do.

Celia said, "Diana thinks it's Skip, I know. I thought it was Marvell for a bit, but I can't see what possible—"

"But, darling, it's got to be," said Lucy. "It's too frightening if it isn't." She sipped her tequila, spluttering slightly as she remembered another thing to add. "Mm—and someone called Johnny did something nasty to Giles this afternoon. He wouldn't tell me what but he was very jumpy and everything. He just came up and asked me which of the Yanks was called Johnny. He was quite flabbergasted that one of them wasn't."

"But don't you think," said Celia, "that Keith— I mean what those boys did to him. And Roxeanne and everything."

"Celia! You said yourself that you found it while Keith was upstairs."

"Oh, I don't *know*. I just want it to be over." Celia's eyes clouded and she reached for a paper tissue. "Can't it just be over?"

"If it was Keith it would be." Lucy moved to the window, drawn by the sounds from below. "Keith's out of action now. No. It's worse than Keith." She swiveled, hooking her elbows backward on the sill. As she returned Celia's gaze the two girls became aware that Diana had withdrawn from the conversation, had indeed withdrawn her presence from the room.

"Diana?" they both asked.

Diana tried to say something but the words were submerged. She sat up—no, she was slipping back, slipping back to . . . to *cry again and please the black road as intensely sad fireflies winking to a thickening presence of dew and sleeping bags in the starched chill of night fatigue every day lassitude and disgust from the pink retreat it's brief and pleasureless being alone without knowing why letters a day in hanging-garden avenues the first of many summers the time it is hating everything time wondering* Diana.

She exhaled heavily and her jaw went square. She said, "I think it's Andy."

LX: ANDY

Andy, on being asked his age, can reply with veracity and more or less without self-consciousness that he's fucked if *he* knows. "Around twenty, I guess," it suits him to say, gesturing with a slack-wristed hand, "—give or take a year."

He is twenty-four. Today is his birthday. As he sprawled in the adjacent meadow, as he counted the extinguishing stars and nuzzled close to the crying grass: so, twenty-four years earlier, a swarthy girl drew the wet sheet from her face and asked, "Ten little tiny fingers? Ten little tiny toes?"

"He's cool, I think," the baleful hippie said, running a sleeve over his beard. "I think he's cool."

He was cool. His mother moved on two weeks later and for the first years of his life Andy crawled the mattress land of the dark, high-ceilinged, communal flat in Earl's Court, hunter of the spare breast, on the lookout for warmth, invader of unminded sleeping bags, growing up on cereals and old fruit. He was the foster child of a hundred postnatal waifs, the cossett of a dozen itinerant rhythm guitarists, the darling of scores of provincial pushers, the minion of a thousand sick junkies.

They called him Andy, on account of the unnatural size of his hands. He called himself Adorno, after the German Marxist philosopher whose death had brought so much despondence to the commune in the summer of 1972, when Andy was just a boy. *Andy Adorno*—it was the most exquisite name he had ever heard.

.   .   .

In the course of a routine raid by the local Hygiene and Sanitation Board operatives, the young Adorno's existence became known to the authorities. Mr. Derek Midwinter, the inspector under whose care Andy fell, is on record as describing his dealings with the boy as "a complete bloody nightmare." Originally proposing to remove Andy from the flat, register him with the censors, enroll him at a Child Care Unit and get his education underway, Midwinter ended up paying Andy £5.50 a week to leave him alone. (Adorno continued to hold sway over many representatives of authority with a trick-or-treat system he had devised; it featured complicated sexual blackmail and brute force.) When he was good and ready— in his own fucking sweet time—Andy dawdled up to Holland Park Comprehensive and asked to speak to its principal. After a five-minute interview Andy was talking to girls in the playground while a pallid headmistress backdated his entrance forms. It was understood that he would study nothing but the Modern American Novel, and also that this specialization would not necessarily be reflected in his examination results. That afternoon Andy was voted form captain.

Earl's Court was his country.

A twenty-four-hour land. At nine, huge panting coaches were voiding four thousand aliens a day into its dusty squares. Drainpipe-latticed houses like foreign legion garrisons, their porches loud with penniless Greeks and tubercular Turks. Men in vests gazed from behind stagnant windows. By night half a million youths spilled from the electric pubs; dirty girls paraded and dirty boys cruised along the jagged strip; the darkness was hot with curry smells from the neon delicatessens. Tramps dozed behind nude-mag vendors' stalls. Dying Pakistanis hawked into dimly lit shop windows. At five in the morning, a windy threadbare silence would lapse on the spent districts. Food boxes and cigarette packets spun end over end among the fruit skins and beer cans. Hairnets of doped flies mantled the puddles and dogshit. From between railings old cats stared. Ramshackle buildings of rubbish lolled against the dark shopfronts, like collapsed dreams of the city's sleep. Through the air came the whisper of the quickening town, plaintive music over choppy water.

By day and during the early evenings Andy supervised his

drugs consortia, looked after his fringe business concerns, bought records, played music, saw films, kicked dogs, watched TV, read, drank, ate, fucked. He was everywhere, a familiar and revered figure in the crowded landscape.

Late at night, just before the stillness came, he scaled condemned fire escapes and explored the roofs and skylights, lay on the sooty grass behind the Underground station, sat on swings and sang, climbed trees in the dark squares, screamed until the dawn went misty with tears, raced like an animal through the dying streets.

A radically telescoped *résumé* of Andy's sex life.

An early developer, he started not sleeping with girls at the age of seventeen. Intense, confusing, sudden, strange—it was a revelation to him. "She was a casual girl, too," Andy broods. Looking in at Life on Mars for a nightcap one autumn evening, he had selected and duly approached a girl to take home. "Round eighteen, long blond hair. Dutch or something, nice face, good fig. All over me, quivering like a blender. Had to slap her down a bit, as I recall. There you are—I can even remember her name. Irma—something like that. Wilma. No. Norma. No. Hang about . . ." He escorted her to his door and preceded her up the cabbage-damp stairs. He led the way into his room, pitched himself onto the double mattress, and advised her to take off her clothes and join him. "Well. We're sort of talking and stuff. I get the scotch out and so on. She's nude, I'm nude, she's practically sitting on my face, and—you know—we're starting to get friendly. And then, well, Christ, it just sort of . . . happened. I didn't fuck her."

Hard-on trouble, Andy? "Nah. Onna contrary. The prong I had on me—I could of mugged an eight-foot boogie with it. I tell you, when I went to the bathroom to lose the scotch, I hadda practically stand on my head if I wanted to piss in the can and not up my own fuckin' nose. Nah. Wasn't anything at all to do with that. Listen, anyhow. I can tell something awful's gonna happen, but I sort of give it a go. I mean, you have to, don't you? You do. It's only polite. She's practically got both my legs in her mouth by this time anyway, and I don't want to seem like some sort of pervert or fuckin' sex maniac—lean over and say, 'Sorry, kid, I don't feel like it.'

Fuck that. So I gave it a go. Christ. It was . . . I don't know what it was. It was . . ."

It was canceled sex. It was a feeling of vast but theoretical weariness combined with acute and local foreboding, petty irritation arm in arm with cosmic disgust, vexed fussiness married to apocalyptic fear. How did she fit in? What were these—her breasts, her ankles, her hair—her *eyes*? What was her role and what were he and his body for? He felt like a bit player in some far-flung organization, the servile motor of another's body.

The girl was making a lot of noise now. The boy turned her onto her back and knelt between her spread legs. The girl closed her eyes and his broad hands smoothed and kneaded her thorax. The boy twitched. The girl glanced up to see that an expression of almost preposterous loathing had come over his face. He fell brokenly on to his side, wretching and shivering in the gray sheets. She inched away from him, crying silent tears.

Looking past her, Andy glimpsed a third body on the mattress: a young, athletic, olive-skinned figure in sawn-off jeans and white shirt, reclining on striped pillows, two beer cans resting on his stomach: a long-ago Andy. Thirteen years old, lithe and predatory, he waits smiling in the quarter light as one by one they appear and kneel for a moment at his side. A melancholy girl with distant eyes, an older woman with deep, maternal breasts, someone his age with impossibly tiny shoulders, witch-like hippies, black-leather blondes, nervy urchins, schoolgirls, widows, shop assistants, divorcees, traffic wardens, bus conductoresses, policewomen, girls from Tehran, Dorking, Massachusetts, Slough, Montego Bay, the Earl's Court Road, spicks, frogs, huns, sprouts, boogies, the one with damp hair that smelled of nutmeg, the one that kept her shirt on although her tits were casual, the one from downstairs, the one that bit his rig, the one from upstairs, the very pregnant one, the not so pregnant one, the twelve-year-old, the fifty-seven-year-old, the one that liked him beating her up, the one that hated him beating her up, the tall Pakky that had no snatch hairs, the short Geordie that had no hair, the one that gave him four kinds of venereal disease, the one he'd given four (different) kinds of venereal disease, the one with the ear-to-ear gobbler's mouth, the blind one, the one that screamed the house down, the bald one, the one with

the six-foot legs, the fucking fat one, the one with breasts like
airships, the one with the turn-off dog-end nips, the one that
wouldn't go down on him, the one with the flash bum, the
melancholy girl with distant eyes . . . : they're all forgotten
now, as their memory turns on the changing boy.

"Course, it comes and goes, this gimmick. I've only ever had
the fuckin' thing about twenty times, really. Maybe thirty
times. The way you handle it is— the minute it starts, just
pretend it's a drug. Oh, look— I'm sweating, I'm weak as a
chick, my heart's like a fuckin' tom-tom, and I feel like Frank's
monster. Then it passes, is all. If you want, ten minutes later
you can even fuck.

"You know, sometimes I think I was born just in time. I
mean, I'm fuckin' glad I'm not younger than I am, born later.
Some of the kids I knew at the flat . . . kids around fourteen
or fifteen. Yeah, they get hard-on troubles same as the next
guy, and they get things we get like false memory and street
sadness. Night fatigue, things like that. Course. But they get
this canceled sex thing the whole time. They get the shudders
inna cot when they try and fuck. I tell you, they'll all be
cock-choppers by the time they're eighteen. I'm just glad I got
out before it could all catch up on me. Born in the middle, just
right—when you don't go mad but still get lots of fucks. I
suppose that's basically why I'll always vote Conservative. I
don't know, mind, how the next lot of guys are going to make
out, the lot that come after me. I'm just glad I'm not one of
them, is all. Check?"

61: INTO THE MIDDLE AIR

He took eight swallows of Hine, wiped his mouth and offered
the flagon to little Keith. "How you feeling, kid?" Andy asked.

Even as Marvell protested that an intake of brandy was
hardly Keith's top priority, the soapy dwarf shook his head,
or at any rate permitted his eyes to roll slightly. He was
finding all movement more complicated than usual—i.e., very
complicated indeed, unbelievably difficult, quite extraordinarily
recondite—but he was still entirely compos mentis. Whitehead
was in fact congratulating himself once again for electing

such a civilized and agreeable way to die. He shut his eyes softly—and his body disappeared! Never in his life had he felt *so light,* free, however illusorily, from that heaving, viscous, fudgy torso, with its cumbrousness, its demands, its noises, and its smells. He completed a tactile reconnaissance of his body. Nothing. He had finally escaped into the middle air.

"On your fuckin' feet, Keith," said Marvell. "Andy. Get him on his fuckin' feet."

Andy put the brandy bottle down sharply on the coffee table. "*You* get him on his fuckin' feet."

Quentin swept across the room. "No time for fun and games now, Andy," he said, dipping his fingers into White-head's yielding flesh.

"Okay," said Marvell. "Rox— Go inna kitchen. Get some mustard, pepper, bad butter, bad lard, bad milk—anything bad—aim it all in the fuckin' blender and bring it right back here."

"Howbout them boiled eggs Celia had?" Skip slowly suggested.

"Great. That oughta do it. Like eating dead babies. right? I have some emetics and laxatives and shit, but they'd make the Venus de Milo set up camp in the john, and we want to take it easy with this kid, you know?" Marvell leaned forward and slapped little Keith quite hard across the face. "Mm-hm. Oughta get him outside. Don't want him throwing up onna carpet."

Requiring a good deal of assistance, Whitehead was steered through the french windows. "Can I sit down? Please. Please let me sit down."

"Nope," said Marvell. "Lean on the wall right there."

"*I* know," said Andy suddenly. He stepped forward, clasped Keith's quadrangular nose with his left hand, and jammed a long right forefinger into his exposed throat.

A wretching quack sprang from Keith's mouth—as, with no less alacrity, did Andy's finger.

"AWW! Little fucker *bit* me!" shrieked Andy as he leaped at the reeling Whitehead.

It was only the remarkable speed of Quentin's intervention and Skip's timely aid that saved little Keith from a more summary loss of consciousness than he was destined soon to enjoy. He was still coughing vilely when Roxeanne reappeared, bearing the full beaker above the heads of the crowd.

Diana's contention, that Johnny was in fact the man whose bed she had shared for the past six months, was put over by her with lucidity and unwonted calm. She talked of Andy's creed of violence: however boastful and erratic he tended to be on the subject, his devotion to that activity was at least partially real. She adduced his murderous daydreams about the Tuckles: even as she spoke, there stood on the garage workbench four crude Molotov cocktails which Andy was proposing to drop down their chimney. She testified to his aberrant and depressive behavior in recent weeks: Andy had admitted to two attacks of false memory that same afternoon. Finally, she disclosed that Keith's pornography collection had been savaged at some point during the day, presumably by Johnny: that made Andy the only resident to have been spared his attentions. And so on.

But was anybody really listening now? The noises from the garden had become loose and intermittent, like the sound of a megaphone down a windy street, and Diana's words seemed to get nowhere, seemed to fuse in the light of the colorless room. Celia and Lucy had glazed over and as soon as Diana fell silent she felt herself slip back into the same slow, watery retrospection. One by one the girls were wandering through the door.

"Slam him against the wall," said Marvell, accepting the frothy jug from Roxeanne. "Skip— Hold him hard. He's gonna drink alla this and he's gonna fuckin' hate it. Hold his nose, Rox, and keep his mouth open."

As soon as the noisome fluid touched his lips Whitehead's whole body seemed to fizz with revulsion. Marvell's hirsute thumb had been planted on Keith's deep Adam's apple, which he tweaked and depressed in order to regulate the flow. When the last third of the beaker emptied over his shoulders, chest, neck, nose, and drowned mouth, both little Keith's legs seemed to bend up into the air. When Quentin and Skip released him, he remained soggily upright against the wall.

Nothing happened.

Crouching on the grass a few yards away, Andy looked up

from nursing his bitten forefinger. "See, I told you," he said. "*I* know." Unhindered, Andy swooped up in front of Keith, half knelt sideways on, circled his arm like a baseball pitcher, and swung his fist full force into Keith's solar plexus. It seemed to dive wrist-high into his stomach before bouncing back.

If Whitehead had been in a cartoon (which is probably where he belonged), he would simply have imploded to a third of his mass and drifted up into the air. As it was, he collapsed instantaneously, his legs snatched from beneath him as though they had been lassoed by a cantering cowboy.

". . . My *fuck*in' *hand!*" shouted Andy. "You little—!"

"There, there, Andrew," said Quentin, effortlessly containing his struggling friend. "There there."

Twenty minutes later and the uncooperative Whitehead had failed to respond, variously, to swallowing a half bushel of grass, having his kidneys ground and punched, getting his testicles mightily squeezed, and being swung circularly in midair, this way and that, by his arms, his legs and his hair.

Andy stood over Keith's punctured body. "Fuck him," he suggested. "That's what I say."

"Andy, don't be *absurd*," said Quentin. "Unless we can get him through this ourselves we'll—"

"We'll have to call the hospital. Or the police," said Celia, who had appeared from between the french windows. Behind her, in the more tranquil light, stood Lucy and Diana. "Let's just get him out of here, can't we?"

Andy stepped forward and booted Keith negligently in the ribs. The body accepted the blow as might a sack of half-dressed cement. "See? Poor little bastard. He's . . . he's all fucked up."

"Look, er . . ." Marvell knelt beside Keith on the paving stones. "Look, I can't have any law here." He felt Keith's pulse. "Best thing is, I drill him fulla emetics and aperients and stuff and we just leave him here for a time. Or"—he raised his voice—"or on the grass, huh, Cele? Don't want him exploding right here onna patio, yeah, am I wrong?"

Celia swirled back into the room.

"Chicks!" said Marvell indulgently, taking Keith's wrists in his hands. "Try to be helpful and they— hey, Skip, haul his legs, willya? I know Rox'd blow her stack, any guy heaving on her— yeah, thassit, dump him onna lawn. Now here, my friend, we gotta problem. Lie him on his back, he'll gag on his own vomit. Lie him on his chest, he won't shit right. I don't know about you, kid, but I could use a Hine."

After a few minutes Keith was firmly roped to the still-blossoming apple tree; two grimed hypodermics hung from his bloated arms.

62: GHOSTLY PERIODS

Perspective was the next to go. As soon as they were back inside, all the corners in Appleseed Rectory came adrift, swam out of position, and folded back in new and unfamiliar conjunctions. Through its open doorway the kitchen was no more than a displaced rhomboid of light. The stairs concertinaed away in unaligned succession. The hall leaned back and forth like a seaborne doll's house. Everywhere they looked mad angles veered up at their eyes.

Giles lay shivering on his bed, a deep-river creature of his own sweat. His mouth was a hive, his teeth changing position like dancers. If he clenched his jaw they just wouldn't fit, wouldn't fit, crags, tors, ridges, beaks, grinding against each other like the rusty cogs of an old machine. He prayed for them to fly away, white birds escaping this sodden nest. Until then he would be locked deep in this house, this room, this mouth, this mouth, with its marshmallow teeth and its sweet-sherry gums.

He could hear the fridge juddering peacefully at him, but he knew he'd never get to it. There were so many things in the way and anyhow his mind kept slipping back, slipping back to . . . to *gauzy skin and dying pillows oh baby please I enjoyed the swell of the land in ghostly periods with blood she kissed him gorily as saddening dreams the various sunshine off dusty glass and his teeth an old mother old mother and baby* Giles.

"NO!"

Hiring every morsel of his strength, Giles cleared the bed and stormed the fridge. His hands were flapping so extravagantly that he had to refill the glass twice before any of the contents forced its way down his throat. When it did, Giles tried very hard to force it out again. No substance that toxic (he felt certain) had ever entered *his* system before. He lowered his nose to the bottle. It was gin all right—but it smelled as harsh and alien as strong medicine to a delicate child.

"Glug glug glug," he said, and added in a voice suddenly panicky with comprehension, "goo goo goo!"

Within seconds he was out of the door. Behind him the darkness drummed with a thousand mothers.

This dwarf pleasureless and very mad dream girl nothing flash life has its holiday fair enough? terror and confusion for a four-foot box in a cartoon world of sugary tea crying with shame for each . . . It broke off.

Whitehead twitched, jolting the back of his skull painfully against a protrusion in the gnarled apple tree. He was alive and he was awake—he even struggled briefly with his bonds. Assuredly Keith was in great pain, but this stemmed from the beating he had received from his housemates rather than from the barbiturates intended for his suicide, which were at present doing him nothing but good, numbing both the retro-drug and the punishment his body had recently sustained. He still felt vastly better than he would, say, on an average morning, appreciably trimmer, more wholesome, less corporeal.

What, nevertheless, was he doing here? At the best of times little Keith's head was not the most maneuverable of units and it was only with great discomfort and travail that he managed to scrape his chins over the stinging ropes about his neck to get a glimpse of the left-hand quarter of the house. All was dark and worryingly quiet. Why, then, had they done this to him? Was he there for fun, for sex, for target practice? He sensed something flapping against his upper arm, something heavy and metallic. He squinted down and saw the needle point dangling from his right "bicep"; burning his neck, he turned to see its twin dangling from his left.

Then he felt his body start to come alive. The soft machinery stirred: winches creaked, pumps groaned, tubes opened, pipes rustled. Keith arched with the effort of containing himself as once again he became a blast furnace, a forest fire of frantic glands.

63: THE ANTIDOTE

And when the distances went the house was hell at last. Each minute the atmosphere changed radically, boiling up to gas and thinning out to nothing at all. Currents of sweating air slopped through the shrunken rooms. The corridors tapered off into palls of submarine mist. Appleseed Rectory was hell now, and its inhabitants crawled round it with borrowed faces and canceled eyes. If they kicked against the womb, they folded onto the floor and were sucked down into a hot, thudding sleep.

—Skip came across Andy sprawled face down on the stairs. In Andy's palm was a large red pill, half eroded by perspiration. Skip removed it and popped it into his mouth as he crawled over Andy's body.

—Diana knelt in an upstairs closet. She searched through old clothes for yesterday's dolls.

—Giles crouched beneath the kitchen table. If he heard a noise he would scurry behind the cooker. If he heard a noise he would scurry beneath the kitchen table.

—Lucy opened her eyes. Marvell was urinating on her legs. She tried to speak and she could not speak.

—Roxeanne was a starfish on the thick sitting-room cushions. She masturbated caressingly with a chipped hukah pipe beak.

—Celia stood upright on the baronial armchair. Through her tears came snatches of forgotten nursery rhymes.

Now Quentin awoke in the empty hall. He climbed to his knees, holding his head between clenched fists. When his eyes opened to the bruised light he needed all his will to focus them on the fast-escaping outlines. He reeled to the nearest wall and pressed his forehead hard against the cold stone. Inhaling deeply, he summoned his body and his mind.

Quentin found Marvell in the washroom, alone, giggling softly into a pile of soiled underclothes.

Quentin picked Marvell up by the hair and slammed him furiously against the door.

Marvell's eyes stared.

"The antidote," said Quentin clearly. "The antidote. You've got five minutes. Do it, Marvell. Or I'll kill you."

64: HIGH TEA, OR HERE WE GO AGAIN

Enough? Have we had enough? Nothing would be easier, of course, than to give the Americans some food, some sleep even, and pack them off—that would appear to get rid of *Johnny*, and, why, they could even drop little Keith at the hospital on the way. Might be some bother there but, on the whole— yes—it would demand small ingenuity to restore peace to Appleseed Rectory. Unfortunately, though, there is no "going back" on things that in a sense were never meant, things that got started too long ago. These things *go on*. It isn't over. It hasn't begun.

Two-thirty and high tea was served at the Appleseed kitchen in a mood of buzzing, ravenous hilarity. Sipping chilled Hock and a light Mateus rosé, they negotiated vast stacks of toast and gentlemen's relish, cucumber and cress sandwiches, water biscuits spread with celery salt and avocado paste. Celia was still sad about The Mandarin (whom Quentin promised elaborately to bury the next day), but otherwise there was little to regret because there was little to remember. The only sure recollection they had was of an experience of almost vibrant fear coupled with something more numinous, the nudge of a deeper act of memory, a spiritual strain that had filled them all with an exquisite and gentle anguish. They felt like ocean divers after a fascinating and perilous expedition, or, more appropriately, like safely disembarked astronauts who, amid the populous celebrations, were quietly aware that they had known the full pain and tragic isolation of space.

Then Andy dropped his plate with a clatter and got suddenly to his feet. "Little Keith!" he said. "What happened to little Keith?"

"Oh, Christ," said Diana as the boys sped from the room, "here we go again."

In the pewter light from the garage it seemed as if the apple tree had grown a second stump, a squat and knobbed extension at its base.

Skip looked at Marvell. "Jesus. You think he's still alive?"

"Andy?"

"Don't ask me, squire," said Andy. "I'm fucked if I'm going near him while he smells like that."

Quentin buried his nose in a perfumed handkerchief.

"He twitched then," said Marvell, adding more quietly, "I think he twitched then."

"How will we ever know?" said Quentin through his handkerchief.

Andy snapped his fingers. "Got it! The *hose*. Come on, Quent, give us a hand," he said happily. "Like I always maintain—you can do anything once you put your mind to it."

The hose used at Appleseed Rectory had been bought second-hand, on Andy's suggestion, from the municipal fire department warehouses in Catford, SE5. Although of limited utility in the garden—it did not irrigate so much as void any bed on which it was trained—only a heavy-duty implement, Andy had argued, would be equal to such routine domestic tasks as local-yob suppression, Tuckle intimidation, and so on. (Andy had pooh-poohed the objection that pressurizing the tap would cost Giles £2,000, and Giles had stuck up for him.) The mouth of the hose had a diameter of four inches. Experiments had shown that it could flatten a villager from twenty-five yards.

At a little under a third of that distance from Keith, Andy now stood with his restless legs planted wide apart. His right hand was held aloft, while his left gripped the hose's heavy snout. Then Andy chopped his raised arm through the air. "Now!" he yelled.

As the first pole of water hit him in the face, Keith's ragged, wobbling figure found its contours and, as Andy played the hose up and down his body, the slumped form seemed actually to dance free of its bonds. Six minutes later Andy's right arm chopped through the air once more. "Right!" he said. "That oughta handle it."

In a loose semicircle, Andy, Quentin, Skip, and Marvell warily approached the tree.

Quentin and Marvell looked at each other in candid horror.

"Mm. On second thought maybe I should have backed off some with the hose," said Andy, himself noticing the new orange blood that had started to well from Keith's mouth, nose, and eyes.

Marvell felt for Whitehead's still-vibrating wrist. "He's still there! It's faint, but he's still there!"

"Onna other hand," said Andy, "it was probably just what he needed. A good jolt. Just the job."

"Cut him down, Skip," said Marvell.

When Skip had severed the last of the ropes, Keith fell forward like a thick plank into the mud created by the broad wash of the hose. Except for the thin leather belt he was virtually naked, his dressing gown torn away by the force of the water; the remains of his clothes stuck to his white body in thin damp strings.

"Wotcher reckon, Marv?" asked Andy.

Marvell took out his hypodermic wallet and knelt on the grass. "I'll plug some meth up his ass. Then we'd better walk him around some."

"Check. I'll just give him one more go with the hose. Now we've got the bloody thing out. Just to clean him up. Don't want all that mud on our hands."

"Mud? Oh, yeah, right."

"Is he okay?" called Lucy from the french windows.

"Keith?" said Andy. "He's laughing."

65: seems silly now

When Lucy came back into the sitting room, Giles was standing by the door, looking tense.

"They say Keith's okay."

". . . Oh. Good."

"What is it, Giles?"

"Lucy, a friend of mine wants me to ask you something."

"Which friend?"

"Just a friend."

"I see."

"A friend," said Giles.

"Yes, I'm with you. What does he want to know?"

"My friend wants to know if you could ever—if you could marry someone who didn't have any . . . if he had . . ."

"If he had what?"

"No, that's the point—if he didn't have . . . if he had . . . if he didn't have . . ."

"If he *didn't* have what, then?"

"If he didn't have . . . if he had . . ."

"*Say* it, Giles. Christ."

"Well, you see, what my cousin wants to know, actually, is could you marry someone who had . . . who didn't have . . ."

"*Jesus*. WHAT?"

"Who didn't have teeth. Who had false ones. Could you?"

"If I loved him, of course I could!"

Giles sank against the door. "Gosh. I never thought I should marry," he said to steady himself.

Giles poured out a glass of Hock and said to Roxeanne, "They say Keith is well again."

Roxeanne said that she thought he probably would be. "You can get away with most things these days."

Celia stood up and, with Diana's assistance, began to load the dishwasher. "Well," she said, "if he is he's going to have to find somewhere else to live."

"Right," said Diana. "I've got no time for suicides. It's just *too* boring. A schoolfriend of mine was in a crash once and I went to see her every day for three months. A year later the bitch stuck her head in the oven because her guy couldn't kick being queer. Did I go to the hospital once? No way. I told her why not, too."

"I agree," said Celia. "It's selfish, stupid, and utterly boring."

"Well," said Giles. "I don't know, I just feel . . . That drug and everything . . . I just feel terribly *relieved*."

And then Giles Coldstream did something he had not done for five years. He turned full face to Roxeanne and he smiled —not his habitual tragicomic-mask, thin-lipped stripe, but a bright, frank, boyish, ripple-eyed grin.

Roxeanne leaned forward sharply and frowned up at him. "Hey, man, what's with your teeth? They're all, you got *wires* and shit in there—"

Upending his glass and knocking his chair over, Giles backed away from the table, his face stunned with a look of guilty dismay.

"Here, let's . . ." said Roxeanne, bearing down on Giles,

who retreated gesturing with his hands like an entertainer quelling applause. "The fuck, *how* old are you? And your teeth are all *dead*."

Containing his tears, a frightened child, Giles bolted from the room.

"Round and round the garden," sang Quentin and Andy, two prop forwards to Keith's dangling hooker, "ran the teddy bear. One step, two steps, tickly under there. Round and round the garden ran the——"

"Hey," broke off Andy, "it's pretty knackering, this. The fuck are those Yanks? Why can't they have a go for a bit?"

Keith began to groan. It was a reedy, cat-like sound.

"At least he's alive," observed Quentin. "We're not *completely* wasting our time."

"No," said Keith, pronouncing it "Mo" through pulped lips.

"Mo who, you little wreck?" Andy asked.

"Mo," said Keith. "Mot in the well. Doan frow me in the well. Dome drowm me."

"Don't throw you in the well? Quentin, he talks as if we throw him inna well every night. We've a bloody good mind to, Keith. There's gratitude for you."

" 'Don't drown me,' " repeated Quentin. "That reminds me— Keith never got the antidote, did he?"

Keith started crying, crying in painfully snatched falsetto, crying like a baby.

Quentin and Andy turned to each other with bulging eyes.

Giles was crying too. He was doing so at his desk while he assembled his writing paper and pencils. Fat tears smudged the sheet as he wrote:

> *Dear All. God knows I have had a hard enough life since my accident. It has not been easy but I have tried to muck along as best I could. But now, with these remarks of Rocks-Ann's, I really do not know what I shall*

He sniffed wetly. He stood up. There was something else in his gait when he walked toward the drinks cupboard.

·　　·　　·

"Round and round the . . . Jesus. My arm's fuckin' dropping off. Look—Quent—there they are. Hey! The fuck over here, you lazy shits!"

Skip and Marvell merged into the garage light, buckling their belts. They ambled toward the rocking trio.

"What kinda shape's he in?"

Andy unhitched Keith's arm from his shoulder and swung the naked body forcefully at Marvell and Skip. "Where you been? Crapping or screwing or what?"

"What difference does it make?" asked Marvell urbanely.

"Fuck-all to you guys, that's for sure," said Andy, pacing back toward the house with Quentin at his side.

They settled on the steps outside the french windows. Fifteen yards away Skip, Marvell, and Keith marched round in the halflight like jagged clockwork figures in a silent film. Andy produced his hash kit and within half a minute had rolled two one-paper joints. "Hey, man," he said reflectively, handing one to Quentin and lighting them both. "That guy Keats. How old was he when he checked out?" "He was twenty-six," said Quentin. ("Walk *right*, walk *right!*" they heard Skip holler at the crippled Keith.) "Oh, really?" said Andy rather snootily. "I mean, that's not bad. What was all the . . . gimmick?" "I expect people thought he had yet to realize his full potential." Unimpressed, Andy protruded his lower lip and nodded a few times. "Fuck potential," he said.

"Quentin?" asked a new voice.

Quentin turned to the french windows, whence Giles falteringly emerged. "My good friend Giles," he said.

"How's Keith? Is he well again now?"

"He's as well as can be expected. Rather better, as it happens."

"Oh. I see. So you won't be taking him to the hospital."

"We do hope we may be spared that embarrassment, yes."

"Oh, actually. I see." Giles turned to go.

"Why do you ask, Giles?"

"Only that . . . that I've done it too. But I don't want to be a nuisance. Or a bore. I'll simply go back upstairs."

"You've done what too."

"Sort of killed myself, actually. I had, I've just drunk two liters of brandy—in one, well, no, actually in two, cos—"

"Giles, are you serious?"

"Mm. The book says I ought to die in twenty-five minutes, apparently. Seems silly now. But if you're not . . . I mean, I don't . . ."

Quentin leapt to his feet.

"Welcome to the gang, kid," said Andy, flicking his cigarette high into the air.

66: no more games

Within twenty seconds Quentin was on the telephone to Hampstead Central Hospital, where a nurse of Irish provenance assured him that the patient, as described, had no chance whatever of reaching them alive. The only suitably equipped unit in mortal range, she said, was the Psychiatric Casualty Wing of the Blishner Institute, Potter's Bar. She would now ring there herself and ask them to ready a stomach pump in B4, to which ward the patient should be rushed as soon as he arrived. Throughout the conversation Giles sat smiling shamefacedly on the sofa. Lucy was beside him, stroking his hair and saying as little as she could.

Quentin slapped down the telephone.

"Right. Skip—which is faster—the Chevrolet or the Jaguar?"

"The Chev," said Skip. "I tune it. It, it'll hit—"

"Get in it and rev. Lucy, Roxeanne, get Giles in there. Andy, come on. Let's get Keith in there too. No more games."

In noisy formation, the Appleseeders crowded into the drive.

"Dump little Keith in back," said Marvell. "He still stinksa rat."

"It's the mercy-dash express!" said Andy, picking Keith up by his hair and the back of his belt and lobbing him into the trunk.

"Get up front, honey," Roxeanne told Lucy. "Tell Skip the way. I'll take care of Giles."

Andy joined Roxeanne and Giles in the back seat while Lucy ran round to join Skip in the front. The Chevrolet was already in gear when Quentin raced forward from the remaining group on the porch. He put his head through the driver's window and handed Skip an envelope. "Here are the details. I know the head man there and it might speed things up. Open it when you get there." Skip put the letter into his flying jacket and zipped it up. Quentin smacked the car roof twice.

"Now gun it."

With a wide squirt of gravel the Chevrolet ground off into the night.

"Beat me, beat me," said Andy (for Skip had switched on the tape). "Beat me, beat me—aw, chop my head off."

As the car straightened onto the road Giles slumped from his seat to the floor. Andy was about to draw this to Roxeanne's attention when he noticed that her hand was busy on his lap. His eyes swelled.

"You fork off here?" said Skip.

"Fuck off yourself," said Andy.

"Yes. *Here*," said Lucy.

Skip pulled them onto the dual highway at 75 mph. The heavy car rode high up the verge before stabilizing again. Andy looked down at Roxeanne's head, which bobbed rhythmically over his groin.

"Christ," he said elatedly. "We're all dying here. We're *all* dying!"

67: SPRING CLEAN

Quentin allowed Celia to embrace him momentarily before he shooed her back into the house. Diana and Marvell stood nervously in the hall.

"Now," he began. "Incompetent as we know the authorities to be I don't imagine they'll let two contiguous suicide attempts go completely unremarked. So shall we make a start? Marvell, may I make you responsible for the drugs? Round them up and come to me. Don't worry about the hash and whatnot—just the hard stuff. Celia, Diana: could you, as it were, spring clean? Banish, at any rate, the grosser evidences of debauchery. I'll get the lion's share of the bottles into the garage and recky the garden. If we could reconvene in the drawing room in, say, fifteen minutes . . . ?"

.   .   .

By then it was three-thirty. From the one remaining vessel in the room Quentin poured four small glasses of Benedictine. "Splendid," he said. "Now we wait."

Marvell glanced as his watch. "Oughta be there by now."

For a moment they all sat back and let the tiredness pound through them. Then Diana stood up. "I'm going to bed," she announced.

Quentin got to his feet. He kissed Diana deftly on the lips. "Good night, Diana. Thank you for your help." He conferred silently with Marvell and Celia. "I think, however, that we'll stay up and see this through."

"Okay." Diana hesitated as she turned to leave. "Wait . . . isn't there something else? Isn't there—haven't we forgotten something?"

Quentin spread his arms. "I fail to see what."

The effort of recall flickered once more in Diana's eyes.

"The weekend—it's over then?"

"I don't know," said Quentin, "what else it could be."

68: WHITE ROOM

The Chevrolet came to a grilled halt broadside an ambulance in the Blishner Institute Psychiatric Casualty forecourts. As the five spilled from the car a tall young intern with long black hair noosed in a headband promptly wheeled a stretcher from between the sliding doors. "This him?" he asked, levering Giles onto the white sheeting. "Yeah." They had started back to the building when Andy abruptly snapped his fingers. "Fuck," he remarked to Lucy. "We forgot little Keith again."

He ran back to the car, exhumed Keith from its trunk, and trotted back with the body slung over his shoulder.

"What's with this one?" asked the intern, staring at Keith's blood-bubbled face.

"Uh . . ." said Andy. "Uh, he just took this great load of aspirins."

"Like hell he did," said the intern. "You boys had better stick around."

He led them between the automatic doors, through the dim vestibule, along a corridor and into a small white room.

"Stay here," he told them.

Andy watched him go. "That guy wants a fight," he said, letting Keith's body drop from his shoulder to the floor.

"I'm not staying here," said Skip. "That guy means business and I'm loaded."

"Relax," said Andy. "I tellya, he's—"

"Hey!" said Roxeanne, opening a cupboard door to reveal four shelves of bottles and vials. "Get this!"

"Christ," said Andy. "Look. Mandies! Andrenalin! Amyl-nitrate!" He spun around to Skip. "Get inna car, turn it round. We'll be right out." He began loading his pockets, Roxeanne hers. Skip kicked Keith out of the way and hopped into the corridor.

And there was Keith, looking as if he had been dead for a week. And there was Giles, drowning, dying and dying in the white room. Lucy crept nearer the stretcher. She held his limp hand in both of hers. Her face burned with incredulous disgust. *"Andy,"* she whispered.

Andy turned, wide-eyed, a jar of pills held up in either hand. "Yeah?"

"Andy. What are you *doing*?" Lucy's voice trembled. "Get out of here and leave us alone. Get out."

His hands dropped to his sides. "Ah, what the hell, Lucy? I mean, really—what the hell any more?"

69: WRONG YESTERDAYS

In the smaller of the Appleseed Rectory sitting rooms, Quentin reclined on a pink chaise-longue with Diderot's *Le neveu de Rameau* dandled on his thighs. But he wasn't reading. His forefingers placed in either nasal cleft, Quentin's head was tilted backward in a meditative posture.

In the larger of the Appleseed Rectory sitting rooms, unaware of Quentin's presence behind the half-closed partition doors, Celia and Marvell were together on the sofa.

"Yeah, that," Marvell was saying, "that'd be the time I was over here before. When I stayed at a, at Quentin's people's home?"

"Oh. So you visited Tallbury."

"Nah, not 'Tallbury.' What was it . . . fuckin' great country place. It was . . ."

"Tallbury," said Celia. "So you met them before they got killed?"

"They did? *All* of them?"

"In an aeroplane crash," said Celia neutrally.

"What, some sorta charter flight?"

"Probably. They are more dangerous. The brother survived."

"The brother? Oh, right—the 'brother,' yeah. Ah, that's too bad. I liked them really a lot. Quentin never said."

Next door, the book slid from Quentin's thighs. He made no attempt to retrieve it.

"You liked them?" said Celia. "They and Quentin never got on."

"Nah, well—but they liked *him*, huh, Cele?"

"He only put up with them because of the trust money."

"Yeah," said Marvell. "That *was* the gimmick."

"Hardly a gimmick. The money is rightfully his."

"Guess you could put it that way."

Next door, Quentin's eyes closed. A bleached light played on the corners of his eyes.

"When was this?" asked Celia.

"Uh, early last year."

"Last *year*? But Quentin's parents died four years ago."

"Parents? Parents? No, no, Celia. This was a 'people's home'? It was a gimmick Quent had an interest in then. You know, one of the de-luxe old-fag joints? Quent financed it. Get the queers along, screw their cash, and maybe they leave you something when they pop off?"

"Quentin's 'people'?"

"Yeah. Inna home. He never had any parents far as I knew. It was a good gimmick. It was a very good gimmick. We were, I was pulling down four hundred, maybe five hundred—"

"Quentin?"

Quentin's eyes opened. He sighed, and a great weight seemed to slide upward from his body. Then it hit him, like newly fallen snow, all the blank wrong yesterdays.

"Quentin?" Celia called. "Quentin."

"Yes?" said Johnny.

part three
SUNDAY

LXX: JOHNNY

did all kinds of jobs—Mondays he was bucket boy at Greek Charlie's downriver abortion factory, sold OK piss samples Tuesdays for the semilegal immigrants to smuggle into the Health Board Centre, evicted widows and cripples from South London tenements Wednesdays, Thursdays it was petnapping for the paravivisectionists, removed antisyndicate fingernails Fridays, the weekends his own—so then it was drugs, four acid plants run by him, as many trips to Tangier a month, dealt direct with Chinese heroin agents, cornered the coke concessions in three continents—into the sex market full time, so incredibly good looking that when he hit the street courting couples snarled with lust and reached out to steady each other, lorries and girl-driven minis alike mounted the pavement and cannonaded shop windows, people of all ages dropped to their knees in his wake, championed the fuck farms and pioneered the boyhire networks, two hundred a trick by the time he was through—until all these dreams began to slow down on him, all these pornographic, hallucinatory, and mercantile dreams —and suddenly it is not he who sits in a darkened room but flashing this way and that far to go through the night looking for a name, and so—

"Quentin?"

"Yes," said Johnny.

Celia came through the door and with a hideous, inhuman leap Johnny was on her back, a lithe-limbed insect accelerating her fall to the ground. Holding his wife by the hair Johnny smashed her face into the stone floor, smashed until it went all runny and sweet in his hands. Without looking round he jumped and swiveled his right arm backward and upward and shattered the approaching Marvell's jaw with the side of his fist. Johnny kicked. He kicked, and stopped when the twitching stopped.

Diana had felt the disturbance from below and was already in her dressing gown when she heard the gentle footfalls on the stairs and the soft knock.

"Who is it?" she said.

"It's Quentin," said Johnny.

Diana opened the door: "*You,*" she said as he closed it behind him.

"Oh no. Johnny, don't kill me," said Diana. "Please don't kill me, Johnny."

71: THE COMING LIGHTS

Skip tapped his fingers on the steering wheel. He trained the Chevrolet's rearview mirror on the hospital exit. He swore. Then Skip remembered the envelope Quentin had given him. He took it from his jacket. It was, he now saw, addressed to himself, to Skip Marshall, Reg: 87695438, c/o Buzhardt, 20120 South Richmond Avenue, LA, Calif. 90065. The seal had already been broken and the paper was crinkled. Skip took the letter out; he recognized the strained, precipitous hand.

> *Son. I am out of Honkville and I reckon as how we could take another try at it, your Ma's last words to me as I cradled her in my arms was we shuould, she forgived you and I both. I have your bus money home, she said for you to get back be my baby boy when first you colud. You're loving pa, Philboyd Marshall Junior.*
> > PS: Do it boy—JOHNNY

The piece of blue paper fluttered from Skip's fingers as Andy and Roxeanne appeared through the automatic doors and raced down the steps.

Roxeanne got in beside Skip while Andy dived onto the back seat.

"Luce's staying with the deadies but we ain't!" shouted Andy, cupping his hands over his mouth and letting out a high-pitched whoop. "Rox— crack out some of that *Adren!*"

When the Chevrolet pulled out onto the motorway Skip pressed the accelerator pedal to the floor.

"Pull over at the next access, honey," said Roxeanne. "Andy and I want to fuck. Don't we, Andy?"

". . . Yeah," said Andy from the back seat.

Skip did not respond. The car passed the 80 mph speed limit.

"Ah, baby, come on," said Roxeanne. "You can watch. Can't he, Andy?"

"I don't give a shit," said Andy.

Skip did not respond. The speedometer dial jerked up to 90 mph.

"Hey, take it easy," said Roxeanne. "Hey, Skip—slow down!"

Skip did not respond. His dead, spectacled eyes were steady on the unraveling highway.

"Casual," murmured Andy. "It's ton street. Cajjj."

Abruptly Roxeanne's jaw plummeted. She held up the blue paper. "Andy, you crazy fuck! You give him this?"

The car was moving at 110 mph.

"What?" Andy leaned forward. "Nah— Quent did. It's just—"

Roxeanne had begun to pound with her fists on Skip's metallic arms. "Oh, *fuck fuck fuck!*" she screamed. *"Baby, baby, don't kill us! Andy—stop him, stop him!"*

"Quentin," said Andy. "He's Johnny?"

"Andy Andy Andy!"

"Diana . . ." said Andy, and exhaled.

"Andy . . . Andy . . ."

Andy sank back. "Ah, I don't give a shit," he said.

The Chevrolet was traveling at 135 mph when it climbed the flyover exit route ramp. Skip made no attempt to negotiate the thirty-degree turn. The car tore through the roadside trestles and flew up into the coming lights.

72: THAT SAD WELCOME

Keith asked the mini-cabbie if he wouldn't mind pulling over. It was seven o'clock and a bright dawn had begun to show over the luminous hills. Dusky and tumescent though he was with bruises, Whitehead had an obscure desire to walk the remaining five hundred yards to the house. He offered the driver three of the four ten-pound notes Lucy had given him. The driver seemed gratified. "Thank you, sir," he said.

Little Keith tasted the air between swollen lips, smarting again to the tranquil anonymity of the village. Half-tears gathered in his puffed-over eyes. He moved on gradually, in a way relishing the stealth forced on him by his damaged legs, enjoying the sweet and painful integrity of his body. The intern had asked him, with every show of urgency, to stay on for treatment at the Institute, but—no—Keith had wanted to return as soon as possible to his anxious friends. He was, even now, embarrassingly moved that they had—with all that determination and concern—rescued him from the death he had so childishly invited. In his mind he praised also the skills of Marvell, whom he assumed to be responsible for the "unidentified drug" which, the doctors said, had providentially compressed his fat tissues and halted the fatal permeation of the barbiturates. He looked around at the oblongs of graying brick, the unresting trees (what was it they were saying . . . *fresh, fresh, fresh*), the darting birds, the different sky. How, he thought, could he ever have wished to be elsewhere? He felt as if he had undertaken a long journey and had survived to be born again—born again, through the midwifery of this sudden weekend.

Keith felt, moreover, in the know, one of the *cognoscenti*, the possessor of exclusive information, tall with news. Giles was dead. He was dead. Before the stomach pumps could even be made operational his breathing had ceased, and on the application of the respirators his heart had instantly collapsed. Giles's mother had been brought down from the wards above; Mrs. Coldstream had embraced little Keith, bathing his cheeks in her tears. The intern, again, had offered to telephone Appleseed Rectory, but Keith had forestalled him. He wanted all of that sad welcome, the faltering sympathy of his friends. Keith rehearsed phrases, wondering how best to present the melancholy story. He had himself seen Giles laid out on the white stretcher, Lucy weeping over his poor shoulders, his quiet face sullen and babyish in death.

Keith limped steadily over the bridge. He paused at the opening of the drive. Appleseed Rectory stole out from under the morning shadows. Keith blinked. Was it really there? Perversely he thought of turning back, of running away. But then he smiled at his own foreboding. It's all over, he thought, stepping onto the damp gravel.

The Appleseed kitchen: the suitcase, the car keys, the bag of drugs, the roll of notes, the burnished ax. On the wall, the (decoy) excremental G of the Conceptualist Gesture. Johnny was there. He leaned forward eagerly by the window. As he watched Keith move up the drive, his green eyes flashed into the dawn like wild, dying suns.